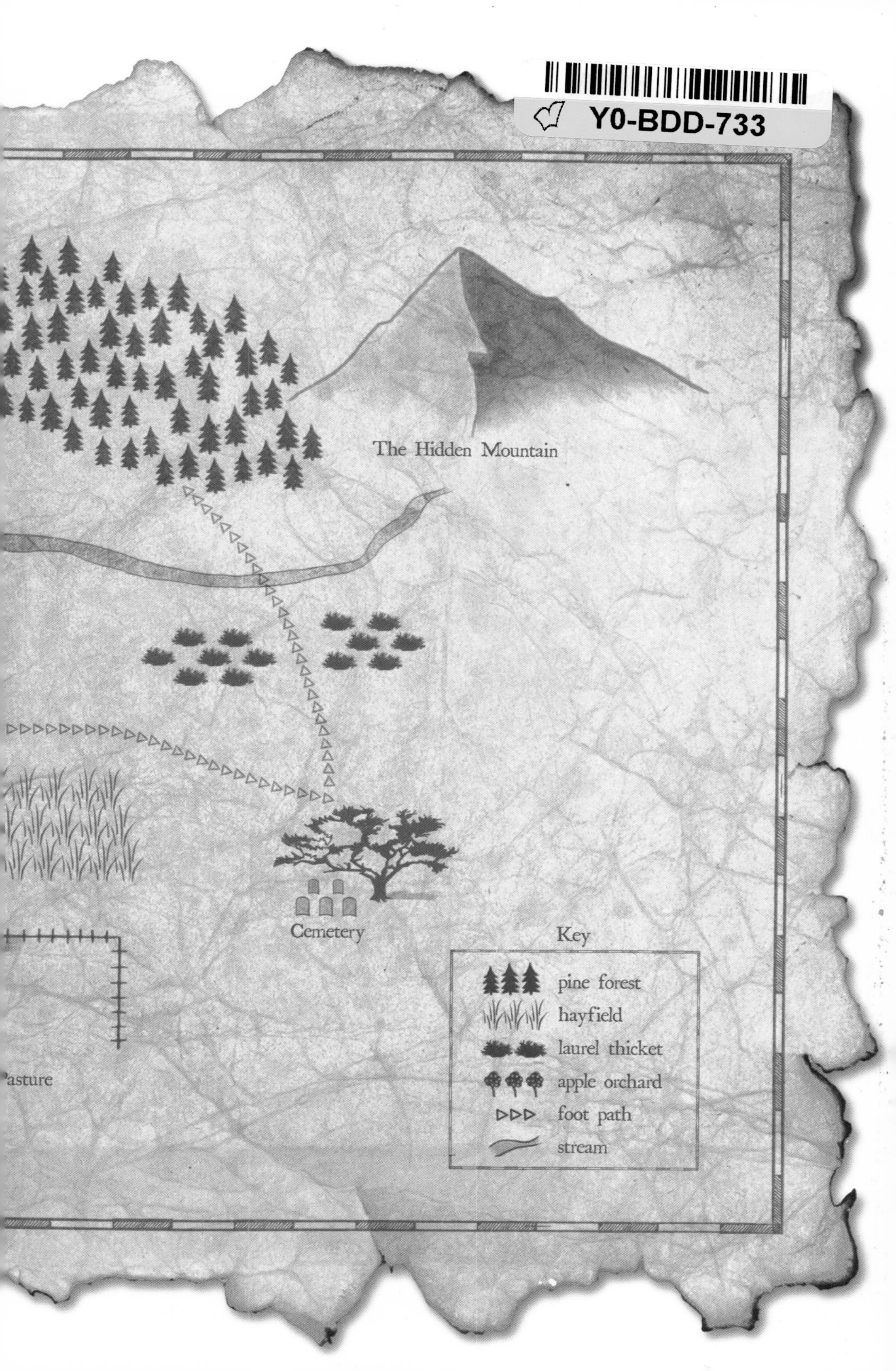
Y0-BDD-733
The Hidden Mountain
Cemetery
asture
Key
pine forest
hayfield
laurel thicket
apple orchard
foot path
stream

Arlo,

Remember who you are.

S L Ruiz

CONTENTS

SWEETWATER ANIMAL SOCIETY

AND

The Hidden Mountain

CHAPTER ONE

THE ROSE OF SWEETWATER

The sky began to darken and a strong gust of wind blew through the middle of the barn. The sorrel-and-white mare paced frantically as Will Sweetwater and his daughter Emily watched through the stall door. They had waited almost a year for this day and now it seemed like their worst nightmare was coming true.

Emily jumped onto a bale of hay to get a better look. "Is she having the baby?"

"Well, she really should've had it by now." Her father sighed. "I'm afraid there might be a problem." Wiping a smudge of dirt off her freckled cheek, he could see the concern in her eyes. He brushed back her long sandy-brown hair and put his arm around her.

"Oh, you mean the foal could be breech?" Emily asked. "I read about that in one of my medical books." Will looked at his daughter in amazement. He couldn't believe how smart she was for a nine-year-old.

"You're right, it could be breech. And because Peaches is a miniature horse, this birth might be real hard on her." He took out his handkerchief and wiped the sweat from his forehead as Spencer ran into the barn and jumped on the bale of hay next to his little sister.

"What's goin' on? What'd I miss?" he asked struggling for enough hay to stand on.

"Hey, quit pushin'!" Emily demanded as she tried to keep the perfect spot she had for herself. "You haven't missed anything yet, except Dad says the foal could be breech."

"What does that mean?"

"It means it could be coming out backwards."

Spencer looked to the stall just as the mare knocked over her water bucket. He jumped off the hay and opened the latch on the door.

Will grabbed his hand to stop him. "Where do you think you're going?"

Spencer gazed up at his father. "I'm gonna get her some more water."

"I don't think so, son. That horse'll kick you into tomorrow if you go in that stall right now. Look, I want to show the two of you something that I don't ever want you to forget." He latched the door and Spencer jumped back onto the bale of hay. "Do you see the way Peaches is pacing around the stall right now?"

Both of the children watched as she walked around the stall, sweating and breathing fast. Then she ran and made a complete turn in the air and kicked out with both of her back hooves. She suddenly stopped to snort at the straw and move it around with her nose.

"That horse isn't here right now," he said.

"What do you mean she's not here?" Spencer questioned.

"Her mind...it isn't here. When you look in her eyes it's not the same Peaches that we all know, she's somewhere else and she doesn't really know what she's doin'. Animals have a sort of protection for the kind of pain that she's goin' through right now. Your grandmother can explain it better—she understands how it is with animals."

Spencer stared at Peaches. "What can we do to help her?"

"Well, we're just gonna watch her for a little while longer to see if she can do this on her own, and if she can't, I'll have to call Dr. Miles."

"What will the doctor do?" Spencer asked.

"He'll have to try to turn the foal around if it's breech." Will looked down at his two children and watched as their faces showed their confusion. "Let's just wait and see."

All three of them looked through the door and watched as Peaches continued to pace. The wind picked up again and—CRACK! All three jumped and turned around just in time to see a bolt of lightning hit the tall chestnut tree outside the barn.

"Good gosh!" Spencer yelled as he lost his balance and fell backwards off the hay bale. Emily couldn't help but laugh at her brother, struggling to get back on his feet.

"You all right, son?" Will asked, bending down to give him a hand.

"Yeah, but, boy, that seemed close," Spencer said as he tried to shake off the tingling in his left arm.

"You guys keep an eye on Peaches—I'm gonna go see how much damage that did."

As they watched their father walk out of the barn they heard the mare make a deep moaning sound.

"She sounds so miserable," Spencer said. "I wish there was something we could do to help her."

"Well, you said you wanted to be a vet, what do you think she needs?" Emily asked.

"If I had to guess, I'd say she might feel better if she could lie down," Spencer said as he jumped down from the hay.

"What are you doing?"

Spencer slid the stall door open. "I'm gonna see if I can help her."

"I don't think that's such a good idea, Spencer. Dad said it could be dangerous. She seems to have a rapid heartbeat and anxiety, and that combination can lead to...well, I'm not exactly sure what it can lead to but I think it might be bad."

"You and your medical books," he said, moving slowly toward the mare. "Sometimes it just takes a nice easy--"

WHACK!!!

Just as Spencer touched her halter the tiny horse pinned her ears back, kicked with both back hooves and hit the wood panel of the stall. Spencer fell against the wall and laid there frozen, not knowing what to do next. Emily screamed and Will came racing into the barn. He saw his son lying in the corner of the stall.

"Spencer, are you all right?"

"Yeah, Dad, she didn't get me—she got the wall."

"Just stay there a minute—I'll be in to get you." Will talked to Peaches in a soothing voice as he made his way over to Spencer. "Easy girl, that a girl, easy baby." He sidestepped his way over to Spencer, picked him up by the shirt and made him walk behind him until they were safely out of the stall. After the door was latched, Will bent down on one knee to take a good look at Spencer. "Are you sure you're all right?"

"Yeah, Dad, I'm fine," Spencer said, brushing some straw from his pants.

After the shock of what had just happened wore off, Will grabbed Spencer by his arms and looked in his eyes.

"Why did you go in there after I just finished telling you how crazy she is right now?"

Spencer looked at Emily and felt somewhat embarrassed. "I thought I could help her lie down."

"Well, here's the deal, Spencer. You could have gotten yourself killed for one thing, and for another thing, what happened to what I taught you about respect for animals?"

Spencer looked up from the floor and right into his father's eyes. "I do respect Peaches, Dad, I love her. I just wanted--"

"You see, son, that's just it—*you wanted*. If you're going to work with animals one day you have to start thinking about things from their point of view."

"I don't know what you mean."

"Son, Peaches is trying to have a baby. Can you possibly imagine how hard that must be for her, not to mention how painful. Even if she was having a normal birth it would be difficult. If we're not careful we could lose both her and the foal."

Spencer looked back at the floor and the tears began to pool in his eyes. He wiped them away with his hand and looked back at his father. "I would never do anything to hurt Peaches or the new foal, Dad, I would never..."

"It's okay, son. She doesn't seem any worse off, but try to remember; we have to take care of our animals."

"Hey, look at the cats!" Emily cried.

Their two barn cats, Dudley and Gerri, were sitting on the sill watching Peaches. The brother and sister were both gray tabbies but they didn't look a bit alike. Gerri had a solid black stripe going down her back while Dudley was light gray, a lot bigger and had four white paws and a white spot on his nose.

"Do you think they know that Peaches is having a baby?" Emily asked.

Will nodded. "I'll bet they do. They've been there all afternoon, ever since she went into labor."

"Maybe they're scared like us," Spencer said anxiously. Will put his hand on his son's shoulder and they all continued to watch the little horse.

❊ ❊ ❊ ❊ ❊ ❊ ❊ ❊ ❊ ❊ ❊

After a few minutes passed, Will walked to the front of the barn and looked at the chestnut tree and up at the sky. "That sure was weird," he thought, "just one bolt of lightning."

The two children followed him and they watched as the clouds parted and the sun began to shine. "Well, it looks like it's clear for now and I don't think we can wait any longer," Will said. "Emily, go tell your grandmother what's goin' on and tell her to call Dr. Miles. Spencer, go and get Roberto. We're gonna need all of the help we can get."

The two children ran out of the barn and up the gravel road toward the main house. "I'll meet you back at the barn!" Spencer yelled to Emily as he took the path that led to Roberto's house.

When he got to the wooden bridge that went over the stream he stopped for a moment to catch his breath. He looked down at the water and could see his reflection. His copper-colored hair looked murky brown as he brushed it back from his face. His blue eyes once again glazed over as the familiar feeling of fear came over him. His father's words about losing Peaches and the baby made him feel the same as when his mother had died two years earlier. The pain returned to his arm and his stomach felt like it was flip-flopping back and forth.

As soon as he started to feel better he remembered where he was going. He began to run up the path to the little farmhouse near the edge of the tree line. When he reached the house he jumped the two porch steps and landed at the front door.

"Roberto! Roberto!" he yelled.

A woman with light brown skin and dark hair came running out onto the porch. "Spencer, what's happening? What's wrong?"

Spencer could hardly get out the words as he struggled for every breath. "Sofia, where's Roberto? Peaches is having the baby and Dad says it could be backwards and he needs his help."

"He's in the orchard," she said. "You'll have to go there to find him. I can't leave the house, Anna's sick again."

Spencer had already jumped off of the porch by the time she said orchard. He headed back down the path and across the bridge, down the gravel road and past the barn. The road took him by the hayfields, back over the stream and through a grove of walnut trees. It opened on the other side to a huge apple orchard which was split right down the middle by the road. Against the backdrop of the blue sky Spencer could see a faint trail of smoke. He ran off the road and weaved in and out of the trees until he came to the tractor.

"Roberto!" he yelled waving his hands in the air. "Hey, Roberto!"

He ran around to the front of the tractor to get his attention. Roberto stepped on the brake and the engine backed down to a faint hum.

"*Qué pasa* little man? What's up?" he asked.

"Dad needs you in the barn!" Spencer was doubled over and holding his stomach. "It's Peaches!"

"Is she having the foal?"

"Yeah, but there's a problem and Dad needs your help."

"Climb up," Roberto said. "It'll be faster if we take the tractor." He put it into high gear and the engine wailed as he turned it toward the barn.

❊ ❊ ❊ ❊ ❊ ❊ ❊ ❊ ❊ ❊ ❊

"Is there anything we can do for her?" Roberto asked Will as he watched Peaches.

"Well, the vet should be on his way so we'll just wait until he gets here."

Emily came running back into the barn with her grandmother close behind.

"What did Dr. Miles say?" Will asked his mother.

"She's on her way and will be here in a few minutes," Kate said looking into the stall.

"What do you mean she? Where's Harry?"

"He's out on another call so they're sending his niece. She just graduated from the university and started working in his practice a few weeks ago."

"Oh, great," he grumbled. "We probably know more than she does!"

CHAPTER ONE

"Let's just give her a chance, Will." Kate moved in closer to get a better look. "Oh, poor thing, we've got to get her to lie down."

Spencer smirked at Emily. "See, I told you."

Will looked at Kate. "Mom, do you think you can get her to relax a little?"

"Well, we'll give it a try. Roberto, will you please go and get Abbey from the pasture?"

"Sure thing, Miss Kate. Should I leave Rio and Blue out there?"

"Yes, for now," she answered. "I'll go and feed them later."

Roberto grabbed a lead rope and halter and ran out of the barn. In just a few minutes he was back with the big, bay mare. She blinked her eyes as she moved from the bright light of the afternoon sun to the darkness of the barn. She looked like royalty as she glided her large frame through the barn and into the stall next to Peaches. Kate went into the stall and took off Abbey's halter. She ran her fingers through the thick velvet coat that was such a dark brown it almost looked purple. Her mane and tail were black and she had a white spot on her forehead in the shape of an arrowhead.

"Well, old girl, Peaches needs our help."

Spencer and Emily could tell that their grandmother was whispering something into Abbey's ear but they couldn't hear the words. Kate slid open a wooden window between the two stalls so she and Abbey could see Peaches. Spencer and Emily watched as their grandmother placed her hand on Abbey's forehead. Both Kate and Abbey lowered their heads and closed their eyes.

Spencer hit Emily in the ribs with his elbow. "What are they doing?"

"I don't know," Emily replied. "It looks like they're praying."

Roberto overheard them and put his finger up to his lips for them to be quiet.

Kate gently ran her hand down Abbey's long neck and moved quietly into the stall with Peaches. The little mare let out a whinny and moved to the far corner. Kate closed her eyes again and knelt down on the straw. After a few moments, Peaches walked over to Kate. She made a low moaning sound and Kate reached out and stroked her soft, red mane. Finally, the little horse began to lower herself onto the straw.

Spencer and Emily couldn't believe what they were seeing. Spencer tapped his father on the shoulder. "Can Gram talk to horses?"

"No, Spencer. I told you—she just understands them," Will said in a whisper.

They heard the sound of car tires on the gravel outside the barn. Emily jumped off the hay and ran outside.

Seconds later she led the doctor through the barn. "She's back here, in the last stall."

Jessie Miles was still young enough to look like a college student but carried herself with the assurance of an experienced doctor. She had long blonde hair and soft features. When she spoke, her blue eyes danced and her smile warmed her words.

"Hi, everybody," she said as she came closer to the stall. "I'm the other Dr. Miles, but you can call me Jessie."

Everyone smiled but Will. He had already made his mind up he wasn't going to like her. She made the rounds and shook everyone else's hand before coming to him. She sensed his uneasiness about her and gave him her apologies instead of her hand. She explained her uncle was out on a call at the far end of the county so, if it was all right, she would take a look at the horse.

"We would be very appreciative," Kate said as she rose up. "I'm Katherine Sweetwater, and we're very happy you could get out here so quickly and on such short notice. Aren't we, Will?"

"Yes, ma'am, we sure are," he said reluctantly. "That little mare is having a heck of a time delivering that foal."

"Well, let's have a look at her." Jessie stepped into the stall. Peaches was still lying in the straw as Jessie reached down and slowly stroked her neck. She lifted her head and Jessie looked into the soft brown eyes of the little horse. "She still seems pretty alert. How long has she been in labor?"

"Almost three hours now," Will said.

Jessie laid Peaches' head back down on the straw as she whinnied again and kicked out with one back hoof.

"I'm gonna need someone to help hold her while I check and see what's goin' on with the foal," Jessie said.

"I'll help you," Spencer said. "I'm gonna be a vet too."

"Oh, is that right? And what about you, Emily? What do you want to be?" Jessie asked.

"A molecular biologist!" Emily exclaimed without hesitation.

"Good gracious, that sounds like a very important job. You'll have to tell me about it sometime, but for now, Emily, can you show me where I can wash up?"

"Sure!" Emily jumped down from the hay.

"And, Spencer, I'll need your dad and Roberto to help me hold Peaches, but can you go to my truck and get the blue canvas bag for me?"

"All right," Spencer said, happy to have a job to do.

❊ ❊ ❊ ❊ ❊ ❊ ❊ ❊ ❊ ❊ ❊

Will and Roberto held Peaches on each side of her halter while the doctor moved into position behind her.

"Now try and keep her as quiet as possible," Jessie said, "I'm gonna have to see if it's breech." Fascinated, Spencer watched as the little horse just lay in the straw while Jessie checked her out.

"Gram, do you think Peaches understands that Dr. Miles is here to help her?" Spencer asked.

Kate smiled. "I know she does."

"How do you know?"

"Because I told her," she whispered and gave a little wink. Spencer and Emily just stared at her. "Now, Spencer, pay attention to what Dr.

Miles is doing. You'll need to know how to do this one day."

"Well, I have good news and bad news," Jessie said. "The good news is that the foal isn't breech."

"What's the bad news?" Will asked.

"It's a very big baby," Jessie said, wiping the sweat from her forehead onto her sleeve. "This isn't going to be easy."

Spencer felt a pang of panic as he jumped off the hay and slid the stall door open.

"You can help her though, right?" he pleaded.

"We're gonna give it our best shot," Jessie said. "Don't worry, Spencer, I've done this before."

"Get back up there, Spencer, and close that door!" Will shouted.

Spencer slid the door closed and jumped back up on the hay. "Sorry, Dad, I forgot."

"If I could only tell her to relax and not to push right now that would be great," Jessie said. "If she does any pushin' at all then the shoulders could get stuck."

Kate quietly opened the stall door and went back in with Abbey. She again placed her hand on Abbey's forehead and whispered. Spencer and Emily watched as Peaches rolled over in the straw onto her side. Will and Roberto let go of her halter so she could get more comfortable.

"Perfect position! That's exactly where I need her!" Jessie exclaimed.

Everyone stood still and watched as the foal began to show itself. First, two little hooves, one in front of the other. Next, they saw the head which was a beautiful sorrel color.

"We've got ourselves a redhead!" Kate said as she and Abbey looked on from the other stall.

Peaches stayed on her side but kept trying to look around to see her foal.

"You just keep up the good work and you'll see your baby in just a minute," Jessie said as she moved Peaches' head back onto the straw. "Now, if we can just get these shoulders out we'll be home free."

Right then, as if the little foal was tired of waiting, it came out in a burst onto the straw.

"Oh!" Emily exclaimed. "She looks like a little cow!"

"That's 'cause she's solid red," Spencer said. "There's not one white spot on her!"

"Can you tell if it's a boy or a girl?" Emily asked.

Upon further inspection, Jessie said, "It's a girl!"

"She couldn't be more perfect," Kate said. "She won't hurt for love around this farm. Right, kids?"

Spencer and Emily answered as one: "No, ma'am!"

"I'll stay for a while longer to make sure she's nursing," Jessie said from the corner of the stall where she stood with Will and Roberto.

"We can't thank you enough," Will said. "I thought we were gonna have a real problem on our hands."

"Oh, it was my pleasure. It's fast becoming my favorite thing about being a vet."

"I can see why," Will said and gave her a smile.

Spencer and Emily stood on the bale of hay and watched Peaches clean the foal.

"Why is Peaches pushing her around?" Spencer asked.

"She wants her to get up and start walking," Jessie said.

"So soon? She was just born!"

"Spencer, if you'd take time to read a little bit more you'd know that the mother wants the foal to start nursing right away, and she needs her to walk to do it," Emily said.

"Hey, guys, what are we going to name her?" Will asked as he walked out of the stall.

"Well, we'd decided on Flash when we thought she was gonna be red and white like Peaches, but now that name doesn't seem to fit her," Emily explained.

"I have an idea," Will urged as he looked at his mother and smiled. "I don't know if you guys remember but my grandmother was named Rose. She was your grandpa William's mother. Emily, you were probably too young but Spencer, do you remember when she came here for a visit?"

Spencer cocked his head trying to recall.

"Anyway, she was very special to me and I thought maybe we could name the foal after her. Since the foal is solid red, like a rose, we could call her Rosebud. What do you think?"

Emily grinned. "I like it!"

"Perfect!" Spencer added.

Kate walked over and kissed Will on the cheek. "I'm sure she would have been proud to have her name given to such a special little lady." They all looked back into the stall as Will's voice filled the barn:

"Welcome to Sweetwater Farms, little Rosebud!"

❊ ❊ ❊ ❊ ❊ ❊ ❊ ❊ ❊ ❊ ❊

Kate went into the stall and put the halter back on Abbey. "Roberto, would you mind taking Abbey back to the pasture?"

"No, ma'am, just leave her there and I'll take care of her. I'll go ahead and feed Rio and Blue while I'm out there too."

Kate stroked Abbey's neck and whispered in her ear. This time Spencer could hear what she was saying.

"Good job, old girl. We can always count on you."

She stepped out of the stall and latched the door behind her. "Well, now that all the excitement's over, I'm gonna go and start supper. Oh, Roberto, I almost forgot—how's Anna feeling? Sofia had to leave the office early today to get her out of school. They said something about a stomachache."

"Yeah, her stomach's been bothering her and she felt the same way two weeks ago. Sofia's going to take her to the doctor--maybe tomorrow after school if she can get an appointment."

"Well, that's good. I can cover in the office until she gets back. Just tell her we'll talk in the morning," Kate said as she walked out of the barn toward the white pickup truck. Jessie was at the back of the truck putting her supplies away. "Well, Jessie, we can't thank you enough for your help today."

"Oh, it was my pleasure, Mrs. Sweetwater."

"Please, call me Kate."

"Well, Kate, you sure do have a nice family. I enjoyed meeting everyone."

"Are you sure you mean everyone?"

"I do. I can certainly appreciate why your son might have been upset when he saw me—after all, he was expecting my uncle."

"Well, thank you for being so understanding," Kate said. "Have a safe trip back to the office and I hope we see you soon!"

Kate headed up the road toward the main house. Will came out of the barn and saw Jessie standing by the truck.

"She's drinkin' real good now," he said. "It took her a little while but once she found what she was lookin' for she was all business."

"That's great," Jessie said closing up the truck.

"Listen, I want to apologize for the way I acted when you first got here. I was a little nervous about the foal and…well...I'm sorry," Will said as he looked down at the gravel road.

"No apology necessary," she said. "Maybe you can make it up to me by letting me take some of my uncle's calls when he has to come out here. This sure is a pretty place."

"Thanks. The farm's been in my family for generations. My great-great-great grandfather came here from Scotland and thought it was so pretty he never left."

"Do you farm anything other than apples?" she asked.

"No, we never had any reason to. We've always been blessed with good crops. The Native Americans used to say this land was special and the water that ran through it made anything grow. I believe it, too. The apple business has been real good to us."

"Well, from the looks of your kids it's been real good to them, too. They seem to be very happy."

"Yeah, they are. It was hard when their mother died a couple of years ago."

"Oh, I'm sorry. I didn't know." Jessie murmured, a bit embarrassed.

"It's all right," he said trying to ease her. "It's been real hard but we're all getting along better now. Roberto and his wife came to work here when my father died four years ago and they have a daughter the same age as Emily. It's helped Spencer and Emily to have all of them here. And Roberto and I have been friends since college. He helps me in the orchard and his wife Sofia runs our office. My mom trains the horses and takes care of the other animals. So, if we have any problems with Rosebud, you'll be hearing from her."

"Hey, Dad!" Spencer yelled as he ran out of the barn. "Do you think Jessie could look at Sully before she leaves?"

"Where is he?" Will asked.

"He's in my room. Can I go and get him...please? He still doesn't feel good."

"Would you have time to look at another patient, Dr. Miles?" Will asked.

"Sure. What kind of a patient is Sully?"

"He's my son's yellow lab. Go to the house and get him, Spencer. We'll wait here."

Spencer ran up the gravel road toward the house.

"What's going on with Sully?" Jessie asked.

"He's got some sort of stomach problem. He eats real good but he always seems to feel bad."

In a few minutes Spencer came running back down the road with the yellow dog following behind. Sully went right up to Jessie to check her out. His nose was trying to take in all the smells she had on her from the clinic.

"He likes you!" Emily said as she came out of the barn.

"Well, he either likes me or the hundreds of cats and dogs I smell like," Jessie bent down to rub his ears. "Spencer, can you tell me a little bit more about how Sully's been feeling?"

"One thing I know is he loves food," he said. "We feed him a lot but he never seems to get fat."

Jessie looked down at Sully and could see his ribs showing through his yellow coat. "What about his energy, does he like to play with you?"

"He used to. Now all he wants to do is lie around." At those words they all watched as the dog made a place in the flower bed outside the barn and lay down in a tight ball.

"Oh, I see what you mean. Do you think you could bring Sully into the office so I can run some tests?" Jessie asked, looking at Will.

"Can we, Dad?" Spencer begged.

Will nodded. "Sure, we'll call tomorrow and make an appointment."

Jessie went back over to Sully in the flowerbed. She looked into his eyes and stroked his head. She lifted up his lip and looked at his teeth.

"Why are you doing that?" Emily asked.

"I wanted to check his gums," Jessie said. "Sometimes the answers to things are in places we would never think to look."

"Well, we've already taken up too much of your time." Will reached out to shake her hand. "Thanks again, it was nice meeting you."

"Like I said, just call me anytime." She headed for the truck. "Bye, Spencer and Emily."

"Bye, Jessie," they said at the same time.

"Dad, can I sleep in the barn tonight to keep an eye on Rosebud?" Emily asked.

"No, Em, I don't think so. Peaches will do just fine without any of us. Why don't you check on the foal one more time and then head up to the house? I'm sure your grandmother's got supper ready, and you have to finish your project for school tomorrow."

"Oh, yeah, I'm almost done though, which is more than I can say for Spencer." Emily laughed as she gave Spencer a tap on the arm and skipped into the barn. He started to hit her back as his father grabbed him.

"Son, I want to talk to you a minute."

"I wasn't gonna hit her," he swore as he pulled his arm back.

"Yeah, sure you weren't," Will said. "No, listen Spencer—I want to talk to you about Sully. I'm going to call tomorrow and make an appointment with Dr. Miles like I said, but there's something I want you to understand." He sat down on the gravel and began to rub Sully's head. "Son, this dog is only two years old and I think he's real sick. If Dr. Miles says there's nothing she can do for him, then we're going to have to do the right thing. Do you know what I mean?"

Spencer sat down in the gravel and began to rub Sully's head too. The big dog looked up at the two of them, enjoying the attention.

"Yes, Dad, I know." Spencer looked into Sully's big brown eyes. "Don't worry, Sully, Dr. Miles is gonna make you feel better."

"You heard what I said—right, son?"

"Yeah, Dad, I heard. But I'm gonna believe that she can help him, okay?"

Will looked down at Spencer as he hugged Sully. "Sure, son, that's okay." Will watched Spencer for a moment, reminded of how much compassion he had and what a good boy he was. "I'm glad you're my son," Will said softly as he got up from the gravel.

"What?" Spencer asked.

"Nothing, just finish up in the barn and you and your sister come up for supper," Will said heading up the road.

CHAPTER TWO

THUNDER & LIGHTNING

The two-story white farmhouse took on a pinkish glow as the sun began to set. The leaves on the magnolia tree in the front yard started to shake as the wind picked up. The little concrete birdbath, which sat under the tree, was full of water from rain the night before. On the front porch by the swing, wind chimes danced back and forth in the breeze.

Emily scooped up the last bite of her cherry pie. "Dad, can I go check on Rosebud and Peaches after dinner?"

"No, you have homework, and besides, Roberto said he'd look in on them."

"Do you think when Rosebud gets older we can train her to pull a cart like Peaches?" Emily wondered.

"Sure, in a couple of years," he said. "In a month or so you can put a halter on her and lead her around. If you want you can include her training in with your summer chores." Will watched as Spencer moved the pie around on his plate, not paying attention to the conversation. "Do you want to work with Rosebud too, Spencer?" No reply. "Son, did you hear me?"

"Oh, sorry, Dad. Sure I'll work with Rosebud. It'll be fun," Spencer said without looking up. "Can I be excused now? I'm gonna do my homework."

"Can I finish his pie?" Emily asked as Spencer got up from the table.

"Sure, son, and no to you, Em. One piece is enough before bedtime."

"Yes, sir," Emily agreed reluctantly as she got up from the table and took the dishes to her grandmother at the sink.

"Spencer, did you feed Sully?" Will hollered as Spencer was climbing the stairs to his room.

"Yes, sir, but he didn't want to eat," Spencer yelled back. Will stared at his empty plate now knowing why his son was so quiet during dinner.

"Looks like we're in for a bad one," Kate said as she looked out the kitchen window.

The sun was almost completely gone, and in its place were gray and black clouds that were rushing through the dark sky. "Emily, when you go upstairs shut your window and tell Spencer to do the same. I don't want it to rain on my new curtains."

Emily grabbed her backpack off the counter and headed up the stairs.

"And, Emily, one hour on the computer and only sites for your project. And tell Spencer too!" Will shouted.

"Yes, sir," she said dragging her backpack behind her.

"What's wrong with Spencer?" Kate asked.

"I think this thing with Sully is really getting to him. I had to talk with him about the possibility of putting him down."

"Oh, no," Kate gasped, "surely there must be something we can do."

"I told Dr. Miles we'd bring him to her office for tests. If she can't find anything wrong, I don't know what else to do. Right now he's suffering," Will said and walked into the den.

Kate turned back to the window as the sky lit up with lightning.

CHAPTER TWO

It fell dark again and she could see her reflection in the glass. Her once brownish hair now had a hint of gray and she looked at her face remembering the younger version that used to look back. "Amazing," she thought. "I still feel as fit as I did when I was a teenager."

She could see the moon as it started to faintly show itself through the clouds and it brought her back from the past.

"A full moon!" she exclaimed.

She ran to the refrigerator to look at the calendar. "It can't be," she said in a low voice. She ran back to the window and just as her eyes fixed again on the moon, lightning struck! It lit up the sky and showed the moon like a big ball of crystal-white light.

"It's Lakena's moon!" she exclaimed in a quiet voice to herself.

"Could it really be tonight?"

❊ ❊ ❊ ❊ ❊ ❊ ❊ ❊ ❊ ❊ ❊

"Come in," Spencer said as Emily pushed the door open.

"Dad said only one hour on the computer and I get it first," she said.

"He didn't say you get it first. You added that yourself. I heard him," Spencer said as he lay on the floor petting Sully.

"What are you doing?" Emily asked. "Why aren't you doing your homework?"

"I'm just thinking," he said. "You know, you're starting to look more like her all the time."

"Who?"

"Mom. The older you get the more you look like her. I was just thinking about her today. Do you ever think about her?"

"Yeah, but I have a hard time remembering stuff. So instead, I think about where she is now and what she's doing."

"What do you mean where she is now?" Spencer asked. "Dad says she's in heaven with Grandpa."

"I know but I wonder what heaven is like. Jonas Walker says that heaven is space."

"Like outer space?" Spencer asked.

"No. Like all of the space around us."

"Well, Jonas Walker lives in outer space if you ask me," Spencer sneered. "I don't even know why you're friends with him."

"Because he's a genius and you're just jealous," she said. "Anyway, he says that our bodies are made up of matter and energy and when people die it's only their bodies that are gone and their energy is still here. Maybe that's why Dad says Mom will always be with us."

"Whatever," Spencer groaned, not really knowing what she was talking about.

Emily looked down at Sully lying on the floor. "Is he sick again?"

"Well, he didn't eat any supper and that's weird for him. Even when he's felt bad before he would still eat."

"Maybe Jessie can do something to help him," she said as she ran her fingers down the full length of his yellow tail.

"Yeah, maybe," Spencer said, pulling himself off the floor. "I sure do hope so."

Kate was listening to their conversation outside Spencer's door.

"Hey, did you kids close your windows like I told you to?" she asked as she walked into the room.

"I did," Emily said, looking over at the curtains blowing from side to side in Spencer's window. Kate looked at Spencer with a frown as she walked over to the window and slid it down.

"No fair! She didn't tell me," he said, shooting Emily a dirty look.

"Emily, can I talk to Spencer for a moment?" Kate asked as she sat down on the bed.

"Okay. I'm going to get on the computer now anyway." She left the room.

"One hour!" Spencer insisted as she shut the door.

"Come over here and sit by me, Spencer," Kate said holding her hand out for him. "Your dad told me he talked to you about Sully." At the sound of his name the dog lifted his head and looked at the two of them.

"Come here, boy!" Spencer patted the bed for Sully to jump up, and it seemed to take all of his strength to make it up on the bed to lie beside Spencer. "Yeah, I told Dad I was gonna believe Dr. Miles could help Sully but now it seems like he's worse and I don't know what to believe." Spencer looked down at his bedspread and played with a loose thread while trying to fight back his tears.

"Spencer, I'm going tell you a story that your grandfather told me about our ancestors who once lived on this land." She took his hand in hers and raised up his head so their eyes would meet. "I want you to listen to my words and believe in them."

As she held his hand he looked past her and could see the moon through the window. It was big and perfectly round and had a very odd glow to it. Then he saw lightning streak across the glass followed by a loud clap of thunder. He jumped and squeezed his grandmother's hand.

"Ouch, that one hurt!" he exclaimed, grabbing his arm in pain.

"You can feel the electricity coming from the lightning, can't you?" she asked as she rubbed his arm. "There, does that feel better?"

"Yes, ma'am. But why does it make my arm hurt?"

"Well—you're just very sensitive to it," she answered trying to avoid the question. "Now, where was I? Oh, yes—did you know that your great-great-great-great grandmother was a Native American Indian?"

"Yeah, Dad told us about how she and her family lived on this land. She married Sir Benjamin Howell, the guy who came here from Scotland. Aren't they buried in the cemetery where Grandpa and Mom are?"

"Yes, they are. Well, her name was Lakena and her father was a great chief in this valley. Her mother died when she was giving birth to her. As she grew, the people of her village told her that her mother was the sun and that she had gone back to the sky. And, everyone loved Lakena so much they started calling her the 'princess of the sun.' That's when they changed her name to Suri Lakena, because Suri means princess. So, when Suri Lakena died, the people believed that she actually went back to the sky to be with her mother, the sun. They believed Suri Lakena became the moon and would always look after them."

"To this day, they believe in the springtime there will be a special full moon. The legend says on the night of Lakena's moon, if there is something you want and you wish for it with your whole heart and soul, it will be given to you."

Spencer was glued to her every word.

"Now," she said, "look out the window."

Spencer looked beyond her and saw the moon again with the clouds drifting by.

"You see, Spencer, this is the night of Lakena's moon and you can make a wish for anything you want." She patted his leg and kissed his head. "Anything you want."

❊ ❊ ❊ ❊ ❊ ❊ ❊ ❊ ❊ ❊ ❊

Will knocked on Spencer's door. "Are you getting ready for bed, son?"

"Yes, sir," Spencer said in a garbled voice as he came out of the bathroom brushing his teeth.

"Did you finish your project?"

"No, but mine's not due until the last day of school."

"Isn't that next week?" Will asked.

"Yeah, but I'm almost done."

"Okay, but I want it finished by the end of *this* week," Will said and kissed Spencer on the head. "Now, I want you to get some sleep and try not to worry about Sully. Good night, son," he said as he pulled the door closed.

CHAPTER TWO

"Good night, Dad."

Spencer pulled down the covers on the bed and jumped in. Sully moved from the bottom of the bed up to the top to lie beside Spencer, groaning and rolling over on his side. Spencer put his hand on Sully's stomach and closed his eyes.

"Well, Gram said I could wish for whatever I want and it has to come true. So, here goes—I want to make a wish for you, Sully. I want to know what's wrong with you so Dr. Miles can fix you and we can be together...forever."

With those words he drifted off to sleep. The moon began to change from crystal-white to a yellowish-orange color. It looked like it was breathing as the colors seemed to interchange, yellow, orange and back to white again. Sully raised his head and turned to look out the window. He could sense something strange was happening. He whimpered, jumped to the floor and crawled under the bed. Spencer rolled over and pulled the covers up around his neck. The moon cast a fiery red shadow on his face as he repeated the words, "Together... forever."

❊ ❊ ❊ ❊ ❊ ❊ ❊ ❊ ❊ ❊ ❊

Kate poured a cup of coffee. "Another beautiful spring day."

Will flipped the morning paper to the sports section. "It sure is."

"Can I get you some breakfast, son?" she asked, reaching for the sugar bowl on the table.

Will shook his head and looked at his watch. "No, ma'am, I've already had some cereal. I need to get ready to meet Roberto in the lower orchard."

"Good morning, Gram. Good morning, Dad," Emily said cheerfully.

"Wow, look who's ready to go this morning. You must have slept well." Kate kissed Emily on the cheek.

"I slept great! But best of all, we only have one week of school left. Just one more week and I'll be in the fifth grade," she said smugly.

Will put the paper down and looked at his daughter. "Did you get your project done last night?"

"It's over there on the counter and ready to go."

"I should have known. And let me guess—it has something to do with science."

"Yep, I did it on Newton's Law of Universal Gravitation. I applied it both to falling objects on Earth and to the moons and planets orbiting the solar system. I simply compared the force of gravity with the force that keeps objects in orbit."

"Of course you did," Will said, smiling at his mother.

"Did you hear your brother stirring around up there?" Kate asked.

She slurped her milk. "No. Hey, Dad, when I finish breakfast can I go and see Rosebud?"

"Anna will be here any minute. Why don't you wait and see if she wants to go with you?" he asked as he walked to the bottom of the stairs. "Spencer! Time to get up for school! Spencer, did you hear me?"

Spencer stretched and pulled off the covers. "Yes, sir. Be right there," he yelled back. He lay in bed for a moment as he got his thoughts together. "Sully, you down there boy?" He jumped to the floor and found him snuggled up under the bed. "That storm really scared you last night, huh?" Walking to the bathroom, he rubbed his eyes. And when he went by the mirror a flash of yellow reflected back. He stood at the sink, splashed water on his face and dried it off with a towel. He hung the towel on the hook behind the door and on the way out he didn't notice the face in the mirror wasn't his own.

He put on the jeans and shirt his grandmother had laid out for him and gave Sully a quick kiss on the head. He lifted his nose in the air. "Mmm, Gram must have made bacon and eggs. Come on down, Sully, and I'll get you some breakfast too. You must be starved." Spencer grabbed his backpack and headed down the stairs.

CHAPTER TWO

"Good morning, Spencer," Will said. "I'm glad you could join us."

"Mornin'," he said as he put his backpack by the door.

"I'm off to meet Roberto so you guys have a good day at school. Mom, call me if you need help in the office when Sofia takes Anna this afternoon." Will grabbed his truck keys off the counter. "And, Em, don't upset Rosebud and Peaches if you go to the barn."

"Hey, did I miss breakfast?" Spencer said as he looked around the kitchen.

"No, why?" Kate asked, pouring another cup of coffee.

"I could've sworn I smelled—oh well, I'll just look in the fridge for something. I'm so hungry I could eat a..." His words vanished as he came out of the refrigerator with a chicken leg in his mouth.

"Spencer!" Kate shouted. "You can't have fried chicken for breakfast—put that back and get some cereal." She grabbed the chicken.

"Oh, but it tastes so good." He licked his lips. "It's like I've never had it before!"

"You look like a dog with a bone!" Emily said, laughing.

"Emily, hush up or you're gonna make matters worse."

There was a knock on the door and Sofia stuck her head in the kitchen. *"Buenos días."*

"Good morning." Kate smiled. "Come on in."

Anna was a smaller version of her mother with smooth light brown skin and long black hair. The only difference was Anna's hair was pulled back in a single braid tied at the end with a bow.

"How are you feeling, Anna?"

"A lot better today. It's weird. Yesterday after lunch I felt really bad but today I feel okay. Mom even made my favorite breakfast--bacon and eggs--and I ate everything on my plate."

"So, *you* had my bacon and eggs," Spencer complained. "I knew I smelled them from somewhere."

"I don't think it's possible that you smelled them all the way from their house unless you grew a bigger nose in your sleep," Emily said, and she and Anna giggled.

"You guys are hilarious," Spencer said, grabbing the box of cereal.

"Anyway, it's really been strange," Sofia said. "She felt the same way two weeks ago, so I thought it best we get her to the doctor today. We have an appointment at two o'clock."

"But we're presenting our projects this afternoon," Emily said.

"Miss Sloan said I could turn mine in next week," Anna replied.

"But you won't be there to see me present mine. I did it on Newton's Law of Gravity."

"Oh, I'm sorry I'll miss that." Anna smiled at Kate. "You can tell me all about it tomorrow."

"What did you do yours on?" Emily asked.

"Well, since I was sick my mom helped me. We made up a real business. We invented a product to sell. Then we figured out how much money it would take to make the product and we compared it to how much money we could sell it for. Right, Mom?"

Sofia smiled. "That's it exactly."

"That sounds very interesting," Emily said laughing.

"Well, what's interesting to me may not be to you," Anna said.

"I think you hit the nail right on the head," Kate added. "It's amazing to me that you two are friends—you're as different as night and day. One thing's for sure though, you're both just like your mothers."

"Well, this mother better get to work if I'm going to leave early today." Sofia kissed Anna on the cheek. "Now, you be in the school office at one-thirty sharp and I'll pick you up there. *Te amo, Anna,*" she said as she walked down the hall.

"I love you, Anna," Spencer groaned theatrically as he took his last bite of cereal.

"That's not nice, Spencer," Emily said. "Gram, Anna and I are gonna go to the barn and see Rosebud, okay?"

"We leave in ten minutes, so hurry up," Kate said, heading into the den.

CHAPTER TWO

Spencer finished his breakfast and put his bowl in the sink. He lifted his nose in the air and got a passing whiff of sweet flowers, fescue grass and the bitter aroma of chickweed. "What's going on?" he wondered as he grabbed his backpack and went out the door.

Now the smells were coming through loud and clear—everything was HUGE! It was like someone turned up the volume on his nose—and his ears! He turned around and could hear his grandmother washing out his bowl in the sink. He could hear the tractor from Ennis Tucker's farm three miles up the road. "That must be why I smell fresh-cut grass," he thought to himself. He turned in the direction of the barn. He heard little giggles and could just barely make out Emily's words:

"He hasn't even finished his project yet—I don't know how he ever expects to go to vet school."

Kate came out of the house and headed for the car. "Come on, Spencer, we'll pick up the girls at the barn."

"Good morning, Spencer."

Spencer looked up as he was about to get in the car but didn't see anyone. He looked past the row of hedges that bordered the pasture and could see Rio and Blue grazing in the distance.

"Who said that?" he asked.

"What did you say?" Kate asked as she was getting in the car.

Spencer looked around again and thought he must be going crazy after the morning he'd already had. "Um, nothing, Gram I just thought..."

He looked around one more time and there, standing by the fence, was Abbey staring at him.

CHAPTER THREE

SULLY, IS THAT YOU?

"Gram, could you please roll the window down?"

"Sure," she said, glancing in the rearview mirror. "Are you okay? You look like you've seen a ghost."

"Yes, ma'am, I'm all right—it's just been a weird morning."

She pulled up to the barn and the girls came running out. They piled into the car and Kate drove back up the gravel road, past the house and onto the main road.

"Oh, that Rosebud is so cute!" Anna exclaimed to Emily, who was sitting in the back with Spencer.

"I know, my dad says we can start training her this summer. You can help if you want," Emily said.

"Yeah, that'd be fun. Spencer! What are you doing?" Anna shouted when she saw Spencer hanging his head out the window.

"What?" he sounded agitated.

"What are you doing with your head out the window?" Emily asked.

"It just feels good," he said, "and the smells this morning are unbelievable! I feel like I can't get enough of just...air."

Kate watched in the mirror as Spencer stuck his head back out the window. His straight red hair was pinned flat against his head but the smile on his face and the squint of his eyes reminded her of...a dog! She was beginning to piece together Spencer's strange morning and what it all meant. With her thoughts wandering, the front tire slipped off the road and she had to fight with the steering wheel to get control again.

"Sorry about that, kids," she said, glancing again at Spencer. "There was something in my eye. Anna, tell me how you've been feeling. What are your symptoms? Do you know what that word means?"

Emily jumped in. "It means, you know like...did you throw up or did you have a fever or something like that."

"Thank you for explaining it, Emily," Kate said.

"Well, my stomach hurt a lot," Anna said, "and I felt like I wanted to throw up but I never did. I just wanted to lie on the sofa and watch T.V."

"Oh, you were tired all of the time?" Kate asked.

"Yes, but then by the next day, I was okay again. It's been the same both times."

Emily was listening carefully from the back seat. She hit Spencer and he pulled his head back into the car.

"Em, you really should try this," he exclaimed. "It's great!"

"I don't want to. It's silly, and besides, I'll mess up my hair. Hey," she whispered, "did you hear what Anna just said about her symptoms?"

"No, in case you haven't noticed I've been busy," he said as he tried to brush the hair out of his eyes.

"Well, from what she described it sounds just like Sully."

"Can dogs have what people have?" Spencer asked.

"I don't know. Let's wait and see what her doctor says today and then we can ask Dr. Miles."

"Oh, that reminds me—hey, Gram, would you mind feeding Sully when you get home?" Spencer asked.

"Sure but I have to stop by Tucker's store first. Will that be okay?"

"Yeah, he was sleeping when I left anyway."

She looked at Spencer again in the mirror. "Was he still feeling bad?"

"I don't think so—he just wasn't ready to get up."

The car pulled up to the curb in front of the school. Spring Valley Elementary was a single-story red-brick building with a flagpole at the front entrance. There were other children being dropped off at the same time, scurrying around in every direction trying to get to their classes. They all seemed the same—bogged down with backpacks that looked like they weighed more than their owners.

"Thanks, Gram, tell Mr. Tucker hello!" Emily teased as she made kissing noises while getting out of the car.

"You're very funny," Kate said, "but I love you anyway. Have a good day, Spencer and Anna."

"Bye, Gram. Bye, Grandma Kate," and they shut the doors behind them. The three children walked together to the flagpole and said their goodbyes.

"There he is—the redheaded sapsucker!"

Spencer turned around to see Dwight Fitch standing behind him. He was a tall, husky boy with thick, dark hair. He could look down on Spencer by about five inches and took the opportunity every chance he got. He was flanked on each side by the Pitsner twins. You would never have known they were brothers, much less twins. They both had blonde hair, but Todd's was straight and hung in his face, which led to a constant habit of him flicking it back with two fingers. Shawn's was curly and cut close to his head as if to disguise its wiry appearance.

At the sound of Dwight's voice Emily and Anna turned around just in time to see Shawn grab Spencer's lunch bag.

"Oh, let's see what Granny fixed the poor sapsucker today," he sneered, looking into the bag.

"Give it back!" Emily demanded, snatching it back from Shawn.

CHAPTER THREE

"Oh, that's it, sapsucker. Get your little sister and her south-of-the-border friend to fight your battles for you," Todd taunted. "You're a real brave man."

At this, Spencer couldn't help himself. He turned his head slightly and gave them a cutting glance. He could feel himself stiffening up. His lip rose slightly showing his teeth. He knew what he was doing but there was no stopping it. He was growling at the three of them! Emily and Anna stared at him, confusion on their faces, and the boys burst out laughing.

"Now the little bird thinks he's a dog!" Dwight chuckled, doubled over leaning against the flag pole. Spencer's face turned red with embarrassment. He breathed a sigh of relief when the bell rang, signaling the start of class. The three boys walked away with Todd howling like a wolf while the other two continued their rounds of laughter.

"What are you doing, Spencer?" Emily asked, hand on hip.

"I don't know," he said, his voice still quivering, wanting to slip back into a growl. "I can't control it. There's definitely something weird going on."

"Well, you better start to control it or those boys are going to make sure you have the worst day of your life. Come on, Anna, let's get to class." Emily handed Spencer his lunch bag and the two girls set off across the front lawn of the school.

* * * * * * * * * * *

Spencer found his seat near the back of the class and pulled out his American History book, notepad and pencil. He glanced over at Dwight laughing with another boy. Spencer was sure the morning's episode would be spread around the whole school by lunchtime. His only consolation was the twins were not in any of his classes. So, basically it was his word against Dwight's. His teacher had already started writing the morning's assignment on the blackboard by the time he arrived.

She wrote ten questions and turned to the class. "These are the questions that will be on your final exam next week. I suggest you write them down."

Spencer began to write but was distracted by a sweet aroma coming from the girl that sat in front of him. Her name was Nicole Darling. They had gone to school together since kindergarten, but as Dwight Fitch liked to put it, she was definitely out of Spencer's league. Most days she wore her long, wavy, blond hair pulled back in a ponytail. Today, however, she had a simple blue barrette on one side which held back her bangs. The smell was so strong that Spencer couldn't concentrate. He found himself leaning forward in his chair trying to get a better whiff. He had his eyes closed, trying to pick out the changing fragrances that were caught in the air whenever she moved her head. He was paralyzed. It was like all his other senses had stopped working and had decided to focus their energy on one enjoyment: the smell of Nicole's hair.

"Spencer," he heard the voice but couldn't open his eyes. "Spencer, is there something I can help you with?"

It was Nicole. She had turned all the way around in her seat and they were now face to face. He slowly opened his left eye and then his right: his brain followed. He realized he was leaning so far forward in his chair there was no going back. He lost his balance and toppled forward, landing in the aisle between the desks. Stunned, he lay on the floor for a moment.

The teacher was now standing over top of him. The entire class was roaring with laughter, led of course, by Dwight Fitch. Spencer struggled to get to his feet. His face, for the second time that day, was red from embarrassment. As he pulled his chair and desk back upright he looked at Nicole, who was smiling, not laughing, at him.

"Are you having a problem today, Mr. Sweetwater?" his teacher asked, helping him put his desk back in place.

"No, ma'am, no problems—but could I be excused for a moment?" he asked, looking down at the floor.

"Yes," she said, "that's probably a good idea. Get the hall pass off my desk—I'll give you ten minutes."

"Thank you." Spencer walked to her desk, tripping over his backpack and almost falling again.

Dwight was still snickering as he passed by his desk and Spencer could hear him say "sapsucker" under his breath. He felt his lip getting set in the growl position again and put his hand over his mouth until he was safely out of the room. He wandered down the hall in a daze talking to himself all the way to the bathroom. Once there, he looked under the stall doors to make sure he was alone. He paced in front of the mirrors looking down at the floor. Every time he passed a mirror the same reflection of yellow would flash back, and when it finally caught his eye, he stopped. He slowly looked up and stared at the face looking back at him.

"No way!" he yelled out. "Sully, is that you?"

A little voice from inside his head whispered, **"I think so."**

Spencer couldn't believe what he was seeing; the same big brown eyes and the same black nose and floppy yellow ears of the dog he had just left at home. "Why am I seeing you when I'm looking at me? It can't be!"

"But I think it is," said the little voice again.

The door began to open and Spencer ran into a stall. He could hear someone washing his hands and decided he might as well make use of the time he had. He raised the lid.

"That's not how I do it."

"Be quiet!" Spencer blurted out. He put his hands over his mouth but it was too late.

"Spencer Sweetwater, is that you in there?"

Spencer waited for a moment before answering in a low voice. "Yeah, who wants to know?"

"It's Jonas...Jonas Walker."

Spencer thought for a moment. "Hey, Jonas, could you stay there for a minute? I need to ask you something."

"Sure, you know it always takes me a while to go anywhere."

"Now, you keep quiet," Spencer pleaded. "I need to ask him some questions about how and why this could be happening to us."

"Are you talking to me?" Jonas asked.

"Ah—no, just to myself." He whispered to Sully. "Remember, quiet." He pulled himself together and opened the stall door. Jonas was still washing his hands when Spencer came out.

"Could you hand me a couple of paper towels?" Jonas asked. Spencer handed him the paper towels and watched as Jonas pushed the control switch which moved his black, metal wheelchair toward the trash can. "Now, you said you had a question for me."

"Yeah, it's a hypo-ledical question."

Jonas couldn't help but snicker a little over the mangled word.

"Just tell him already!" Sully urged.

"I told you to be quiet and let me handle this," Spencer said. It was then he realized he was having this conversation in his head and not out loud. "Awesome!" Unfortunately that was out loud.

"Oh," Jonas said, "you mean my new chair? Yeah, it is awesome. I don't have to push my wheels anymore. Everything's controlled by this little switch. Watch this!" He turned the switch to the right which made him go around in circles. "Sweet, huh?" He gradually came to a stop in front of Spencer. "Sorry, so what is your...*hypothetical* question?"

"You know a lot about molecules and cells and stuff, don't you?"

Jonas began to laugh.

"What's so funny?" Spencer asked.

"What's funny is that we've been in the same class together our whole lives and you don't even know me. Well, I guess you've figured out that I'm African-American and I wear glasses, but besides that, I think your little sister knows more about me than you do."

"Well, that's because she's into the same things as you and you're in that weird club together."

CHAPTER THREE

"You mean the science club?" Jonas noticed Spencer looking at his wheelchair while he was talking. "Are you sure that's why or is it maybe something else?"

Spencer looked clueless. "Like what?"

"He thinks you're afraid of his wheelchair," Sully said.

"I'm not afraid of the wheelchair!" Spencer said out loud.

"I didn't say you were. I wouldn't be in it if I didn't have to be, believe me."

"Why do you have to be?" Spencer asked. "I've heard it has to do with your spine or something."

"I have spinal muscular atrophy. It's a genetic disorder that affects my muscles. That's why I study molecules and cells and stuff. Maybe one day I'll be able to find a cure—and walk!"

"I'm sorry," Spencer said. "I didn't mean to make you talk about it."

"No, it's okay. I wish more people would ask me instead of acting like they're afraid of me."

"What's he saying?" Sully asked.

"He thinks we're afraid of him," Spencer said in his thoughts.

"I'm not afraid of him. He seems nice." Spencer had the sensation of wagging his tail. He pulled at the seat of his pants and shook one leg.

"Oh!" he said to Sully, "that tickles."

"I know! Isn't wagging your tail fun!" Sully exclaimed.

The bell rang.

"Oh, my gosh! My teacher is going to kill me." Spencer started for the door.

"Hey, what was your question?" Jonas asked.

"Later! I have to get this pass back to my teacher," Spencer shouted as he ran out of the bathroom. A second later the door opened again. Spencer stuck his head back in. "Sorry, Jonas," and held the door open for him.

* * * * * * * * * * *

Lunch couldn't have come quickly enough for Spencer. He bypassed the long line for chocolate milk and headed outside to the lunch tables. He reached in his pocket and pulled out his cell phone to call home.

"You're only supposed to use that for emergencies," Sully said.

"Wouldn't you say this is an emergency?" Spencer asked. "Why do I keep doing that?" he thought, "I've got to stop talking to him. This isn't real...this isn't real!" He dialed the phone and his grandmother answered.

"Gram, I'm glad you picked up."

"What's wrong, Spencer?"

"Nothing, I'm fine but could you do me a favor and check on Sully? Um—I just want to make sure he's all right."

"Hang on a minute." He waited for a moment and then she came back to the phone. "Well, I guess he's all right. He's not in your room. He's probably fine, Spencer. I'm sure he's just out with your father in the orchard. Is there anything else you wanted?"

"No thanks, Gram, I'll see you later." He put the phone back in his pocket, sat down on the bench and pulled the sandwich from his bag.

"I don't understand this at all," he thought as he took a bite.

"You know I can hear everything you're thinking," Sully whispered.

"Okay," Spencer said. "If you're really here, then what am I thinking now?" Spencer thought really hard and finally Sully said:

"You think your sandwich is delicious but you wish Gram would have cut the crust off for us."

"Wrong, wrong, wrong!" Spencer protested. "Ha! I wish she would have cut the crust off for me!" Spencer was standing at the table, shaking his fist in the air when he noticed everyone was staring at him. He sat down and focused on his sandwich again.

"Spencer?"

"Spencer?"

"I'm not talking to you," he snapped to Sully.

"Remember the wish?"

"What?"

"Remember the wish you made last night on Lakena's moon?"

"Yeah, what about it?" All of a sudden it hit him. "Oh, my gosh!" He stood up from the table. "It came true!"

"I think so," Sully agreed.

"Okay, let's pull ourselves together," Spencer glanced around. "We'll just get through the rest of the day and then Gram will pick us up and she'll fix this." He finished his lunch and walked over to the trash can. "You just keep quiet, Sully."

"Hey, Spencer, can I say one more thing?"

"Yeah, boy, what is it?"

"I love being with you."

Spencer could feel the tickling again as he walked down the sidewalk. He pulled at the seat of his pants and shook one leg—he knew Sully was wagging his tail.

CHAPTER FOUR

WHAT'S FOR DINNER?

The drive home from school that day was the longest of Spencer's life. He needed to get home, check on Sully and talk to his grandmother about the wish he made on Lakena's moon. When they pulled into their driveway from the main road they could see a shiny, red sports car sitting in front of the house.

"Whose car is that?" Emily asked.

"I don't know but it has out-of-state license tags," Kate said, pulling up behind it.

The kids jumped out of the car and Emily went running into the house. Spencer waited for his grandmother by the front steps. She had stopped to pull a few stubborn weeds growing in her flower bed.

"Gram, can I talk to you about the story you told me last night?"

"I think that would be a good idea, Spencer. Let's see who's visiting us, then we'll go up to your room."

They both went into the house and found Will in the living room with a tall, rugged man wearing a cowboy hat. The man stood up and took his hat off when Kate came into the room.

"Mom," Will said, "this is Billy Wynn."

CHAPTER FOUR

"How do you do, ma'am?" he asked.

"Nice to meet you, Mr. Wynn," Kate said as she stuck out her hand to shake his. "This is my grandson, Spencer, and that was Emily, my granddaughter, who just went running through here."

Billy had on shiny black boots that caught Spencer's eye. "They're genuine alligator," he said to Spencer. "You ever seen anything like 'em?"

"No, sir," Spencer said when he pulled his eyes away from the boots and looked up.

The man was GIGANTIC and had jet-black hair. When he talked his voice was powerful and echoed throughout the room. His black suit matched his dark eyes and Spencer immediately felt uncomfortable.

"Well, I've heard a lot about you, Spencer. Your dad tells me you're in the sixth grade over at Spring Valley. Maybe you know my nephew."

"What's his name?"

"It's Dwight, Dwight Fitch."

"Yes—um, I know him." Spencer swallowed hard, choking on his words.

"Great!" Billy said. "When I get settled into my new house I'll have you and Dwight over." Spencer tried to produce a smile, but all he could manage was a scrunched-up face that looked like he had smelled something really bad.

"Mr. Wynn is buying Ennis Tucker's farm," Will said.

"Yes, I know," Kate replied. "I was at his store this morning and he told me all about it."

"Mr. Tucker can't sell his farm!" Spencer insisted.

"Well he can and he did, young man—or at least it'll be mine by the end of the month," Billy said as he sat back down on the sofa. "Once I get through with that land it's gonna look entirely different."

He crossed one leg over the other as he twirled his hat in the air. He was sweating and took his handkerchief out to wipe his forehead. Spencer could see something high on his boot that looked bright and shiny. He took a step closer and saw two swords, crossed at the blades, with a snake winding between them. Billy noticed Spencer staring at the boots and pulled his pant leg down to cover the swords.

"You're not gonna farm?" Kate asked.

"No, Mom," Will interrupted. "Mr. Wynn is going to tear everything down and build a resort. He was just telling me about it when you came in."

"A resort! What kind of a resort?" she asked. "I don't think we have many folks around here that would be interested in swimming or playing tennis."

"No, no," Billy said smugly, "all of our guests will be from out of town. My plan is to keep the main house for myself, with some fixin' up of course, and then build a hotel. I do it all the time. I've bought farms from Maine to Florida and as far west as Texas. People come from all over to stay at my world-famous resorts."

"World-famous, huh?" Kate laughed. "Seems to me you might be upsettin' the turnip truck if you build that resort in this part of the county. People around here don't really like a lot of change."

"Yeah!" Spencer shouted.

"That's enough, Spencer," Will demanded. "Go upstairs and start your homework."

"Yes, sir."

"Good to meet you, son," Billy said. "Remember, I want you and Dwight to come over to the house." Spencer was already halfway up the stairs and knew no one could see him roll his eyes.

"Oh, Spencer, I forgot," Will shouted, "Sully has an appointment with Dr. Miles on Monday."

"Thanks, Dad!" he yelled back.

Spencer got to his room and threw his backpack on the desk. He looked around for Sully and didn't see him anywhere. He said in a quiet whisper to himself. "Are you in there boy?"

There was no reply.

"Sully, I know I told you to keep quiet but it's okay. Now you can talk." Spencer waited, but there was nothing. He heard laughter coming from down the hall. He walked down to Emily's room and pushed open the door—and there, on the floor, were Emily and Sully. He was on his back and she was rubbing his tummy.

"There you are. You had me worried," Spencer said.

Emily giggled. "I was right here."

"Not you, I mean Sully." Spencer sat down on the floor and began to pet him too. Sully gave a little bark, rolled over and started to chew on Spencer's shoelace.

"He seems to be feeling better," she said. "You see, it's just like Anna. She said that all of a sudden she started to feel better too."

Anna came bouncing into the room. "Hey guys, whatcha doin'? How was your project, Emily? Did the class like it? I mean did the class understand it?"

"Very funny," Emily said. "It was wonderful, of course."

"What did the doctor say is wrong with you?" Spencer asked anxiously.

"Why, Spencer! I didn't know you cared," Anna said, batting her eyes at him.

"I just want to know because maybe Sully has the same problem you do. So what did he say?"

"Allergies," she replied.

"Like to trees and stuff?" Emily asked.

"No—to food!"

"You're allergic to food?" Spencer questioned.

"Some kinds of food," she said. "They did some tests and I'm mostly allergic to corn."

"Well, that doesn't sound so bad," Spencer said. "So what, like you just can't eat corn on the cob?"

"No!" she exclaimed, "I can't have anything with corn in it—and just about everything my mother makes has corn in it. Like my favorite—enchiladas, and my other favorite—tortilla chips."

"You can't ever eat them again?" Emily asked.

"Maybe, when I get older. The doctor said I might out grow it." She looked down at Sully lying on the floor beside her. "So, do you think he's allergic to food too?"

"Yeah, he has the same symptoms as you," Emily answered.

"He seems to be feeling okay now," Anna said as she rolled Sully over again to rub his tummy.

"I don't think he's eaten today," Spencer said.

"Well then, it *would* make sense that his problem could be food," Emily said.

"What do you mean?" Spencer asked.

"Because he didn't have supper last night and he didn't have breakfast this morning. He hasn't had anything in his stomach to make him feel bad."

"Hey, you're right," Spencer agreed. "Dad told me he made an appointment for him on Monday to see Dr. Miles, but maybe we should check the food he eats to see if there's anything in it that could make him sick."

"That's a great idea," Emily said. "Let's go downstairs and look at the bag."

"How about you guys go and I'll stay here," Spencer said hesitantly.

"Why?" Anna asked.

"Because the man that's buying Mr. Tucker's farm is still down there and he's Dwight Fitch's uncle. He thinks Dwight and me should be best friends. But besides that, there's something weird about him. Maybe you could just bring the bag of food up here."

"Okay, I'll go," Emily said. "I'll be back in a minute."

As she tiptoed down the hallway she heard car tires spinning in the gravel outside. She looked out the window by the stairway and saw the red sports car heading up the driveway toward the main road. She started down the stairs and could hear her grandmother and father talking in the living room. From the sound of her father's voice she could tell there was something wrong. She made her way down the steps and stopped by the last post in the banister. Even though she'd been told not to eavesdrop on private conversations she couldn't help herself.

"He can't take it if he doesn't have proof," she heard her grandmother say.

"Well, maybe he does have proof," Will argued. "Mr. Wynn said he had clear title to the land."

"How could he?" Kate asked. "This is ridiculous! No man can just come into your house and say that he's gonna take your land! Well, I'll tell you one thing: I'll never give up Sweetwater Farms to some smooth-talkin', sports-car-drivin', alligator-wearin' cowboy! And it'll be over my dead body that somebody turns this beautiful land into a golf course!"

"Mom, just take it easy. I'll call our lawyer and see what he has to say about this."

"I'll tell you what he'll say—he'll say, where's the original deed to the land? And we'll say we don't know. No one's seen it for two hundred years. And he'll say—oh my, that could be a problem."

Emily heard the front door slam and she knew her grandmother had left. Then she heard her father say, "I need to speak to Mr. Daggett please—yes, I'll hold."

She quickly ran into the kitchen and opened the pantry door. She grabbed the bag of dog food and began to tiptoe back up the stairs. Once she reached the top step she ran to her room.

"That took you forever," Spencer complained. "Is Mr. Wynn still here?"

"No, he's gone. But listen to what I just heard." She sat down on the floor and said in a whisper, "That man wants to take our farm."

"No, he doesn't," Spencer argued. "He's buying Mr. Tucker's farm. You must have heard wrong."

"No, I didn't. Dad and Gram are real upset and they said something about him turning Sweetwater Farms into a golf course. I heard them say they don't know where the deed is. What's a deed?"

"I don't know," Anna said.

"Me either," said Spencer, "but I knew I didn't like him as soon as I saw those boots."

"What was wrong with his boots?" Emily questioned.

"They were made out of alligators!"

"YEWWW," Anna squealed. "That's yucky!"

"I know. Weird, huh?" Spencer replied.

"Well, I don't know anything about his boots, but I do know what I heard. Dad's on the phone right now with Mr. Daggett and he only calls him when there's a problem."

"I've got an idea!" Anna said excitedly. "Let's get on the computer and see what a deed is."

"Good thinking," Emily said.

"Hey, while you guys do that I'll check out the dog food," Spencer said. "Let me see the bag."

"Do you know what you're looking for?" Emily asked.

"I'm gonna look at the ingredients and see if there's any corn in it."

"Well, just because Anna's allergic to corn, doesn't mean that Sully is too."

"Yeah, but isn't that a good place to start?" Spencer began examining the bag.

The girls ran out of the room and into the playroom where the computer was. Sully rubbed his head on Spencer's leg trying to get his attention.

"Oh, you want to talk now?" Spencer asked as he rubbed Sully's ears. He looked into his eyes and remembered seeing that same face in the mirror at school just a few hours before. "Was it all just my imagination? Did it really happen?" He shrugged. "Well, whether it was real or not, we have to get you feeling better."

Sully's head tilted from side to side as if trying to understand what Spencer was saying.

CHAPTER FOUR

"I can't find the darn ingredients," Spencer thought to himself. Sully stood up and sniffed at the bag. He gave a little bark and placed his paw on the lower part of the bag.

"Oh, you think you found them?" Spencer asked with a chuckle as he lifted Sully's paw. Spencer jumped to his feet with a startled look on his face. There, under Sully's paw were the ingredients he'd been looking for. He stood back from the bag and looked at Sully. Sully stood back from the bag and looked at Spencer.

"We're still together!" Spencer shouted. "You still know what I'm thinking!" Sully barked and ran around in a circle. He jumped on Spencer and knocked him to the floor. As Sully was licking Spencer's face, the girls came running back into the room.

"Why are you two playing at a time like this?" Emily snapped.

"We're not playing—we were looking for the ingredients. And what do you mean at a time like this?"

"We could be losing the farm!" she shouted. "We looked up the word deed on the internet and the definition is—*legal paperwork that shows ownership.*"

"So what does that mean?" Spencer asked.

"It means that Gram and Dad don't own Sweetwater Farms! I heard them say that they don't have the deed!"

"Well, who has it then?" Anna asked.

"I don't know. Maybe Mr. Wynn has it, and that's why Gram and Dad are so upset."

"They *have* to own this farm," Spencer insisted, "it's been in our family for generations. Gram was just telling me last night about our great-great-great-great grandmother who lived on this land two hundred years ago!"

"Well, that doesn't prove anything," Emily argued, "and Gram told Dad we need proof." The grandfather clock in the hallway chimed four times and Anna jumped up from the floor.

"I have to go," she said. "My mom told me I have to help her with supper. More like we have to figure out what I can eat for supper. I'll see you guys tomorrow."

"Hey, since tomorrow's Saturday, do you want to help me clean Rosebud's stall?" Emily asked. "We can play with her too."

Anna's voice trailed back from down the hallway: "Oh, yeah, that'd be fun. I hope you find out what's making Sully sick."

"Yeah, let's get back to it," Spencer said as he grabbed the bag of food again. "We'll have to wait 'til later to see what Dad says about the deed thing. Besides, you were eavesdropping and weren't supposed to hear it anyway." He read out loud to Emily: "Chicken byproducts, water, animal fat—that all sounds gross!" He stopped reading. "Why do dogs eat this stuff anyway? Why don't they eat what we eat?"

"I don't know, just keep reading," she said, somewhat annoyed.

"Egg product, corn, wheat flour--"

"Hey, stop! You just said corn!"

"I did? Everything was starting to sound the same."

"So, here's what we can do," Emily said, gazing at Sully. "We can make a controlled experiment, just like Isaac Newton did!"

Sully looked at Emily and cocked his head to one side.

"Oh, boy," Spencer complained, "here we go."

"But not with gravity," she added. She began to pace around the room, talking to herself as if Sully and Spencer weren't there. "If we isolate the volatile conditions and remove all of the other possible variables then--"

"Um—excuse me," Spencer said waving his hand in front of her to get her attention. "Remember us? In English please."

"Okay, we'll stop feeding Sully his regular dog food, at least until he goes to see Dr. Miles on Monday. If he doesn't get sick we'll know the dog food was his problem."

Spencer raised his hand as if he were in school. "I have a question, Professor Sweetwater."

Emily grinned. "Yes, student."

CHAPTER FOUR

"If we don't feed him his dog food, what *will* we feed him?" Spencer rubbed Sully's ears.

"Great question, Student Sweetwater!" she thought and then it came to her. "We'll feed him what we eat. We'll fix his supper the same as ours—the same breakfast and the same lunch too."

"But I like salami sandwiches for lunch," Spencer argued.

"Well, then he'll have salami sandwiches too!" She sat back down on the floor and scratched Sully's head.

"Hey, what's going on in here?" Kate asked as she came into the room. She saw the bag of dog food on the floor. "What is *that* doing up here?"

"Um...er," Spencer tried to think of something to say. He knew she wouldn't like the idea of Sully eating salami sandwiches.

"We were trying to get him to eat a little," Emily blurted out trying to save her brother.

"Well, did he?" Kate asked.

"No." Spencer sighed. "But he does seem to be feeling better."

"Well, good," Kate said. "Your dad tells me he's going to see Dr. Miles on Monday. That's a good thing for our little boy," she said in a baby voice as she bent down and kissed Sully's nose. He took it as an opportunity for a belly scratch and rolled onto his back. "Emily, can I talk to Spencer?"

"Sure. I need to look up something on the computer anyway. By the way, Gram, what's for dinner tonight?" Emily asked as she was leaving the room.

"Pot pie—isn't that your favorite?"

"Yes, ma'am. And I'll probably eat enough for two!" She said looking back and winking at Spencer.

"Spencer, before you say anything, I think I know what's going on," Kate confessed as she knelt down on the floor by Spencer and Sully.

"You do? But how?"

"It has to do with the story I told you last night about the spring moon and Suri Lakena, right?"

"Yeah, but how'd you--?"

She interrupted, "Never mind." She looked down at Sully who was falling asleep. "We're all going over to Mr. Tucker's farm tomorrow morning to look at a tractor your father wants to buy. When we get back, I want to take you somewhere. There's something I want you to see. Do you think you can wait until then?"

"Yes, ma'am," he said reluctantly as he looked at Sully, "we'll wait." Kate looked toward the door. "Emily, you can come tomorrow too. You might as well come in—I know you're there."

Turning pink, Emily pushed the door open and peeked in the room. "I just happened to be walking by." She plopped down on the floor. "So, what's the big secret?"

"That's for Spencer to tell, if he wants." Kate rose up from the floor, grabbing the bed for support. "Supper will be ready in an hour. You kids finish your homework; then you should have just enough time to see Peaches and Rosebud before we eat." She left the room closing the door behind her.

"So, tell me the secret," Emily begged.

"Okay, but if I tell you, you have to promise not to tell anyone."

"I promise."

"No, I mean really promise like you've never promised before in your life."

She nodded enthusiastically. "I do. I really promise. Now, what is it?"

"Gram told me a story last night before I went to bed."

"Yeah, so?"

"Just be quiet and listen. I know that's something new for you—but try."

"Okay, sorry."

"Well, the story was about our great-great-great-great grandmother—gosh, that's a lot of greats! Anyway, her name was Suri

Lakena and she was a Native American Indian. She was very special and the people of her village loved her very much. When she died, they said she became the moon and that every night she would watch over them. They also believed in the spring there would be a full moon with special powers. They said if you made a wish on that moon, then it had to come true—and well, the full moon was last night."

"So, did you make a wish?"

Spencer was hesitant. "Yes, I did."

"Well, what was your wish?"

He sat down in the chair by her desk and looked at Sully as he slept on the floor.

"Well, the first part of it was that I wanted to know what's wrong with Sully."

"That's a good wish," Emily said trying to relieve his noticeable tension.

"Yeah, but that's not all. I wished that we would be together... forever."

"What's wrong with that?" she questioned. "Sully can be your dog forever or at least for as long as he lives."

"Well, I think something got a little mixed up as I was making my wish. When I said the word together, it actually happened."

"What happened?"

"We got put together," Spencer said, relieved to have it out. "Sully's inside me, I mean, he's not really inside me 'cause he's lying on the floor, but we got connected somehow. He knows what I'm thinking. And, there's something else—he can talk!"

"Okay, now I've heard everything." She rolled her eyes and got up from the floor. "If you don't want to tell me what's going on between you and Gram you don't have to. But you don't have to make up some silly story either—I'm not *stupid*, you know."

Spencer stood up and grabbed Emily's arm as she was turning toward the door. "No, it's true, I swear! I'm telling you because I need your help."

Emily looked at Spencer. "Well, if you're telling the truth, then show me something."

"What?" Spencer asked unsure what she meant.

"Prove it to me. If you want my help I need to see what you're talking about." She sat down in the chair, crossed her legs and folded her arms across her chest. "I'm waiting."

Spencer thought for a moment and pulled a piece of paper out of Emily's notebook. He wrote something on the paper and stuck it in his pant's pocket. He stood back from the desk and looked at Sully. The yellow dog lifted his head, looked at Spencer and then at Emily. He got up from the floor and walked over to her. He sat down in front of her and lifted one paw for her to shake. Emily reached down and grabbed his paw.

"What does that prove?" she argued. "He does that all the time."

Spencer reached for the piece of paper in his pocket and gave it to Emily. The words written on the paper were *Sully, say hello to Emily.* "Okay, wait a minute," she said, flustered "let me think about this."

She looked down at Sully still sitting in front of her. His gaze seemed to almost mesmerize her as she stared into his eyes. Then, all of a sudden, she jumped up from her chair as if she'd seen a ghost.

"What's wrong?" Spencer asked, even though he already knew the answer.

"He—um," she paused thinking about her words for a moment, "he just winked at me!"

Spencer fell to the floor laughing. "Did you tell him to do that?" Emily demanded, her hands placed firmly on her hips.

"You should have seen your face!" He howled again as he gave Sully a big hug. "Great work, boy, we got her good!"

"Okay," she said, "I guess you did get me. Maybe you're telling me the truth after all." She sat down in the chair and took a deep breath. "Now start at the beginning and tell me everything, don't leave out a single detail."

Spencer began the story again and Emily clung to every word. She asked question after question until Spencer was so tired he finally lay down on the bed. After she was completely satisfied she'd gotten all the information she could, she began to look through her science book.

"What are you looking for?" Spencer asked.

"In the science club we did some research on molecular physics."

"What's that?"

"That's when atoms or particles of matter, like you and Sully," she explained, "are pulled together by electromagnetic waves."

"I'm sorry I asked."

"It could explain everything!" she exclaimed. "So, Gram knows about this?"

"I think so," he said, "and that's why she said we'd talk about it tomorrow. She said there's somewhere she wants to take me. Maybe she'll explain it then."

"I know, tomorrow when you go over to Mr. Tucker's farm, I'll go and talk to Jonas."

"Do you think he can figure out what's happening to us?" Spencer asked.

"I'm not sure, but don't tell anyone else about this for now, at least not until I've had a chance to talk to him."

CHAPTER FIVE

PEE WEE & SWEETIE PIE

"S*pencer...Spencer.*"

He heard the words and could feel someone gripping his shoulder but he was too deep into his dream to wake up. They were walking at the edge of the hayfield near the barn. The sun was shining on her long, blond hair. He felt as if he were floating and Nicole kept repeating his name "*Spencer...Spencer...*"

"Spencer, wake up!" Emily shouted.

"What? Huh?" he mumbled trying to open his eyes.

"I've got Sully's breakfast," Emily whispered as she waved the plate of scrambled eggs and toast under his nose.

Spencer sat up in bed. "Um—I'll take some of that too!"

"It's not for you. I got up early, before Dad and Gram, so I could get Sully something to eat." When Emily put the plate on the floor Sully jumped off the bed and headed straight for it. He gobbled up the toast before she could even break it apart. "Wow, I think our experiment's going great so far. He loved his dinner last night and his breakfast this morning. He's a member of the Clean Plate Club!"

CHAPTER FIVE

"What's not to love about breakfast in bed?" Spencer rolled over and pulled up the covers. He glanced at the clock on his bedside table: six o'clock. "I can't believe you got us up so early!"

"That shows how much you know about doing an experiment," she said, pulling the plate away from Sully. "You have to be prepared. How would I have gotten his breakfast if Gram had been in the kitchen?"

"I never said I knew anything about experiments." Spencer yawned and stretched out his arms. "I'm going back to sleep now. Wake me in two hours."

"Wake yourself!" she snapped. "I don't know why I'm doing all this work if you're not going to help." On her way out the door, Emily bent down to pet Sully's head. "Don't worry, Sully. I'll make sure you get better—*all by myself.*"

Spencer called for Sully to jump up on the bed. The big dog took one giant leap and landed on top of Spencer. "You're right, Emily," Spencer admitted as he held Sully's face between his hands. "You've been doing all the work and Sully and I thank you very much. Don't we, boy? I'll tell you what, I'll get his lunch and supper today."

"Okay, that's a deal," she said. "But forget the salami and just give him the leftovers from dinner last night. He liked that a whole lot." At the door, she turned around and whispered, "Remember the plan today—you go to Mr. Tucker's farm and I'll go see Jonas. I'll meet you back here at the house." She pulled the door closed and Spencer and Sully went back to sleep.

❊ ❊ ❊ ❊ ❊ ❊ ❊ ❊ ❊ ❊ ❊

Spencer awoke to the sound of Roberto beeping the horn of his pickup truck. He ran to the bathroom, splashed some water on his face and brushed his teeth. He threw on his jeans from the day before and pulled a tee-shirt from the dresser by the window.

"Come on, Sully, let's go," he said excitedly as he patted his leg for

Sully to follow him. He ran down the stairs, grabbed a biscuit from the kitchen and went out the front door. "Good morning, Roberto!" he yelled as he jumped the steps of the porch and landed on the sidewalk.

"Good morning, Spencer," Roberto answered as he stepped into the house.

"We're almost ready," Will said as he came into the living room. "You know how women can be when they're getting ready to go somewhere."

"I heard that," Kate grumbled as she came in from the kitchen. "I had to gather a few things together for Ennis. Did I hear Spencer go through here already?"

"Yes, ma'am," Roberto said. "He's in the truck with Anna."

Anna and Spencer had already found their places in the back seat with Sully sprawled out between them.

"Spencer, let's leave Sully here," Will said, opening the door of the truck for his mother.

"Why can't he come?" Spencer pleaded. "He'll be a good boy. I'll watch him."

"Like you watched him at Mrs. Langford's house last Sunday? After he jumped on her and knocked the chocolate pound cake out of her hands, I don't know why she would ever invite us back."

"He only ate a couple of bites," Spencer pointed out as he and Anna laughed.

"Come on, son," Will urged. "I want to get over to Mr. Tucker's sometime this morning."

Spencer pulled Sully up from his comfortable spot on the seat and made him jump out of the truck. He slowly made his way to the front porch and curled up under the swing.

"We'll be back in a little while, boy," Spencer yelled out the window as they drove off.

❋ ❋ ❋ ❋ ❋ ❋ ❋ ❋ ❋ ❋ ❋

CHAPTER FIVE

The Tucker farm had been around almost as long as Sweetwater Farms. Ennis Tucker raised cows and grew some vegetables and hay but he spent most of his time at his little store over on Route 3. He mostly sold gas at the store but kept a few items stocked for the local farmers. Kate always knew if she ran out of milk or needed a loaf of bread Tucker's Store would save her from making the thirty-minute drive into town. He also kept basic hardware supplies so if Will and Roberto had a problem with a hose connection on the watering system or they ran out of nails to fix the roof on the old storage shed, Tucker's Store would have whatever they needed. Ennis Tucker prided himself on being an important part of the community. He didn't have any children, and since his wife's death six years earlier, he liked working at the store and talking to all of his neighbors more than he liked farming.

Ennis peeked out the bedroom window when he heard the sound of the truck pulling into the driveway. He went to the dresser and took the gold and silver ring off his finger. He gently placed it in the top drawer, and as the sun came through the window the light reflected off the emblem of the two crossed swords. He shut the drawer and went to meet the truck.

When he came out of the house he waved at Roberto and pointed toward the barn. He walked behind the white pickup truck as it slowly made its way down the gravel road. Ennis was a tall, thin man with the sun-weathered look of a farmer. His brownish gray hair was parted neatly on one side and it reached down just far enough in the back to touch the collar of his blue-and-white plaid shirt.

"I didn't see any sense in you parking all the way at the house when the tractor is in the shed behind the barn," he said pleasantly as they all piled out of the truck. He shook hands with Will and Roberto and opened the door for Kate.

"Good morning, Katie," he said in a soft voice as he reached for her hand to help her out of the truck.

She took his hand and offered a smile. "Good morning, Ennis."

"Can Anna and I go in the barn?" Spencer asked, jumping down from the truck.

"If it's all right with Mr. Tucker," Will agreed on his way to the shed.

"Can we, Mr. Tucker?"

"Sure kids. Maybe you can take a couple of the animals home with you. Since Mr. Wynn's buying the place, I have to get rid of everything, including the animals."

"Can we, Gram?" Spencer asked, almost breathless.

"I think we already have our hands full with a newborn foal," she argued. "Don't you think, Spencer?"

"Yes, ma'am," he said reluctantly.

She smiled. "But that doesn't mean you can't look."

"Go around to the back of the barn," Ennis said. "I've left the doors open for you."

The two children walked along the path by the split-rail fence until they came to a large wooden gate. Spencer unhooked the chain and they walked through. The barn doors were open, but because of the bright sunlight they couldn't see what was inside. Just as Spencer took a step into the barn he heard a loud screeching sound and something flew at his head, knocking him to the ground.

"Wow, what was that?" he cried out as Anna stood over him laughing.

"It was just a rooster," she said, pulling a piece of hay from his hair. "Come on, Spencer, let's see what else is in here."

Spencer pulled himself off the ground and followed her into the barn. It was big and very old. The front doors were opened just a little which let in a cool breeze. It disturbed the stillness and allowed the smells of hay, leather harnesses and sweet molasses grain to float through the air. As their eyes adjusted to the darkness they could see four stalls on the left side and three on the right. At the back corner, on the right, there was a wooden ladder that led to a loft where hay was stored. There were large milk cows in the first three stalls on the left and a few chickens were clambering around. Spencer and Anna moved over to the stalls on the right, and in the first one they saw a nanny goat with two kids.

"This must have been what Mr. Tucker wanted us to see," Anna said as she opened the wooden gate that kept them in the stall. "Look how cute they are! Maybe my dad will let me have one of these."

"Don't count on it," Spencer said, walking into the stall, closing the gate behind him.

They both sat on the stall floor and the little goats crawled all over them while their mother watched suspiciously from the corner.

Spencer looked up and turned his head toward the back of the barn. "What was that?"

"I didn't hear anything," Anna answered through her giggles at the goats.

"Yeah, there it is again." He stood up and looked down the row of stalls. "It sounds like crying."

"I still don't hear anything."

"I'm gonna check it out." He walked back through the wooden gate and slowly walked past the stalls, looking in each one as he went.

"Do you see anything?" Anna yelled from the first stall.

"Nothing, they're all empty--but I know I heard crying." He started back toward the goats, stopped and raised his nose in the air. A peculiar smell was coming from the back of the barn.

"I'm gonna check out one more thing," he hollered back to Anna.

As he made his way back to the last stall on the left he could hear the crying again. He peeked over the gate and there, standing in the corner of the stall, was the oddest-looking little animal he had ever seen. It was gray-brown and looked like it was part mule and part miniature horse, with a big head and huge ears flopping back and forth.

"Anna, come here, quick!"

Anna left the little goats and ran to the stall where Spencer was. She wasn't tall enough to see over the top of the gate so she looked through two boards on the side of the stall.

"It's a Sicilian donkey!" she yelled out.

"How do you know?"

"I've seen pictures. My grandparents have donkeys on their farm in Mexico. It's so small, it must be a baby." She opened the gate and Spencer followed her into the stall. "Look at his back," she said in a whisper. "He has the shadow of the cross."

"What do you mean?"

They both looked at the little donkey as he walked around in the corner of the stall. They saw a chocolate-brown line going down the center of his back and another line going across his shoulders, making a cross.

"Why do they call it the shadow of the cross?" Spencer questioned.

"Well, my grandfather told me that donkeys have always been used to help people carry things. He said there are many legends about the cross but he believed the donkey loved people so much that he wanted to carry all of their burdens. But instead of the people giving him their burdens they gave him the cross as a symbol of how much they loved him. I know Emily would say that it's just a silly story and the real reason is genetics. I guess it's whatever you want to believe."

"That's amazing!" Spencer exclaimed. "I can see it perfectly."

As he tried to move closer to get a better look, the donkey moved further away into the corner of the stall. Spencer began to hear the faint sound of crying again. It was coming from the donkey.

"He's crying," Spencer whispered to Anna.

"How do you know?"

"I hear him."

She looked amazed. "How can you hear him? Do you speak donkey language?"

"It's a long story," he said. "I'll tell you later."

He moved close to the little donkey. "What is it, little guy? What's wrong?"

CHAPTER FIVE

The donkey turned around and looked at him.

"I think he understands you," Anna said.

All of a sudden Spencer started hearing all kinds of words in his head. They were all jumbled and made no sense at all.

"Slow down, little fellow. I can't understand what you're trying to tell me." Spencer moved closer and stroked the donkey's neck. "Now take a deep breath and start over."

"He says he has to sell me! I just moved here and now he says he can't keep me and I have to find another home all over again! Where will I go? What will I do?"

Spencer continued stroking him. "Now, now, just calm down."

"Spencer? Did you hear me?" Anna asked. "I said I think he understands you."

Spencer looked at Anna. He realized the conversation he was having with the donkey was all taking place in his mind. She couldn't hear anything they were saying.

"This is so cool!" he shouted.

Anna made a face. "What are you talking about?"

"Okay, I have something to tell you but you have to keep it a secret."

Spencer began his story about the moon and Suri Lakena. Anna and the donkey seemed to hang on every word until he finished: "And so now I can understand what the animals are saying. I thought it was just Sully, but now I can hear the donkey too!"

Anna was kneeling on the floor of the stall stroking the donkey's long, floppy ears as he lay beside her in the straw.

"It's true," Spencer added. "I swear. That's why Emily didn't come with us this morning. She went to Jonas's house to explain everything to him so they could figure it out. She thinks it might have something to do with molectro, electro something or other. I don't remember what she said exactly."

The donkey let out a sigh and had stopped crying. Spencer could hear the sound of tiny footsteps walking above him. He looked up and saw a small black-and-tan cat. It had the black stripes of a tabby mixed with patches of tan like a calico. It stared at Spencer with piercing green eyes as it walked along the hay bales in the loft.

"Fiddle-dee-dee," said the little voice. **"I'm quite certain that you can't understand what I'm saying."**

"I sure can," Spencer hollered up to the loft. The cat stopped dead in her tracks and turned around to stare at him.

"Who are you talking to?" Anna asked.

"That little cat—see it?"

Anna strained her eyes and saw the little furry creature that now sat next to a bale of hay. "Can you really talk to her?"

"Yeah, but she seems to have a little attitude."

"Well, you'd have an attitude, too, if you were a domesticated house cat that was made to live in these unsightly conditions."

"What's she saying?" Anna inquired.

"She says she's supposed to be a house cat."

"Ask her why she's in the barn then?"

Spencer turned his words into thoughts and the cat jumped onto a bale of hay and began to lick its paws.

"Well, you see..." she said in a garbled voice.

"Wait," Spencer begged. "I can't understand you when you're giving yourself a bath. Could you please stop for a moment?"

"Oh, if I must. They do say, however, that cleanliness is next to godliness. And cats are the cleanest animals in the world!"

Anna pulled on his pant leg as he carried on his conversation with the cat.

"What'd she say?"

"Wait a minute," Spencer answered. "She's talking about cleanliness and godliness and stuff."

The little cat lay down and slowly waved its tail back and forth in the air. **"Continue asking your questions, young man."**

"First of all, what's your name?"

"Oh, let me just say that it was not my choice and it certainly does not reflect my truly unique qualities."

"Why do you talk so funny? I mean with all of those big words."

"Why whatever do you mean? I speak the King's English perfectly well. Unless, of course, you're referring to my purr-fect accent. It's my heritage of course. My ancestors were royalty in the court of Queen Victoria herself. So, it is purely by accident that I find myself here with these commoners in this barn. Why, the smells alone are, at times, more than I can endure. But, I suppose it's destiny, because here I am, one of the most beautiful examples of the feline species and they had the presumption to give me a perfectly ridiculous name like...Sweetie."

Spencer waited a moment for his thoughts to catch up to what she had just said.

"That's not such a bad name," he told her.

"Oh, if they would have left it at that I certainly wouldn't have a quarrel, but I'm ashamed to say they also added a—Pie."

"What? I don't understand."

"My name is Sweetie Pie!" She turned her back to Spencer and hid her head in between two bales of hay.

"Hey, come back! I think your name is kinda cute. So, tell me Miss Pie," Spencer couldn't help but smile as he said her name. "Why are you here in the barn if you're a house cat?"

She backed out from between the hay bales and sat at the edge of the loft with her tail curled around her.

"I really belonged to the missus and when she died the sir put me in the barn. I don't blame him really—he thought I would fare better out here with all of the rodents to keep me busy. But I simply detest rodents—they're certainly as far as one could get from cleanliness."

"So what's her name, Spencer?" Anna asked.

Spencer looked at Anna. He seemed stunned to see her. He was so wrapped up in the conversation with the cat he'd forgotten she was even there.

"Her name's Sweetie Pie."

"Well," Anna smiled, "that's an interesting name."

"So, tell me about the baby donkey," Spencer asked of Sweetie Pie.

"Well, first of all, he's no baby. Well, maybe a little crybaby." She chuckled a bit.

Anna moved away from the donkey as he jumped to his feet and shook the straw off of his back.

"I'm three and a half years old!" he insisted, **"I'm a full-blooded, miniature Sicilian donkey and I'm no crybaby!"**

"What's he so upset about?" Anna asked.

"He's mad at the cat 'cause she called him a crybaby. But you're right, he said he's a donkey—and he's almost four years old. He's a miniature like Peaches and Rosebud."

Anna gently squeezed the donkey around the neck. "Oh, I wish we could take the cat and the donkey back home to Sweetwater Farms with us."

Spencer petted the donkey's long ears. "I do too."

"Gee, that would be great, mister," said the donkey. **"Do you think we could go home with you?"**

"Oh, yes, I quite agree," said the cat. **"As long as you remember that my preference would be the house instead of the barn."**

"Well, first things first, donkey," Spencer said. "My name is Spencer, not mister, and this is Anna. Now what's your name?"

Spencer heard a little squeak of laughter float down from the loft. "I don't think you have any room to talk, Sweetie Pie," Spencer called.

The donkey's long ears became limp and fell to each side of his face. His head drooped down so low it almost touched the straw. Spencer was straining his ears trying to hear what the donkey was saying.

"Donkey, I'm sorry, I can't hear what you're saying."

The donkey let out a big sigh. **"I said my name is Pee Wee. And I don't want to hear one more word out of you, Sweetie Pie!"** He stomped his front hoof.

CHAPTER FIVE

Spencer turned slightly away from Pee Wee so the little donkey couldn't see him laugh.

"Well, that's a fine name," Spencer said, trying to get the donkey's ears to stand back up. "Let me talk with Anna now. I think it's gonna take some planning to get her father and my grandmother to let us take you back to our farm."

❊ ❊ ❊ ❊ ❊ ❊ ❊ ❊ ❊ ❊ ❊

Kate and Ennis had walked back to the house and were sitting in two rocking chairs on the front porch.

"Now don't forget, Ennis, you'll want to reheat that pie in the oven and not the microwave. I swear that just zaps the life out of food."

"You don't have to worry, Katie—I'll take good care of your apple pie."

"Don't make fun of me," she argued. "I'm only looking out for you. Oh, I almost forgot, we're having a party next week for the kids. I guess you'd say it's a little end-of-school party. I'd like for you to come—that is if you're not too busy at the store."

"Why Katie, are you asking me on a date?"

"Yes, I'm asking you on a date," she countered. "How about it?"

"Sounds great! I might have a lot more free time for dates once Mr. Wynn takes over the farm. Yep, I'll be a man of leisure then." Ennis stretched his long arms back behind him and locked his fingers behind his head.

"Oh, speaking of Mr. Wynn, what do you think about him?"

"He seems all right I guess. Why do you ask?"

"There's just something different about him. I think even Spencer noticed it. Anyway, he said he wanted our farm so he could build a golf course to go with his resort."

"How can he do that unless you sell it to him?"

"It's a long story, I'll tell you all about it later--after Will and I get it figured out."

"Maybe he thinks a resort and golf course will be good for the community. I'm sure everything will work out fine."

"Well, we'll see. Anyway, I think there's definitely something fishy about Mr. Wynn," Kate replied, "and I'm gonna make it my business to find out what it is."

❊ ❊ ❊ ❊ ❊ ❊ ❊ ❊ ❊ ❊ ❊

"Where are your parents this morning?" Emily asked.

"They left early to help at a community event, something about raising money for clothes for the homeless," Jonas answered. "My mom's in more clubs than I can count and my dad always gets dragged along to help her."

Jonas wheeled himself down the hallway from the living room to the kitchen of their one-story ranch-style house. Emily couldn't help but look around as she followed him to the kitchen. All of the rooms were very large and the hallway seemed as wide as the ones in school. She noticed all of the electrical outlets were higher, and when she came to the kitchen the countertops and cabinets were lower, which seemed perfect to her.

"Wow," she blurted out, "your house is really cool!" When she realized what she'd said, she felt embarrassed. "I'm sorry, Jonas, sometimes I don't think before I speak."

"Don't worry about it. It actually is a pretty neat house. But do you want to see something really cool?"

She grinned. "Sure."

They kept going through the kitchen and out the other side. They entered a room that looked like it was once a screened porch and there was a ramp leading down to it. In place of screen there were huge windows that made everything bright and shiny. Emily looked around and couldn't believe what she was seeing. It was a perfect replica of their science room at school. There were test tubes and beakers with some weird-looking liquids and on the wall there were charts of compounds and a full-size poster of the human body.

"You're right!" she exclaimed. "This *is* cool."

"My parents helped me fix it up," he said. "It has everything I need to conduct my own experiments, including a good amount of sunlight which I need for my bones."

"Why do you need sunlight for your bones?"

"Well, the condition I have makes my muscles deteriorate. So, the doctors told me to get plenty of sunlight, because the vitamin D will strengthen my bones. Since my muscles aren't doing very well, they want to make sure that my bones stay as healthy as possible."

Emily squinted her eyes as if trying to understand what he had just said.

"You know, we get vitamin D from sunlight," he added as if she ought to know that fact.

"Oh, sure, I knew that, I just forgot," she said, trying to cover up.

"So, when you called you said you needed my help. Something about Spencer?"

"Yeah," she replied. "Something's happened to him and we think you might know how to help us. You see it all started the other night when…"

She told him the story just as Spencer had told it to her and when she finished Jonas didn't say a word. He pressed the lever on the arm of his wheelchair and moved forward to a bookcase. He scanned the books and pulled out a large, thick book with a binding made of old leather. He flipped open the cover, scrolled down the contents and placed the book back on the shelf, muttering to himself about DNA and genetics and fusion.

Emily couldn't wait any longer. "Well, what do you think?"

"There!" He pointed to a book in the far corner on the top shelf. He stretched as far as he could and was just barely able to pull it down with his fingertips. The book was big and brown and the title in gold lettering read *Universal Transcription and Decoding.*

He laid the book in his lap, pushed the lever again and rolled over to the long work table in the middle of the room. He placed the book on the table and moved his finger down the different chapter headings.

"There it is," he said, "*Basic Laws of Molecular Structure and Electromagnetism.*" He flipped the pages until he came to the chapter and began to read.

Emily waited for him to finish reading and to tell her what he was thinking—but he didn't. It felt like he had forgotten she was even there.

"Jonas?"

"Jonas?" she asked again.

"Huh," he said still looking at the book.

"Maybe I'll go now and let you read."

"Yes, that's a good idea," he said, looking up from his glasses. "I'll call you tomorrow."

"Okay," she said, heading for the kitchen door.

"Oh, Emily!" he added, "I need samples."

"What?" she questioned.

"I'll need samples of their hair—Sully and Spencer that is."

Emily gazed at him with a questioning look.

"For a DNA test."

"Oh, yeah," she acknowledged, "for a DNA test. That's a great place to start. No problem—I'll get the samples today!"

❊ ❊ ❊ ❊ ❊ ❊ ❊ ❊ ❊ ❊

Will and Roberto finished with the tractor and put it away in the shed. They headed back to the pickup truck and met Ennis and Kate as they came walking down from the house.

CHAPTER FIVE

"Well, what'd you think of my old girl?" Ennis asked.

"She ran real good," Will said as he handed the keys back to Ennis. "It sure would be great for us to have two tractors over at Sweetwater. I'll tell you what, let me go back and talk to Sofia. I need to make sure the funds are in order before I write you a check."

"That sounds fine," Ennis replied.

Spencer and Anna came running up from the back of the barn.

"Hey, you two, did you see those baby goats?" Ennis asked.

"Yes, sir," Spencer replied, "but we have a question."

"What is it?"

"We wanted to know if the donkey and the cat can come home with us."

"Now wait just a minute, son," Will said.

"You have a donkey in there?" Kate questioned.

"Yeah, I don't know what I was thinking when I bought him at the county auction last month. It was before the deal with Mr. Wynn and I thought it might be real cute to see him out in the pasture with those cows. The little fellow just stole my heart. I guess he stole yours too," he said as he looked at Spencer and Anna.

"He sure did," Anna acknowledged, "and the cat too! Please, Dad, can I have the cat? I'll take real good care of her."

"Well, maybe she can live in the barn with Gerri and Dudley if Miss Kate doesn't mind," Roberto finally said.

"Oh, no, Dad," Anna explained, "she has to live in the house. She's not a barn cat."

"You're right, Anna," Ennis agreed. "But how'd you know that?"

Spencer stepped in. "What Anna means is that she just looks like a house cat."

"Then I'll have to ask your mother about that," Roberto said.

"Can we call her now? Please?"

Roberto took a deep breath and looked at his daughter. He reached in his pocket for his keys and started walking to the driver's side of the truck.

"Come on *hijita*. Let's get my phone."

Will laughed. "You're a pushover, Roberto."

"Yeah, yeah," Roberto called back over his shoulder, "I guess I am."

"Now, tell me about this donkey," Kate said to Spencer as she started to walk to the barn. "Let's go have a look at him." Spencer followed her, telling her all of the important details about Pee Wee as they walked. Will watched them go through the gate and into the barn.

"They are certainly two peas in a pod," he said to Ennis. "I swear they'd have every animal in the world if they could."

CHAPTER SIX

THE HIDDEN MOUNTAIN

Emily cut through the woods behind Jonas's house and eventually came to Sweetwater property. She was riding the new bike she'd bought with the allowance money she'd saved last year. It was black and pink with the name Titan Trailblazer 500 in big white letters on the frame. She came to an old barbed-wire fence and had to get off the bike. It was just a single strand of wire so old and loose she could step down on it and roll the knobby tires of the bike right across. After clearing the fence, she climbed back on the bike and pedaled through the meadow and around the pond.

It was actually a small pool of water fed by an underground spring but the horses used it for drinking. Rio especially loved to splash and roll in the cool water on a hot day. She noticed as she rode by that there were bubbles in the water. It looked like a pot boiling on the stove. She stopped her bike and watched as the bubbles came up from the bottom of the pond. They would stay on the surface for a second then tumble over and shoot back to the bottom. "That's weird," she thought. "It's almost like there's a whirlpool in the water." She laid the bike down on the path and walked over to the pond to take a better look. She watched the bubbles dance in a circular pattern and sink back to the bottom again. She stuck her hand in the water and moved it around, trying to check the temperature. It was cold—freezing cold! She quickly pulled her hand out and dried it on her jeans.

"Okay, this it too weird for words!" she exclaimed. "I need to tell Dad!"

She ran to the bike, jumped on the seat and began pedaling as fast as she could. She went up the road through the grove of apple trees and over the wooden bridge. As she rounded the bend, she could see the house. Once in the driveway she jumped off the bike, leaned it against the house and threw her pink helmet into the basket. Spencer was sitting on the top step of the porch with Sully.

"Hey, how'd it go at Jonas's house?" he asked.

"Great! But I need to find Dad. There's something strange going on over at the pond."

"He went to take a check to Mr. Tucker for the tractor he's buying. What's happening at the pond?"

She grimaced. "There're some weird bubbles and the water's really cold."

"Maybe the fish Dad and I put in last year are real big now and they're making the bubbles," he said grinning at the thought.

"I don't think so. But even if it were the fish, why's the water so cold? I mean like freezing cold!"

"I don't know but Dad said he'd be back in a few minutes; you can ask him then. So, tell me what Jonas said."

"He wants me to get some samples from you and Sully."

"What kind of samples? I hope it's not like at the doctor's office when they give you that little cup."

"YEWWW, gross!" she exclaimed. "He just needs some hair samples. He wants to do a DNA test."

"Oh, that's easy enough, huh, Sully? Hey, guess what happened at

Mr. Tucker's farm?"

"What?"

"Well, for one thing, we got ourselves a new donkey. His name is Pee Wee and Mr. Tucker is bringing him over in a couple of days."

"A donkey? What will we do with a donkey?"

"He'll keep Rosebud and Peaches company in the lower pasture. He's a miniature just like them. He needed a good home so Gram said we could bring him here. But listen to this—when Anna and I were at Mr. Tucker's barn I could hear Pee Wee and Sweetie Pie talk!"

"Who's Sweetie Pie?"

"She's Anna's new cat. But she's not really a barn cat 'cause she actually prefers the house. Anyway, I could hear them talk! It's not just Sully—I can hear ALL the animals." Kate was listening to the children's conversation from inside the house. She thought about the pond and Lakena's moon the other night. She knew if she took them to the mountain it would change their lives forever, but she had no choice. Everything was happening so fast it had to be done.

"Hey, kids," she hollered, "come on in and get some lunch."

"Lunch!" Emily cried. "We didn't get Sully any lunch. What are we going to do? Now Gram will be in the kitchen."

"Don't worry" Spencer smiled innocently. "I already fed him. I said I would, didn't I?"

"I can't believe it," Emily confessed. "I thought for sure you'd forget."

❊ ❊ ❊ ❊ ❊ ❊ ❊ ❊ ❊ ❊ ❊

"Just put your plates in the sink when you finish," Kate said as she scurried around the kitchen. "I'm going to go cut some flowers so we can drop them by the cemetery on our walk. I'll be right back." Kate went down the long hallway between the kitchen and the living room and out the back door.

"Does Gram seem nervous to you?" Emily asked.

"Yeah," Spencer said, laughing. "She reminds me of Peaches the other day when Dad said that her brain wasn't there."

Emily laughed and took their plates to the sink. "I wonder what she's nervous about. Has she said anything about where we're going today?"

"No, but I sure do hope I find out what's going on—once and for all."

They heard the back door open and their grandmother came into the kitchen with an armful of fresh-cut flowers.

"Spencer, I think it would be best if Sully stayed here. By the way, I didn't even ask—how's he feeling today?"

"He's doing a lot better," Spencer said, a big smile on his face. "When we got home from Mr. Tucker's he actually brought me his ball and we played until Em got home."

"Oh, well, maybe he'll feel better tomorrow," Kate said as she pruned the flowers over the sink.

Spencer and Emily stared at each other knowing their grandmother hadn't listened to a word Spencer had just said.

"Gram, are you all right?" Emily asked.

"Huh—what?" she answered. "Ah—yes, I'm fine. I'm just thinking about our walk. Come on now, are you two ready to go?"

"Yes, ma'am," they both said.

They headed out the kitchen door and started down the gravel road toward the barn. They could see Sofia working in her garden as they walked by the path that led to her house. When they went by the hayfields they turned to the right staying on a narrow foot path that followed the stream. They started up the hill and as they rounded the bend Emily turned around to see the farm fade out of sight. She looked to the right and could see their three horses grazing in the lower pasture.

"Why are the horses in Peaches and Rosebud's pasture?" Emily wanted to know.

"Oh, I had Roberto move them this morning because of the pond."

CHAPTER SIX

As they came to the family cemetery Kate opened the iron gate and walked in. Emily grabbed Spencer's shoulder and held him back. "I didn't tell Gram about the pond, did you?"

"No."

"Then how'd she know about it? And why didn't she tell us?"

Spencer shrugged his shoulders and followed his grandmother, leaving Emily to ponder her question.

The family cemetery had always fascinated Spencer and Emily. It seemed like a magical place where they could run and play, never really giving thought to it being—a cemetery. Ever since they were small they had come with their grandmother to bring flowers for special occasions or to pull weeds to keep it tidy. On the Fourth of July and Memorial Day they would bring little flags to place on the headstones of their relatives who had fought in wars. There was an old oak tree that stood proudly in the middle. It had sprawling branches that nearly stretched from one side of the cemetery to the other. The tree was so big it took Spencer and Emily both, locking their hands together, to reach around its trunk.

In the far right corner were the grave sights of Sir Benjamin Howell and Suri Lakena. Next to them was their son, Thomas Benjamin and his wife Sarah. Thomas Benjamin had died in the Civil War, and since he was the first soldier in the family, Kate always insisted he should get the first flag on holidays. When the cemetery was first built it was fairly small but through the years the black wrought-iron fence had been expanded to accommodate all of the Sweetwaters it could. Kate had always considered herself lucky to have married into a fine family like the Sweetwaters, and she knew her spot was waiting for her right next to her husband, William Thomas. She always went to see his grave first while Spencer and Emily visited their mother, Jenny's, grave.

Spencer started to clear the leaves and other debris away from her headstone and Emily turned to watch her grandmother. Even though Kate had her back to the children, Emily could tell she was talking to their grandfather. She watched her place the flowers lovingly on the ground in front of his headstone before removing a dead tree branch that must have fallen from the oak tree. She strained to hear what her grandmother was saying but decided it would be best not to eavesdrop. She bent down and began to pull weeds with Spencer.

"I sure do wish you were here to help me today," Kate murmured, brushing some acorns off to the side. "I remember when you first took me to the mountain and how well you explained everything. I have faith, though, that everything will turn out fine 'cause they're very special children. And you wouldn't believe how big they've gotten, William. You'd be so proud of them. Spencer loves animals so much—but we could have guessed that. And Emily, she's so much like Jenny sometimes it's scary. She wants to be just like her too. That's why I've decided to bring her today. I think she can help Spencer through this. Well, we'd better get going while we still have daylight. It's time young Spencer finds out who he really is."

Kate took some of the flowers and put them on Jenny's grave. She kissed her fingertips and gently touched the top of the headstone. She put her arms around the children and gave them a big hug.

"Are you kids ready to start our adventure?"

"Yeah!" they both yelled, and walked out of the cemetery, closing the iron gates behind them.

They started back down the hill toward the lower pasture but instead of turning to the right, which would lead them back to Sweetwater Farms, they went to the left. As they walked Spencer noticed they always seemed to be following the stream. They went through tall grass which gradually changed over to a grove of laurel bushes and dense thickets with tangled underbrush. It grabbed at their clothing with its thorny branches as they walked by. Eventually they came to the tall trees of the forest and Kate stopped by a huge rock to get her bearings.

"This way," she said, moving deeper into the forest. The sweet smells of spring honeysuckle gave way to the heavy aromas of moist black soil and musty wet leaves.

CHAPTER SIX

"Is this still our property?" Spencer asked knowing he had never been here before.

"Yeah, remember Dad said this was land we owned but it was bottom land. We can't grow apples on it because it's too low and it could flood. Isn't that right, Gram?"

"That's right, Emily. That's why we don't want you kids playing over here. There might be sink holes."

"What are sink holes?" Spencer asked.

"They're holes in the earth," Emily said, "and they could suck you up and no one would ever know where you are—ever again!"

"No way!" Spencer yelled out.

"Emily, don't scare your brother." Kate was working on navigating her way over a couple of rocks in the stream. "Both of you stay close to me and you'll be just fine."

"No problem there." Spencer moved closer to his grandmother. Emily had actually scared herself a little too, and she moved closer to Spencer.

After they crossed the stream, the path took them through a maze of pine trees that seemed as tall as the sky. Their needles were so thick on the ground that it felt as if they were walking on air.

Emily sniffed. "Mmm, it smells good in here!"

"Yeah," Spencer added, "it smells like that fancy can of spray Gram keeps in the guest bathroom."

Both children laughed and stopped behind their grandmother. It seemed like they were surrounded by at least a thousand trees. They couldn't see the stream anymore or the path or anything but pine trees. Spencer watched as a bird flew through the trees and landed on a low hanging branch.

"Are we lost?" Spencer asked—afraid to hear the answer.

"Anything but!" Kate exclaimed just as she saw whatever it was she was looking for. They headed off again and after a few minutes they began to see other types of trees. The pine-needle floor started to disappear and both children seemed relieved to put the tall pines behind them.

"Are we almost there?" Emily asked, trotting to keep up with her grandmother.

"Just about," Kate answered. "We have to climb that mountain up there and then we'll see it."

"See what?" Spencer asked.

"Never mind, just keep walking."

Spencer looked up from the path and saw a huge mountain in front of him.

"Where did that come from?" he thought.

As they started their climb he looked over and saw the stream again. It ran down the mountain and spilled over large boulders covered in moss. It splashed into a calm pool and continued on its way down the hill and on to Sweetwater Farms.

Kate made it up the mountain first and waited for Spencer and Emily at the top. Once there, the kids took a minute to catch their breath and look around. There was an area that had been cleared out and had stones neatly placed in a circle. On one side of the circle were huge squared-off rocks stacked on top of one another as if someone had been trying to build a wall. It was surrounded on each side by a dense overgrowth of hemlock trees. The rocks had an opening cut into them and Spencer and Emily ran over to look through it.

"What is this place?" Spencer asked.

"The Native Americans used the top of this mountain as a sacred gathering place. They'd bring their gifts of harvest here in gratitude to Mother Earth for her blessings. They also believed they could predict the weather from up here."

"How'd they do that?" Spencer asked.

"Well, it all had to do with the way the sun would shine through this window at different times of the year. They were able to tell if it would be a good planting season by the way the shadows fell in the ring of stones behind us."

"Wow," Emily announced. "That's very cool! Hey look, Spencer—you can see our house from here."

"Yeah—and the horses and apple orchard too!" He pointed through the window in the rock. "No wonder you wanted to bring us here, Gram. It's really neat! But I don't remember seeing this mountain from our house. How come we can see Sweetwater from here but we can't see the mountain from Sweetwater?"

"That's not to answer now," she said as she started walking again.

"Where are we going?" Emily asked, running to her grandmother's side. "I thought this is what you wanted to show us."

"Almost," Kate answered. "Now stay close to me."

They left the cleared area and found the path again on the other side of the rock window. Kate followed the narrow trail as it began winding back through the trees and then sharply turned to the left. She waited for the children to catch up before heading down a flight of rock steps carved into the side of the mountain. She took Emily's hand and together they carefully made their way down the steps.

"You okay back there, Spencer?"

"Yes, ma'am," he shouted.

The steps stopped at a large flat area that seemed like it was carved right out of the side of the mountain. Spencer jumped the last two steps and fell to his knees. He laughed at himself as he stood up and brushed the loose dirt from his jeans.

He looked around. "Whoa! What is this place?"

In the side of the mountain there was an opening to a cave that was draped with long-forgotten vines. A huge rock sat right in the middle of the open area in front of the cave entrance. On top of the rock was a stone carving of a bird. It had a small head and long pointed wings spread out like it was about to fly. It was perched with its talons firmly clutching the rock below as if it were its prey. Spencer and Emily studied the detail in the feathers and the eyes and the beak.

"Look!" Emily shouted, "Around its neck!" Both children leaned in closer.

"It's wearing a silver chain," Spencer said. "And look—a coin or something." Spencer reached out to touch the coin. "It's a lion holding a sword and look at the name under the lion—Howell!" He turned the coin over and on the other side was a tree. "Hey, it's the tree from the cemetery--and another name: Sweetwater!"

Spencer turned to his grandmother. "Did this belong to Sir Benjamin?"

Kate walked over to the children and put her arms around their shoulders. "It did indeed. It's a medallion of the family crest."

"What is this place anyway?" Spencer looked around at the cave and the mountain and back at his grandmother.

"This is what I wanted to show you," Kate answered in a soft voice.

"So, what's *in* the cave?" Emily asked from the entrance, where she began to move the vines away from the opening.

Spencer raised his eyebrows. "Um—are we going in there?"

"Wait a minute, Em," Kate said, pulling her away from the vines. "Spencer, I'll take you in *only* if you want to go."

"Well," he peeked in through the vines, "what's in there?"

"The answers you've been waiting for." She looked into his eyes. "Trust me." She kissed his forehead. "I'd never let anything happen to you or Emily."

"Well, then," Spencer said as he took a deep breath, "let's see what this cave thing is all about!"

"Okay—wait here." Kate disappeared into the cave but was back in a few seconds with a lit torch. "Now, follow me."

❊ ❊ ❊ ❊ ❊ ❊ ❊ ❊ ❊ ❊

CHAPTER SIX

Kate re-entered the cave while holding the torch out in front of her. The children had each grabbed onto her shirt as they moved through the small opening in the rock, pushing the vines out of the way. Once inside, Emily kept her hand on the smooth rock wall to keep her bearings as her eyes adjusted to the darkness. Spencer was trying to bat away a stray spider web with one hand, still holding onto his grandmother with the other.

"It's cold in here," he whispered as he scuffled his feet along the rock floor.

"Duh, Spencer," Emily taunted, "it's a cave, in a mountain. What do you expect? And why are you whispering?"

"I don't know, maybe there's something else in here besides us. Is there Gram?" he asked.

"Just be patient, and you'll find out soon enough."

They could hear the sound of running water and could see light up ahead. They came to a big open area that had lit torches on the walls and they could see two other passageways just like the one they had come through. In the middle of the room was a small pool of water, calm and clear. All at once it shot up into a fountain which caused the water to run over the edge. After so many years of spilling over, the water had cut a channel through the rock floor. It carried the water from the fountain through the cave and out an opening in the wall. Then the pool became calm again as if nothing had happened. The children ran over and looked into its still waters.

"You'd better be care--"

Kate had barely gotten the words out when then fountain shot up again, spraying Spencer and Emily. They backed away from it and laughed as they wiped the water from their faces.

"Hey," Spencer said, "this water tastes good! It tastes like--"

"Cotton candy!" Emily blurted out.

"Yeah," he added, "just like cotton candy!"

"This is the mineral spring that gave us our name," Kate said.

"You mean Sweetwater?" Emily asked.

"That's right," she said. "This is where the stream begins that runs through our valley. This is why our apples have always grown so well. There's something special in the water that makes it taste like, well... cotton candy. The Native Americans believed it was a magical fountain. They believed this cave was a special place where spirits and man could communicate with each other, and that spirits would reveal themselves here."

"Okay, now you're creeping me out, Gram," Spencer admitted as the fountain blew again.

"I'm just telling you what they believed," she said.

"Hey, what's this over here?" Emily had walked over toward one of the torches on the wall. "It's an old trunk. Can we open it?"

"Sure," Kate answered, "just be careful. It was Sir Benjamin's trunk and it's very old."

Gently she turned the latch and unbuckled the leather straps that held down each side. As she opened the lid Kate held the torch down lower so they could get a better look. On one side of the trunk were old books and papers that were bound together with string. On the other side was a wooden box with the name *Royal Society of Edinburgh* carved on the top.

"Can I open the box?" Spencer asked.

Kate nodded. "Go ahead."

Inside was an old microscope and some slides stacked neatly in a little black case. There were little bottles of colored liquids strapped along the inside of the lid. The labels on the liquids were so old and faded they couldn't make them out.

"Was Sir Benjamin a doctor or something?" Spencer asked.

"No," Kate answered, "he was a scientist."

"Like me!" Emily exclaimed.

"Yes," Kate said, "he was a lot like you—and your mother."

"What?" Emily questioned. "Did Mom know about this place too?"

CHAPTER SIX

"Yes, look in the trunk again."

Spencer closed the wooden box and they both looked back in the trunk. They pulled out the books and papers that were close to the top and found three old maps—one of Edinburgh, Scotland, which was stamped with the seal of the Royal Society, one of the Carolinas and one that said Sweetwater Valley. They put them with the other papers and looked back in the trunk.

"Hey," Emily said, "this is Mom's chemistry kit. What's that doing in here?"

Kate helped Emily lift it out of the trunk. "Your mother was doing some work up here."

"What kind of work?" Spencer asked.

"Well," Kate took a deep breath, figuring out exactly how to explain it. "She was working on genetics."

"Like me and Jonas!" Emily blurted out, forgetting it was a secret.

"What?" Kate questioned.

Emily shook her head. "Nothing."

Kate walked over to the rock wall and placed the torch in a holder, then she looked at Spencer.

"Spencer."

"Yes, ma'am."

"Your birthday is on December twenty-second."

"Yes, ma'am, for eleven years now."

"The Native Americans believed that was a very special day," she said. "It was the first day of the winter solstice."

"What's a sol-stice?" he asked.

"It technically means the sun stands still, but only for an instant. Suri Lakena was also born on that day. Remember, I told you everyone thought she was the princess of the sun?"

"Yeaahhhh." Spencer had no idea what all this meant.

"Well, because of being born on that day and in that very second when the sun stood still, she really was special. And you're special too.

That's the reason you can talk to animals."

"So, you *do* know about that," Emily said.

"Yes, I do, but there's more," she said, sitting down across from the children. "Spencer, you know how it hurts your arm when you feel energy, like from the moon that night?"

"Yeah," he answered, "and like when lightning struck the tree outside the barn!"

"Well, because of being born on that day, you're tied into—nature," she added. "You feel things more than other people. It's all new to you now, but you'll understand what it means in time. It's like learning a new language. You have to figure out what nature is trying to tell you."

"So, let me get this straight," Spencer said. "Are you saying that I was born in that very second when the sun stood still, just like Suri Lakena?"

"I think you were, Spencer." Kate took his hand. "There's no real way of knowing, but you have the same way with animals and nature that she had."

"Just wait a minute." Emily got up off the floor. "Gram, *you* talked to Abbey on the day Rosebud was born and your birthday is in March!"

"Yes, I did. Abbey and I are joined together. She's my animal guide." The children both gazed at her, confused. "Okay, remember the story of Lakena's moon?" Both children nodded. "Well, when I was a little girl, Abbey was my horse and she was my best friend in the whole world."

"Like me and Sully!" Spencer added.

"Yes, just like you and Sully. Well, as I grew up and became older, Abbey did too. By the time your grandfather and I got married, Abbey was very old and had become very sick. The doctor said there was nothing he could do for her, that it was just old age. Well, your grandfather knew how special Abbey was to me so he told me the story of Lakena's moon. He knew I'd do anything to make her better."

"Like when I wished the other night for Sully to get better!" Spencer exclaimed.

CHAPTER SIX

"Exactly like that," Kate answered. "I wished that Abbey would get better so we could be together…forever."

"That's just what I wished for!"

"That's right," Kate said. "So now you're joined with Sully. He's your animal guide just like Abbey's mine. That's why I can hear her talk. But I can only hear Abbey, no other animals. The other day when Rosebud was born I was telling Abbey what Dr. Miles needed—and Abbey told Peaches."

"Wow!" Spencer said.

"Hey, then I've got a question." Emily walked back over to one of the torches. "If you had Abbey when you were a little girl, how old is she?"

Kate stood up from the floor to stand next to Emily. "Well, we're the same age, and that's pretty old! You see, because Abbey and I are joined, she'll live as long as I do."

Spencer jumped up from the floor. "So, Sully will live as long as me!"

"Well, it's what you wished for, isn't it?" Kate asked.

"Yeah, it's exactly what I wished for—except…" he hesitated, looking down at the floor, "how come I can see Sully in the mirror when it's me looking into it?"

"What did you say?" Kate asked as she walked back over to Spencer.

"I said that the first time we, well, *joined*, I didn't just hear Sully, I saw him when I looked in the mirror. He was me and I was he—I mean him," he said, laughing at the slip of his words.

"He *became* you, is that what you're trying to say?" Kate asked.

"I guess," Spencer answered. "Or maybe it's more that we were both—in my body."

"Oh, I see," Kate said, now knowing what Spencer meant. "Well, I need to finish telling you the story of the cave and this mountain, and then I think you'll understand everything a little bit better.

CHAPTER SEVEN

THE GATEKEEPERS

Kate walked over and took the torch off the wall. "Let's finish looking around the cave before I go on with my story." The children held onto their grandmother and they all walked past the fountain to the other side of the cave.

Spencer ran over to the wall between the two passageways. "Hey, look at the drawings."

Kate held the torch up so the light would shine on the wall.

"Cool," Emily said, "they're drawings of animals. There's a wolf and a big cat--"

"It's a jaguar," Kate said.

"Oh, yeah," Emily agreed, "I see the spots."

"And look!" Spencer exclaimed. "It's the same bird that's carved in the stone outside."

"That's a falcon," Kate said, gently placing her hand on the falcon's wing.

"Who drew these pictures?" Emily asked.

"Your grandfather told me they were drawn by Suri Lakena. He said all animals were her guides; she didn't have just one."

CHAPTER SEVEN

Before Kate pulled her hand away from the rock wall, she noticed a slight vibration. The ground began to move beneath their feet and the children reached out for her as the fountain shot up behind them. Kate dropped the torch and grabbed the two children. The pool spewed water to the cave ceiling and Emily held on to her grandmother with one hand while reaching out for the rock wall with the other. After a few seconds the shaking stopped and the water from the fountain returned to the pool like nothing had happened.

"What was *that?*" Spencer's voice was shaky.

"It was an earthquake!" Emily exclaimed. "Well, not really an earthquake—more like a tremor—right, Gram?"

"I'd say," Kate replied, bending down to pick up the torch.

"Hey!" Spencer yelled. "Look at the fountain!"

Kate and Emily turned around to see a shimmering light coming from the pool of water. It started spiraling upward, slowly twisting and turning, growing enormous in size. It was a swirling mix of deep purple and violet with crystal-white shimmers and silvery sparkles that danced and played as it moved toward the ceiling of the cave. The huge cone-shaped vortex lit up the whole room.

"Wow!" Spencer ran up to it and reached out for the light.

"Be careful!" Kate yelled to Spencer. "Stay back and watch it from a distance."

"Why?" Emily demanded. "Why can't we touch it?"

"Because it's a vortex of energy," Kate answered.

"What's a vortex of energy?" Spencer asked.

"I've only read about them in science books," Emily said. "I didn't think they really existed."

"Oh, this one's real all right," Kate said.

The ground began to shake.

"Here we go again!" Spencer yelled, running back to his grandmother.

The vortex began to fade in and out and the colors became faint.

The silver and white sparkles grew dim and the spiraling began to slow down. Its power seemed to be tied into the trembling of the cave. When everything stopped shaking the vortex would spiral up and become fully lit. Whenever the tremors started it would begin to slow its spin and lose its power. As they watched it regain its full strength they could hear the sound of rocks crumbling outside the cave. There was someone coming down the passageway. The children grabbed their grandmother and hid behind her.

Emily looked up at Kate. "What's that noise?" The sound was getting louder and louder and now whatever it was—was in the room with them!

"I can't see anything!" Spencer squatted behind his grandmother's leg. "But it sounds like flapping!"

WHOOSH—WHOOSH!

"Like a bird or something!" Emily yelled.

WHOOSH—WHOOSH!

It flew right at them but turned away at the last minute circling around the cave. Emily could feel a breeze as it flew by, but still couldn't see anything.

Spencer covered his head. "What is it, Gram?"

"Well, stand up and open your eyes," she said in a whisper.

Spencer looked up from his hiding place. "Hey, it's the bird in the drawing on the wall!"

"I still can't see it!" Emily yelled as she ducked her head, narrowly escaping a direct hit from the bird.

WHOOSH—WHOOSH!

"Oh, I almost forgot," Kate said. "Go to the trunk, Emily, and put on the goggles."

Emily ran over to the trunk, still covering her head as the bird swooped down at her.

She pulled out her mother's chemistry set and the maps and the wooden box. She saw a black and silver strap way down deep in the trunk. She tugged as hard as she could and the strap stretched and snapped back. The goggles flew out of the trunk and Emily landed on her rear end. She closed the trunk and ran back to Kate and Spencer, picking up the goggles on the way.

"Now, these should help." Kate brushed the hair out of Emily's face and placed the goggles over her eyes.

"Hey, I can see it!" Emily squealed as the bird swooped down at her. The three of them watched as it slowed its flight and perched on a boulder near the drawing on the wall.

"It *is* the bird in the drawing," Emily said. "And look, around its neck—the medallion!"

Kate walked over to the bird and laid her hand on its soft bluish-gray feathers. It stretched out its wings and nuzzled Kate's hand with its little head.

"This is Ayasha," Kate said, introducing the bird to the children. "It means 'little one' in the language of the Native Americans."

The children walked up to the bird.

"Can I pet her?" Spencer asked as he looked into her little brown eyes.

"Yes, just be very careful," Kate said.

Spencer slowly reached out his hand and laid it on the bird's back. "She's so soft."

"I think she likes you," Kate said as they both petted her.

"Okay, Gram, you have some explaining to do," Emily insisted as she lifted the goggles up onto her forehead. "Hey, where'd the bird go?" She put the goggles on again and could see Ayasha. She took them off and she was gone. "What's up with these goggles?"

"Your mother invented them," Kate said proudly. "She couldn't see Ayasha either, so she figured out how to pull together Ayasha's energy to make a picture. And the goggles let you see that picture."

"Of course!" Emily announced. "Why didn't I think of that? Is that why her chemistry set is up here?"

"Because of that and some other things." Kate looked at Spencer playing with Ayasha. She was lowering her head for him to scratch her neck.

"So you're a falcon," he whispered in a baby voice. "You're a very beautiful falcon...yes you are."

"So, Gram, another question. Well, a few really," Emily announced. "Why did we hear the rocks breaking before the last tremor and why is Ayasha wearing the medallion? Is she the same falcon that was outside the cave?"

As Kate was about to answer, the floor began to shake again. The vortex slowed its spiral and the colors began to fade in and out. Spencer watched Ayasha and couldn't believe his eyes. She was fading in and out just like the vortex. She was there and in the next second, she was gone. Once again the ground stopped shaking and full power was restored to the vortex. Ayasha again lowered her head and nuzzled Spencer's hand for him to pet her.

"What's going on with all the tremors around here?" Emily asked.

"I wish I knew," Kate answered.

Once again they heard a strange sound coming from one of the passageways. The children moved closer to their grandmother as they strained their ears to try and make out what they were hearing.

"It sounds like bells," Spencer said.

"Yeah, and footsteps," Emily agreed, holding on to Kate's pant leg.

They could hear the faint howl of a wolf as if it was baying at the moon. Something came running into the room and jumped onto a large boulder next to Emily. She could feel the aliveness of whatever it was and the warm flow of its breath on her neck made her shrink lower to the floor. The bells became louder and the wolf howled again as the children turned their eyes toward the opening in the cave wall.

"Whoa!" Spencer looked around from behind Kate. "Is that who I think it is?"

"Who?" Emily asked in a panicked voice. "Who is it? I can't see!"

"Put on your goggles." Kate helped Emily pull them down over her eyes.

CHAPTER SEVEN

"Wow!" Emily announced as she adjusted the straps on each side of her head.

Kate left the children and walked over to the other side of the vortex. She put her hands together in front of her and bowed.

"It's very good to see you again, Princess Lakena. And you, too, Takoda," she said, petting the wolf's head.

"It is very good to see you also, Katherine."

Emily could hardly believe what she was seeing. The princess had on a long flowing white dress and she wore a belt of brightly colored strands of fabric. Her long, black hair looked as soft as silk and was woven into two braids that were so long they almost reached her waist. She wore a headband of multi-colored beads with a design of the sun in the middle. Her necklaces were made of different metals—silver, copper and gold--and inlayed with turquoise stones. The sound of the bells had come from hollow brass cones that were tied to each end of the laces on her suede boots.

Emily was captivated by her beauty, almost caught in a trance, but was brought back to reality as she again felt the warm breath on the back of her neck. She turned around and saw a big, beautiful cat sitting on top of the boulder. It rubbed its head with its big paw and waved its long tail back and forth in the air. It was a golden color with black spots and had a big broad head and a powerful-looking jaw. When it yawned, Emily could see its gargantuan fangs and she stood frozen not wanting to move. She couldn't take her eyes off the cat as it jumped down from the boulder and gracefully walked over to Suri Lakena.

"Children," Kate urged, "come over here."

Spencer and Emily looked at each other and started to walk toward their grandmother. Emily lifted the goggles from her eyes just to see if Suri Lakena and the animals would disappear—and they did.

"Very cool," she announced to herself as she put them back over her eyes.

"This is Suri Lakena and this is Takoda," Kate said as she held out her hand to the wolf. "And this is Kuma--"

"The jaguar!" Spencer added as he stood across from the big cat.

"Katherine," Suri Lakena said, moving closer to Emily, "the child looks like Jennifer." She placed her hand over Emily's head. "And she shares her intellect as well."

"Yes, she does," Kate answered. "We're very proud of Emily."

Suri Lakena looked at Emily for a moment longer before turning to Spencer.

"And this must be Spencer." She put her hand out in front of his heart. "Well, Katherine, you were right. He is a child of the sun." She looked into Spencer's eyes. She put her hands together and bowed to him. "We have been waiting for you, Spencer."

He murmured, "For *me?*"

"Yes, we have been waiting nearly two hundred years for you."

Spencer looked confused, not really understanding what she meant.

The Princess walked over to Ayasha and slowly waved her hand in front of her; the bird flew to her shoulder. "We have all been waiting for you," she said as the animals surrounded her. "These wonderful beasts are Guardians of the vortex. Ayasha watches the cave while Kuma and Takoda guard the mountain. The animals can take on many forms, as can I. We can change our energy for the protection of the vortex."

"Like Ayasha was the stone carving outside the cave and now she's a real bird!" Emily exclaimed.

Suri Lakena smiled. "That's right, Emily."

"So, you're a Guardian, too?" Emily asked.

Suri Lakena made another motion with her hand and Ayasha jumped over to Spencer's shoulder. Spencer laughed as the bird moved around and flapped its wings trying to find the perfect spot on which to perch.

"No," she said, "I am the Gatekeeper."

"What's a Gatekeeper?" Spencer asked, petting Ayasha's head.

"Well, the vortex is a very powerful portal, or gate, to the Universe. It's the power source that gives the great planet its life. The power of the vortex makes the trees grow and the flowers bloom in the springtime. It gives us the lightning in a storm and the snows in the winter. Everything in nature is given life through the vortex, including the animals, and even you." She placed her finger gently on his nose. "The energy here is very strong and it needs to be protected to keep life balanced. There are many vortexes on the great planet and they all have Gatekeepers and Guardians. It's our mission to ensure that the positive stream of energy stays strong and continuous."

"How did you become the Gatekeeper?" Emily asked.

"I was born on the day of the winter solstice."

"Just like me," Spencer added. "In the very second when the sun stood still."

"That's right, my dear child—just like you. My father was told by the elders in our village about the vortex and the Gatekeepers. When I was old enough he brought me to this cave and everything was explained to me by the ancient Gatekeeper who was in place before me. You see, Spencer, we are given a choice: we can accept the task of the Gatekeeper or we can refuse it."

"What happens if you refuse?" Spencer asked.

"Then the vortex will go unprotected. It could reverse its spin and produce negative life instead of positive life. It's a very big decision my grandchild but it's also a great gift. The Universe gives you the choice and you have until the second full moon to decide. Once you have made the decision, the vortex will adjust accordingly."

"What do you mean adjust accordingly?" Emily asked.

"It will either continue as it always has, with me in place awaiting the new Gatekeeper, or it could begin the reverse spin, and if that happens it will be out of my control."

"So, who's the new Gatekeeper?" Spencer asked while playing with Ayasha.

All three of them stared at Spencer at the same time.

"What?" he said. "Why are you all looking at me?"

"Because you're the new Gatekeeper!" Emily announced.

"What? No, I'm not. Tell her, Gram," Spencer said sheepishly.

Kate didn't reply: she simply put her arm around him. "We have a lot more talking to do, Spencer. I don't want you to worry about all this right now."

Takoda jumped to his feet and lifted his nose in the air. The mighty wolf howled again just as the ground began to shake. Suri Lakena and the three animals began to fade in and out along with the spiral of the vortex. Spencer grabbed for Ayasha but he couldn't feel her on his shoulder. Kate reached out for Emily and Spencer.

As quickly as the tremor had started, the cave returned to normal and Suri Lakena and the animals came into view again.

"What's going on?" Kate asked. "This has never happened before."

Suri Lakena took a deep breath and looked at Kate.

"We are losing our power," she said softly. "I'm unsure as to why it's happening but for many days now the vortex has been fading. It feels as if the power is being pulled somewhere else."

Once she felt her power restored she knelt down in front of both children. "Now, are there any questions you would like to ask me?"

"Yes, please, answer me this," Emily said. "Are you real? I mean, how can you be two hundred years old?"

"Oh yes, child—I am real. We all are real," she said, gesturing toward the animals. "We walk the great planet in spirit and the reason you can see us is because we are also holograms—in fact, even the mountain is a hologram."

Emily looked at Suri Lakena with a blank stare as if she were searching her brain for information.

"A hologram, a hologram," she repeated to herself while pacing the floor. "You can't be a hologram. You need a laser beam to create a hologram."

"Whoa," Spencer said, "back up just a minute. What's a hologram anyway?"

CHAPTER SEVEN

"Emily, tell your brother what a hologram is," Kate said.

"Well, I think it's a three-dimentional picture, right?" she asked.

"That's right," Suri Lakena said. "And the laser beam you speak of is the vortex."

"Of course!" Emily said, looking at the swirling purple lights. "The vortex would be a perfect energy source."

"But I still don't get it," Spencer argued. "If you're a picture how can I do this?" He reached out to grab Suri Lakena but his hand passed right through her arm. Both she and Kate laughed while Spencer and Emily stared at each other, a bit alarmed.

"You must let me know if it is touch you seek," Suri Lakena said. "Now, try it again."

This time Spencer reached out and felt the soft fabric of her dress and her arm.

Suri Lakena placed her hand over Spencer's. "Touch is indeed a wonderful gift from the Universe, and what a joyous feeling to touch my grandson."

"Wait a minute," Emily protested, "holograms *are* just pictures, so how can Spencer touch you?"

"We pull energy from your matter—your atoms. We can only do it for a brief time, but it's how you're able to pet the head of Ayasha. You see, animals are pure innocent energy, so you're able to touch them immediately. But I needed to have the thought first before you could touch me. So, when Ayasha lands on your shoulder or you're touching my arm, we are pulling from your molecules. Your mother showed us how to do this. She explained how the vortex energy works and how it is the laser, as you call it. I wish we would have had more time with her. She had a beautiful spirit."

"Our mom did all *that*?" Emily asked.

"Yes, your mother was quite a scientist. I would say she was even more intelligent than my own husband."

"Sir Benjamin?" Spencer asked.

"What's that sound?" Emily asked as they all turned around to look at the other passageway. It became louder and louder as it was nearing the room.

"It sounds like a horse!" Spencer yelled as he hid behind Suri Lakena.

They could hear hoof beats and the snorts and blows of a huge horse. The children's eyes were fixed on the opening in the wall when a white stallion burst into the room. He jumped through the vortex and scattered light particles everywhere. When he landed on the other side he reared up, standing only on his powerful back legs. Emily and Spencer were trying to see him through the purple and silver colors of the vortex that swirled around the room. The stallion was adorned with a black leather saddle and bridle accented with pure silver studs that sparkled as the lights from the vortex reflected off of them. The blanket underneath his saddle was dark red and trimmed in a thin, gold edging.

He was a stunning white horse with a flowing silver mane and tail. He walked over to Emily and Spencer and stretched out his front left leg while bending back his right, bowing to the children. When he lowered his nose to the rock floor, the children could see Sir Benjamin Howell riding on his back.

"Did someun' call fer me?" Sir Benjamin asked in his thick Scottish accent.

"Please forgive my husband," Suri Lakena said. "He and Amadeus love nothing more than to make a grand first impression."

The horse walked over and grabbed Spencer's shirt sleeve with his teeth, pulling him out from behind Suri Lakena.

Sir Benjamin winked at Spencer. "Now, take it easy, Amadeus. The lad will warm up en time."

Sir Benjamin's flaming red hair fell down to his shoulders and his long beard was slightly darker in color. He was a big man, but sitting atop Amadeus made him seem like a giant. He wore a shiny silver breastplate embossed with the same lion and sword that were on the medallion.

CHAPTER SEVEN

A swath of tartan plaid wool was draped around one shoulder bound at his waist by a black leather strap that also held his sword. When he dismounted from the stallion he handed the reins to Spencer and walked over to Kate. He kissed her hand and politely bowed.

"Dearest Katherine," he said, "yeh look as beautiful es ever."

"Thank you, Sir Benjamin," she replied. "It's wonderful to see you again. I brought the children to meet you." She struggled to pull Emily out from behind her.

"Aye—Katie," he said, "Jenny's wee babies all grown up, eh." He peeked his head around Kate to see Emily. "Don' be scared, lassie—I'm a bit o' a blowhard."

Emily slowly reached out to shake his hand and Sir Benjamin kissed it and bowed as he had with Kate.

"Sir Benjamin Howell of Edinburgh, Scotland—at yer service."

Emily began to smile at his grand gestures: she was starting to feel more comfortable.

"Tha's it, lassie, we won't hurt yeh," he said. "Now, let's go an' meet yer brother."

He held out his arm for her and they walked across the room to Spencer and Amadeus. The big white stallion was pawing at the rock floor. Spencer was frozen but still holding onto the reins of the majestic animal.

"My husband, this is Spencer," Suri Lakena said, taking Sir Benjamin's other arm.

Spencer swallowed hard as the big man looked him in the eyes. Sir Benjamin took the reins from Spencer and handed them to Emily.

"Would yeh hold me mount, dear lass?"

"Sure!" she exclaimed, looking up at Amadeus.

Sir Benjamin held out his hand to Spencer. Spencer took it and Sir Benjamin put his other hand on Spencer's shoulder.

"We've been waitin' fer yeh laddie," he said as he studied Spencer. "An' yeh 'ave the red hair of a Howell, don't yeh?"

"I guess so," Spencer said, glancing over at Kate. "But my name is Sweetwater."

"Aye—Sweetwater, indeed it tis, but we were all Howells first. An' yeh carry me second name too."

"Your second name?"

"Aye, lad—I'm Sir Benjamin *Spencer* Howell!"

Spencer was stunned as he looked up at the giant man. He studied his silver chestplate. The lion and the sword reminded him of the medallion around Ayasha's neck. "Can I ask you a question, Sir Benjamin?"

"Aye, laddie—yeh can ask me anythin' yeh want."

"Why was your name Howell and our name is Sweetwater?"

"Well, me name is Sweetwater too, lad. Yeh see, when I lived en Scotland I was doin' some scientific work fer the Royal Society of Edinburgh—an' me name was Howell. Me partner was Sir Angus Wynn of Kilkardy, an' he turned out to be a very bad man. He stole me work an' came here to America. So, I followed him. Well, when Sir Angus found out he only had half me work, he was very angry an' came lookin' fer me. But by tha' time I had met Lakena an' we were already married an' had a wee baby on the way. So, to protect them, I changed me name so he couldn't find me."

"Oh, I see—so you picked the name Sweetwater," Spencer said.

"Aye, lad. Lakena's people gave us this land an' they called it the land of sweet water, because of the fountain."

Spencer nodded. "That makes sense."

Emily tugged on the tartan cloth at his waist. "Sir Benjamin, I have a question too."

"Aye, lassie. What's yer question?"

"What was the scientific work you were doing?"

"Ah, well, that would take a bit of explainin', lassie, an' I'm afraid I must save it fer another time."

Takoda let out a howl and the vortex began to slow again. With that, Sir Benjamin mounted Amadeus in one leap, backing the white stallion away from the children.

"Twas me pleasure to make yer acquaintance, me grandchildren—and dearest, Katherine, a pleasure as always. My wife, yeh must return soon. The power es fleeting!"

He squeezed his heels into the flanks of Amadeus and the stallion burst into full gallop, jumping the vortex and heading back through the opening in the cave wall.

"My husband speaks wisely," Suri Lakena said. "If you are to leave the mountain, you should go now."

"But we have so many questions," Emily said. "Like what's happening to the power in the vortex and--"

"Not now, Emily," Kate said. "We can talk about it at home."

The power in the vortex was back to normal again and Suri Lakena walked over and placed her hands on Emily's and Spencer's shoulders.

"We have many days before us for questions, my dear grandchildren. We will be together for a very long time. Now, my animal spirits, we must return. Ayasha, lead the way as protector of the cave!"

Takoda the wolf and Kuma the jaguar took their places beside Suri Lakena and Ayasha jumped from the boulder and took flight. She flew around the cave several times and then up the passageway she had come through. Lakena and the other two animals turned and headed toward the other opening in the cave wall. Kate and the children listened until the sound of the bells had disappeared. The vortex began to spiral back down into the fountain and once again it began to spew water like before.

"Okay, kids, it's getting late," Kate said. "Your father's going to be worried about us, so let's get home."

"But, Gram," Emily said, "what about my questions?"

"I'll explain everything at home. But listen, your father doesn't know about the cave and he has a lot on his mind, so let's just keep this as our little secret. Can you both do that?"

"Yes, ma'am."

CHAPTER EIGHT

ONE, TWO, THREE—JUMP!

"Hold still, Spencer," Emily insisted, holding the scissors close to his neck.

"Why does Jonas still need hair samples if we already know why I can talk to animals?" Spencer asked.

"Well, when I called him and told him about you being a Gatekeeper and about the cave and everything, he said you'd make a very interesting scientific experiment. He thinks you might have weird DNA or something, and I agree. You're a real scientific oddball. You're not natural, you're--"

"Okay, okay, I get it already. Just hurry up!"

Emily finished getting a perfect sample of hair and then held tightly to a few more pieces and pulled hard.

"OUCH!" Spencer yelled. "That hurt! Why did you do that?" He rubbed the back of his head.

"Jonas needs a few pieces that are pulled out from the roots. He said it's the best way to test DNA." Emily slid the hair sample into a plastic bag with Spencer's name written on it. Next she turned toward

Sully sleeping on the rug beside Spencer's bed. She bent down on the floor, but Sully jumped up when he heard the sound of the scissors.

"It's all right, boy, she won't hurt you—much," Spencer said laughing. He sat down on the floor and held Sully by his collar. "Cut it here, on his chest, where it's a little longer—but only cut it I don't want you to pull any out. Jonas will just have to test Sully's the best he can."

"Okay, I don't want to hurt him either."

She worked the scissors with one hand while holding onto the hair with the other. She placed Sully's hair into another plastic bag with his name written on it and put both samples in her pocket. Spencer let go of Sully and the big dog shook and sent loose hair flying in all directions.

"You should have waited for a minute and he would have given you all the samples you needed," Spencer said and they both laughed.

Emily plopped down on Spencer's bed. "He really seems like he's feeling better, don't you think?"

"Well, who wouldn't feel good after having Gram's pot pie for dinner?" Spencer rolled Sully on his back to scratch his tummy. "Look at that big belly." Sully kicked up with his back legs enjoying the game. "Hey," Spencer looked up at Emily, "thanks for helping me with Sully."

"No problem. I love him, too, you know!" She threw a pillow down on top of them.

"Hey, what's going on in here?" Kate asked as she came into the room and closed the door behind her.

"Oh, nothin'," Spencer said.

"Hey, Gram, do you have time for my questions now?" Emily asked as Kate sat on the bed next to her.

"Yes, Emily," Kate said. "Then we'll go downstairs. Your dad rented a movie for tonight."

"All right!" Spencer exclaimed. "Is it the one I asked for? The one about the mummy and the secret tomb?"

"I'm not sure," she said, "but haven't you had enough of tombs and caves for one day?"

"Nope, bring it on!" Spencer said laughing as he gave headbutts to Sully.

"What are your questions, Emily?" Kate asked.

Emily walked to the window and looked out toward the barn. The sun was just slipping down behind the hayfields and Emily knew somewhere out there was the mountain they had been to that day.

"Well, my first question is—where is it?" she asked, pointing out the window in the direction the mountain should be.

"Hey—yeah," Spencer joined in as he jumped up from the floor. "Remember today when we were looking through the window in that old rock wall on top of the mountain? We could see Sweetwater Farms from there but now we can't see the mountain from here."

Kate joined her grandchildren at the window. "You see, kids, the vortex has a way of protecting itself. From a distance it blends in with nature and you'd never know it was there."

"Until you get up close to it?" Emily asked.

Kate nodded. "That's right."

"Okay, question number two," Emily continued. "Why didn't *you* need to wear goggles to see the Guardians and Suri Lakena?"

"Remember when I told you the story of how Abbey and I joined?"

They both nodded their heads.

"Well, your mother told me when I wished on Lakena's moon it must have changed...oh, what did she call it? Oh, yes—my molecular structure. I don't really know how it all works but I've always been able to see them."

"Hmm," Emily thought about her answer. "Well, that brings me to my next question. You said Mom was working on genetics in the cave. What did you mean?"

"Well, when Spencer was born your grandfather and I knew there was a chance he could be the next Gatekeeper—so we decided to tell your mother. She thought it best not to tell your father so things could stay as normal as possible for you kids. Anyway, we took her to the cave and that's when she met Suri Lakena and Sir Benjamin. She began to study Spencer and his DNA because she wanted to make sure when he grew up she could explain everything to him."

"Okay, that makes sense. Now, my last question: Suri Lakena said she and the other animals could take on other forms to protect the vortex. Is it like when Spencer saw Sully in the mirror? Was he actually turning into him?"

"Great question, Emily!" Spencer said, giving her a high-five slap.

"Thanks!"

"Exactly," Kate said laughing at the two of them. She turned to Spencer and gently brushed the hair away from his eyes. "I know everything seems a little confusing right now and you don't know when or how you and Sully or any other animal will join—but in time you will. You'll simply ask and you'll be joined."

"Who will I ask?"

"Well, I don't really mean ask," Kate said. "I guess what I mean is that you'll begin to believe in yourself."

Spencer looked up at her with a funny look on his face.

"Okay, do you remember when your father taught you how to ride a bike?"

"Sure!"

"Well, it works like that. First, you have to build up energy."

"Like when you're pedaling!" Emily exclaimed.

"That's right," Kate agreed. "Then after you build up the energy you have to believe that you can do it."

"Like when Dad let go of the bike and I pedaled on my own?" Spencer asked.

"Just like that," Kate said.

"Hey," Emily was thinking again. "Remember that day in the barn when Peaches was having Rosebud? You joined with Abbey but you didn't look like you had a lot of energy. And I remember Abbey fell asleep."

"Well, she wasn't asleep," Kate said, "she was just resting. Remember, Abbey is very old and we've been doing this for a very long time. It's easy for us because we don't need a lot of energy. Also, Abbey and I can only talk to each other. Gatekeepers are the only ones who can actually turn into other animals."

The door to Spencer's room flew open and their father burst into the room.

"Who's ready for a mummy movie!" he said in a loud, scary voice, startling everyone. All three of them stared at him without making a move toward the door. "Well, you don't have to be so excited about it."

"No, it's not that," Kate told him, "I was just telling the children a story."

"I hope it wasn't a scary story about mummies and tombs and really old stuff," he said as he tickled Emily's neck and grabbed Spencer around the waist.

"No, nothing like that," Kate said, winking at the children. "Come on kids, let's go watch that movie. I'll make the popcorn!"

❊ ❊ ❊ ❊ ❊ ❊ ❊ ❊ ❊ ❊ ❊

"It's a beautiful morning and you kids should be outside playing," Kate yelled upstairs from the kitchen.

Emily was on the computer trying to find out where Edinburgh, Scotland was and Spencer was on the floor in his bedroom, attempting to beat his high score on his video game.

"Yes, ma'am," Spencer hollered down just before messing up on the game and throwing it on his bed. "Come on, Sully, let's go outside."

When he heard the word *outside* Sully sprang to his feet and started jumping on Spencer.

"Oh, you want to go *outside?*" Spencer knew how to get Sully excited and the dog was now barking and running around in circles. "Let's go *outside*! Good boy, Sully! *Outside*!" Sully, still running, headed out of Spencer's room and downstairs to the back door.

Chuckling, Spencer got his baseball and glove from the closet.

"That's one silly dog," he said as he closed the closet door. He stopped and stared at the wall somewhat lost in a daze. "Energy," he said to himself. "That's how we can get energy!" He left his room and ran down the hallway to the playroom. "Emily! Emily!"

Still focused on the computer screen, she snapped. "What? I'm right here, you don't have to yell!"

"Come on, I want to try an experiment."

Her curiosity got the best of her and she looked up at him.

"What kind of experiment?"

"Well, I think I figured out how to get Sully's energy up so we can try and join. Come on, I'm gonna try it in the backyard." His words trailed off as he left and headed for the stairs.

"Wait, I'm coming!" she yelled, pulling on her shoes.

Sully was in the kitchen when Spencer came downstairs. Kate had been cleaning up the breakfast dishes, and as Spencer ran past the kitchen he could see she was about to give Sully one of his doggy treats.

"STOP!" he yelled, catching her before she dropped it into his mouth.

"Spencer, you scared me to death! What's wrong with you?" she asked, pulling the treat back with a jerk of her hand.

"Well, um..." In the nick of time Emily came running into the kitchen. "What's going on?"

"Well, your brother just gave me the scare of my life and all I was trying to do was give Sully his treat." She held her hand out again for Sully to take the treat.

"NO!" Emily yelled this time.

"Okay, what's wrong with these treats and why don't you want Sully to have one?"

Spencer and Emily looked at each other.

"Okay, Gram," Emily said, "just promise you won't get mad."

"Me? Mad? When have you known me to get mad at you kids?"

"Well, remember the other day when I left my new shoes out in the rain?" Spencer said.

Kate sat down at the table. "Okay, never mind. Just tell me what's going on with Sully."

"Well, when Anna got sick and they said she had allergies, we thought that maybe Sully had allergies too," Emily said.

"Yeah, because Sully felt the same as she did," Spencer added.

"Right, so anyway, we looked at Sully's food and the ingredients said it had corn."

"Just like what Anna's allergic to," Spencer inserted.

"Yeah," Emily said. "So we thought we would do an experiment for a few days."

Spencer interrupted again. "Before he goes to see Dr. Miles tomorrow."

"Spencer, I'm telling the story," Emily said.

"Okay, okay—so tell it."

"So, what was the experiment?" Kate asked.

"Well, we did a controlled experiment where we fed Sully only the food that we ate and we didn't give him any of his."

"Yeah, in case it was his food making him sick," Spencer said looking sheepishly at Emily.

Kate looked down at Sully still sitting in front of her waiting for his treat. "So do you think the experiment's working?" Spencer and Emily looked at each other again and Emily spoke.

"Well, I really wasn't supposed to conclude the experiment until tomorrow, but I believe we've proven our hypothesis and the experiment has been a complete success!"

"So, in other words, you two think Sully could be allergic to his dog food and maybe we should find something else for him to eat?"

"Yes, ma'am," they said together.

Kate looked at Sully and rubbed his head.

CHAPTER EIGHT

"You are one lucky dog to have these kids care about you so much." She bent down and kissed his nose. "Did your father know about this?"

"No, ma'am," they both said, still not knowing if she was going to be angry or not.

"Well, I don't know when I've ever been more proud of you two. You did all this by yourselves without telling me or even asking for help."

The two children looked at each other.

"Well, Gram," Spencer said, "you did kinda help. You just didn't know it."

"What do you mean?" she questioned. "I didn't do anything."

"You made all of Sully's food for him," Emily said. "Well, not everything 'cause Spencer and I made his breakfast and lunch but you made his supper."

Kate thought for a moment as the two children slowly backed out of the kitchen.

"You mean to tell me you fed him the extra pot pie I was going to take over to Ennis?"

The kids ran out the back screen door with Sully following behind.

"Remember, Gram," Spencer yelled back, "you've never been more proud of us!"

❊ ❊ ❊ ❊ ❊ ❊ ❊ ❊ ❊ ❊ ❊

"Hey, guys, what's up?" Anna asked coming into the backyard.

"We're trying to get Sully's energy up," Spencer said.

"What Spencer means is that we're trying to see if Spencer and Sully can join together like they did the other day," Emily explained.

"You mean like in Mr. Tucker's barn when you talked to Pee Wee and Sweetie Pie?" Anna asked, looking at Spencer.

"Well, not only can he talk to the animals," Emily said, "but now we know he can actually turn into the animals. It has to do with DNA and energy and where our grandmother took us yesterday."

"Whoa, wait just one minute," Anna said. "You mean Spencer can become Sully? With four feet and a tail and everything? Where exactly did she take you yesterday?"

"Oh, man, you would never believe in a million years!" Spencer exclaimed throwing the ball for Sully to fetch.

"Spencer, you tell her I've got to take these samples over to Jonas. We'll try the experiment when I get back."

"What experiment?" Anna asked sounding even more confused.

They watched Emily put on her helmet and pedal down the gravel road toward the apple orchard.

"First things first." Spencer sat at the picnic table. "How's Sweetie Pie? Does she like her new house?"

"Oh, she's so cute. I just love her so much," Anna said. "And I think she likes the house. She walks around rubbing her head on the furniture and Dad says that means she's getting comfortable with everything. Maybe you could come over and talk to her and make sure she's okay with everything."

"Sure, but first I have to figure out how it all works. Like right now, I don't feel like I can talk to Sully." Spencer looked at Sully playing with the ball under the willow tree. "I mean, I just have this feeling that we're not connected."

"So, how do you get connected?" Anna asked.

"Gram says that I'll learn how to do it. She says that if I'm going to be a Gatekeeper, I'll figure it out."

"Whoa, back up, Spencer. What's a Gatekeeper?"

"Oh, yeah, I almost forgot to tell you where we went yesterday. Well, it was so cool..."

Spencer told Anna the story of their adventure in the cave and about Suri Lakena and Sir Benjamin. He explained about The Hidden Mountain and the falcon and the medallion. When he finished his story, Anna jumped up from the picnic table and started to run toward the stream.

"Hey, what's wrong?" Spencer yelled. "What'd I say?"

She ran through the bushes that lined the backyard and to the path that led to her house. "I'll be back in a minute!"

When she reached the bridge she stopped and lay down on her stomach. She put her hand down into the clear, fresh water and drew it up to her mouth. Spencer watched her jump up with excitement and run back over the bridge, following the path again through the bushes and back to him.

"It does taste like cotton candy!" she exclaimed.

He threw the ball for Sully. "I know. See, I told you."

"This is incredible, Spencer! Do you realize you could be the best veterinarian in the world? And...I could be your manager! I can see it all now," she said, looking out into space. "We'll be unstoppable!"

Spencer looked into space to see what she was seeing.

"Hey, I never thought about this helping me to become a better veterinarian."

"Not just a better veterinarian, the best in the whole world!"

"Well, let's not get ahead of ourselves," he said, feeling a little uneasy. "I still don't know how to join with the animals."

"So, is that what your experiment is about?"

"Yeah. Gram told me when I want to join with an animal, first there needs to be energy. She said it's like when you ride your bike for the first time by yourself. First you start pedaling, that's the energy part, then when the person holding the bike let's go, you have to believe you can do it on your own."

"Oh, I get it. So, Sully needs energy."

"Well, I think I got that part figured out—watch."

Spencer yelled for Sully to come over to him. The dog walked to Spencer and sat down in front of him. "Sully, you want to go *outside*?" Sully cocked his head to one side and looked at Spencer. "Come on, Sully, go *outside*!" Again, Sully just stared at Spencer.

"I don't get it," Spencer said, feeling a little embarrassed.

"Um—Spencer," Anna said softly. "You're already outside."

Spencer thought for a moment and closed his eyes.

"Oh, man," he said, shaking his head, "when we did this before we were in the house. Now what can I do to get his energy up?"

Anna thought for a moment while she petted Sully's head.

"I know!" she exclaimed. "How about running? It's kinda like riding a bike. You could throw the ball a bunch for him and that would get his energy up."

"Great idea. Come here, boy," Spencer said, moving out to the middle of the yard. Sully followed him, jumping in the air trying to get the ball. "Let's go!" Spencer yelled as he threw the ball. It cleared the bushes and the driveway and Sully ran after it. He ran through the backyard and jumped over the bushes in one leap.

"Oh, man, maybe I threw it too far." Spencer stood on his tiptoes trying to see where the yellow dog went. Just then Sully came running up from behind Spencer knocking him to the ground. Spencer laid there looking at the dog panting heavily. "Well, I think his energy is up as high as it can go."

"Do you feel anything?" Anna asked hoping the experiment worked.

Spencer stood up and was silent for a moment. "Are you in there, boy?" he whispered. The dog was back under the tree, playing with the ball. "Nothin'!"

"Well, don't give up, Spencer, I'll help you figure it out."

❊ ❊ ❊ ❊ ❊ ❊ ❊ ❊ ❊ ❊ ❊

"Hello, Mr. Walker," Emily said as she passed through the living room on her way to Jonas's workroom.

"Hello, Emily," he said, continuing to watch T.V. "Jonas is in his laboratory. I guess you know where that is." He looked up and gave her a smile.

"Thank you, sir," she said as she made her way through the kitchen.

Jonas had his back to Emily and didn't hear her come into the room.

"Hey, Jonas, I brought the hair samples from Spencer and Sully," she said as she walked down the ramp.

"Oh, great, Emily, perfect timing. I was just reading up on different cultures and their beliefs about energy systems on the planet. Did you know there are vortexes all over the world?"

"Yeah."

"How'd you know that? I didn't even know that," he said, moving his wheelchair closer to the work table in the middle of the room.

"Suri Lakena told us. Remember, she's the Gatekeeper of the vortex."

"Oh, yeah, your two hundred year old grandmother," he said, laughing.

"What? You don't believe me?"

"Emily, I'm a scientist," he said. "Things have to be proven to me before I actually believe them."

"Well," she said proudly, "I'm a scientist, too, just like my mother, and everything I saw yesterday was true and I *can* prove it!"

"Okay, okay, I didn't mean to make you mad I just want to see the proof for myself."

"All right," she answered. "Let's look at the hair samples and I'll show you proof."

Jonas pulled the microscope over from the middle of the table.

"Hand me those two bottles over by the sink, Emily."

At the sink Emily tried to find the two bottles he was talking about. She saw test tubes with different things in them and two large beakers filled with liquids ready to be heated on the Bunsen burners—but she didn't see the two bottles.

"Bring me those slides too," he said as he carefully opened one of the plastic bags.

She looked further down on the cabinet and saw the small black case. The slides were stacked neatly inside and it reminded her of Sir Benjamin's case in the trunk in the cave. There she also found the two bottles Jonas had requested.

"Hey, this bottle of blue stuff is almost empty," she said as she brought everything to the table.

"Oh, yeah, I forgot," he said, "I need to get some more." He held the bottle up to the light to check the amount. "Well, there's enough to do one of them. We'll start with Spencer's."

He pulled the hair out of the plastic bag using a pair of tweezers. He chose one particular piece and placed it on the slide.

"Great hair follicle, Emily!"

"Thanks!" she said, proud of herself. "I had to trick Spencer but it was worth it."

"Well, I'll just put it on the slide and mix a drop of each of these liquids with it and we'll see what we have."

Emily was so excited she could hardly wait for her turn to look through the microscope.

"What do you see?" she asked.

"Well, it's the typical stuff so far—cells with strands of DNA inside of them."

"May I see?" she politely asked.

Jonas turned the microscope toward her. "Sure."

"Cool, I can see the cells. Is the DNA that spaghetti-looking stuff?"

"That's it," he said, smiling. "That's a pretty good way to describe it, spaghetti."

"So, what's this other stuff in here with the spaghetti?"

"What? What other stuff? Here, wait a minute, I'm going to hook up my laptop to the microscope and we can look at it together." He slid his computer down the work table and attached the cables from it to the microscope. "Now show me what you saw."

CHAPTER EIGHT

"There," she pointed to the computer screen. "It doesn't look like the other stuff."

"No way!" Jonas yelled out. "There's no way that could be in Spencer's DNA! Are you sure this hair sample belongs to Spencer?" He looked at the name on the plastic bag.

"Yes, I cut the hair myself. Why? What's wrong with Spencer's DNA?"

❊❊❊❊❊❊❊❊❊❊❊

Anna sat quietly beside Spencer thinking back over the last few days when Spencer joined with the animals. First, there was the time at school when Dwight Fitch had made him mad and Spencer started to growl. Next, was in Mr. Tucker's barn when he talked to Sweetie Pie and Pee Wee.

"But nothing happened there," she thought. "We simply walked into the barn and went to play with the baby goats."

Spencer walked over to Sully and lay down beside him in the grass and Anna thought how peaceful they looked. Then she remembered. The day Spencer growled at Dwight he was mad, angry, furious! "That's enough to get your energy going," she thought. "But what about the barn? What happened there?"

Just then a strong gust of wind blew hard and the back screen door to the house swung open with a bang. The loud noise scared her so much she jumped up from the picnic table.

"That's it!" she yelled.

"What?" Spencer asked. "It's just the wind picking up a little."

"No, I figured out why you and Sully can't join!"

"Well, how about letting us in on it."

"It's not Sully that needs to get his energy up."

"Huh?"

"It's you!"

"Me? What do you mean? How can I get my energy up?"

"Well, remember when Dwight and the Pitsner twins were trying to take your lunch?"

"Don't remind me," he said, looking down at the ground.

"Well, you got real mad at them. That's energy! And remember the other day at Mr. Tucker's barn when you talked to Sweetie Pie and Pee Wee? Before we went into the barn the rooster flew at you. Remember it scared you and you *fell* to the ground."

"I wouldn't say that I fell exactly, it was more like I tripped."

"Spencer, listen, that's energy too! Being scared."

"It is? Well, then I got lots of energy all of the time!"

Anna sighed, frustrated. "Do you understand what I'm saying?"

"Yeah, I get it. I have to get *my* energy up and not Sully's."

"That's right," she said. "Oh, Emily would be so proud of me for figuring this one out!"

"So, how do you think I should get my energy up now? I'm not mad and I'm not scared."

Anna thought for a moment, and, out of nowhere, she stomped as hard as she could on Spencer's foot.

He let out a yell and fell in the grass. "But now I'm pretty angry!"

"I'm sorry, Spencer. I had an idea and I had to go with it. Are you all right?"

"Yeah, Spencer, are you all right?" said a familiar voice in his head.

❊ ❊ ❊ ❊ ❊ ❊ ❊ ❊ ❊ ❊ ❊

"So what's in his DNA?" Emily asked again while they both looked at the computer screen.

"You see that?" Jonas asked, pointing to the screen.

"You mean that square thing?"

"Yeah. Well, that shouldn't be there," he said, turning the lever on his wheelchair and moving toward the bookcase. He selected a large black-leather-bound book and brought it back over to the table. He opened it to the "Plants and Living Cells" section.

"Is it Sully's DNA?" Emily asked, hoping she would have the proof she needed.

"Well, I'm not exactly sure if Sully's DNA is in there but I do see the DNA of other animals. You see, our cells look just like cells from animals—it's only the DNA that's different. Like, look at this one," he said pointing to the screen. "That's a lizard. And this one here is a mouse."

"How can you tell?"

"Their genetic coding is different—I mean the sequence of their codes in their chromosomes."

Emily stared at Jonas with a blank look.

"Okay," he said, "each strand of spaghetti has information in it telling it to be something—like a lizard or a mouse or a dog or a boy. Well, not only does Spencer have DNA in his cells from different animals, but those square things are plant cells." He studied the cells a moment longer and looked back at the book. "There!" he said, pointing to a page and looking back at the computer again.

Emily looked down at the book on the table. She looked at the computer and back at the picture in the book.

"How can that be? That's a picture of a cell from an oak tree. How did that get into Spencer?"

* * * * * * * * * * *

"It worked!" Spencer ran over to Sully and put his arms around him. "It's great to be with you again, buddy!"

"You too, Spencer! It's my favorite thing in the whole world!"

Spencer rubbed Sully's head and tickled his ears. Sully rolled over for a belly rub and Spencer could hear him laughing.

"I love when you tickle me, Spencer, but let's play some more ball. Come on, throw it for me!" Sully jumped to his feet.

"What's he saying, Spencer?"

"He wants me to throw the ball."

"Hey, maybe that's a good thing," Anna said. "Maybe if we get his energy up, you can totally turn into him, like Suri Lakena said.

Spencer threw the ball over the bushes again. "Okay, boy, go get the ball!"

After a few moments, Sully came up behind Spencer and knocked him to the ground.

"You should have remembered that from the last time, Spencer." Sully was panting hard from the run around the house.

"Oh, you're a real funny guy, huh, boy?" Spencer said, getting back on his feet.

"I don't understand," Anna said. "Why didn't you turn into him? You both have energy."

Spencer was remembering what his grandmother said about riding the bike. Once you have the energy and the person holding the bike let's go, if you believe in yourself, you can do it.

"I know!" Spencer yelled. "I have to believe I can do it! Come on, Sully, I've got an idea." They walked to the middle of the yard.

"What are we going to do now, Spencer?"

Spencer bent down on one knee and faced Sully.

"Sully, Grandma Kate says that we not only can talk to each other but we can also turn into each other. I want to see if we can do it. Do you want to try?"

"Sure, that sounds like fun! How do we do it?" Sully wagged his tail.

"Well, you stand beside me and we'll start running. On the count of three, we'll jump into the air. Now, the most important thing is I have to believe we can join."

Sully jumped up on Spencer. **"Oh, Spencer, that's easy. I believe you can do anything!"**

"Thanks, Sully," he said, moving him over to stand beside him. "Okay, Anna, we're ready!"

CHAPTER EIGHT

Spencer started to run and Sully stayed right beside him.

"Okay, boy—on the count of three!"

They began to run faster and faster and Spencer yelled out:

"ONE, TWO, THREE—JUMP!"

Sully leaped into the air right at Spencer, and in that moment, in the blink of an eye, Spencer vanished and Sully landed firmly back on the ground.

"We did it!" Spencer exclaimed. "We joined!"

Anna jumped up from the picnic table and ran over to the yellow dog jumping around in the yard.

"All right! We did it all by ourselves!" she cried. "Who says Emily is the only one who can do science stuff around here?"

Anna's expression changed. The dog stopped jumping and just stared at her.

"What's wrong, Anna? Why are you looking at me so funny?" Spencer asked.

"Yeah, why's she looking at us like that?"

"This is just so weird," she said. "I'm hearing your voice but it's coming out of Sully!"

"I know! Isn't it great?" Spencer said. "Me and Sully are joined!"

"Um—Spencer. I don't think we really thought this through." Anna sat down at the picnic table. "This is why we should never do science experiments unless Emily is here with us."

"Why, what do you mean?"

"Just look at yourself. You're a dog! How do we get you back to being--Spencer?"

Spencer looked down and saw Sully's two front paws where his own feet should be. He looked behind him and could see Sully's long tail moving back and forth in the air. He and Sully *had* joined and he was—a dog!

"Awww—man, Dad's gonna kill me!"

CHAPTER NINE

WHO'S THE BOSS?

Sofia stood on the front porch of her house looking for Anna. Then she walked down the path that led to the bridge, calling, "Anna…Anna, time for lunch."

"Hey, my mom's coming! What do we do?"

"We should hide!" Spencer exclaimed. "Come on we'll go under the picnic table."

The yellow dog lay on the ground and crawled on his belly like a solider in enemy territory.

"Wait a minute, Spencer. She doesn't know you're here too."

"Hey, that's right."

"Just remember not to say anything."

"Okay, you hear that, Sully? Don't say anything."

"I don't think I'm the problem, Spencer. They can't hear me. They can only hear you."

"Remember, don't say anything, you two. Here she comes!"

"Hey, Anna, what are you doing?" Sofia asked. "Why didn't you answer me when I called you?"

CHAPTER NINE

"Oh, sorry, Mom." Anna picked up Sully's ball. "We were just playing. Here you go, boy, fetch!"

When she threw the ball Sully bolted. Spencer didn't even have a chance to catch his breath. Anna and her mother watched as Sully leaped the bushes.

"Whoa!" shouted Spencer uncontrollably as they flew through the air.

"Who said that?" Sofia asked.

Anna meant to think of a good answer but instead blurted out, "Oh, that was probably Spencer."

Her mother stared at her.

"Um—I think he's on the other side of the bushes," she added.

"Oh, well tell him hello for me. Anyway, I need you to come and eat your lunch. I made *arroz con pollo* and it just came out of the oven."

"Okay, Mom, I'll be right there. Just let me tell Spencer I'm leaving."

"All right, I'm going to find your father and we'll meet you at the house."

Sully came running up behind them and crawled under the bushes with the ball.

"Okay, Mom," Anna said as she watched Sully. "I think Dad's in the barn."

Anna walked over to the bushes, keeping one eye on her mother to make sure she was actually heading in the other direction. "Why did you yell like that? I told you to keep quiet."

Spencer spit the ball out of Sully's mouth. "I couldn't help it, he just took off! Yuck! That ball tastes terrible, Sully. How can you stand to put that thing in your mouth?"

"What's wrong with it? It's the best ball in the whole world!" Sully tried to put it back in his mouth.

"No way, Sully, not while I'm in here! And that's another thing I want to get straight. When we're joined there's only going to be one boss and that's me! No more going after balls or jumping bushes unless I say so. You got that?"

"Got it, boss," Sully said, wagging his tail.

"And don't do that either, it tickles!"

"I can't help it. It happens automatically when I'm happy."

"Well, do you always have to be so happy?"

"Yep!"

Anna could see Sully's head moving from side to side and she knew Spencer must be talking to him.

"I hate to break in on your private conversation but my mother wants me to come home for lunch."

"You can't go now! You have to help us get...un-joined!"

"I'll be back soon. Just hang out here in the backyard and I'll come back as quick as I can."

"Okay, but hurry."

He moved further back into the bushes to keep out of sight.

❊ ❊ ❊ ❊ ❊ ❊ ❊ ❊ ❊ ❊ ❊

Emily and Jonas were still in Jonas's lab figuring out how cells from an oak tree could possibly be inside of Spencer.

"This has to be the oddest thing I've ever seen," Jonas said, studying the picture in the book. "It's interesting enough just to have DNA from other animals mixed with Spencer's, but plant cells too!"

"See, I told you," Emily said proudly. "I guess that gives you the proof you were looking for, doesn't it?"

"Hmm—proof," he said, still unclear about what it all meant. "Well, I still want to look at Sully's hair sample though."

"Well, we need some more of that stuff in the bottle. Where do we get it?"

"At the hobby store in the mall. My dad can drive us. If you need to call home there's a phone in the kitchen."

"Yeah, that's a good idea."

Jonas went into the living room to ask his father to drive them to the store. Emily finished her phone call and met Jonas and his father in the driveway. She watched as Mr. Walker slid the door of the van open for Jonas. He pushed a button inside the door and a metal platform came out and lowered to the ground. Jonas pushed the lever on his wheelchair and rolled onto the platform. Mr. Walker pushed the button again and the platform lifted the wheelchair into the air and back into the van.

"Wow, that's pretty cool! You can go anywhere you want."

"Yeah, pretty much," Jonas said. "My uncle helped us customize the van for my wheelchair. He's an engineer at NASA. He said when I get old enough he'll put hand controls on the steering wheel so I can drive myself."

"I'll probably never get to drive a car," Emily said sadly. "I've had two pretty bad wrecks on my new bike and Dad says I'm the worst driver he's ever seen."

She jumped into the front seat, still talking about her bad driving record as they headed off to the mall.

❋ ❋ ❋ ❋ ❋ ❋ ❋ ❋ ❋ ❋ ❋

Still crouched under the bushes, Spencer heard a truck pulling into the driveway of the house.

"There's somebody coming," Sully whispered.

"I know, just be quiet," Spencer said.

He heard two men talking and could tell they were the voices of his father and Roberto. They walked through the backyard and stopped at the picnic table.

"Well, I'd better get home for lunch. Sofia is making chicken and rice, and I don't want to miss that." Roberto started to leave but stopped. "Oh, Will, I almost forgot. Have you heard anything else from that man, Billy Wynn?"

"No, not a word and it's got me a little concerned. My attorney says that it's plain and simple: Whoever has the deed to the property is the owner."

"And you don't have any idea where it could be?"

"No, and my mother doesn't either. I went through all of my dad's files too, and I didn't find anything. The only thing I can think of is when my great-great-great grandfather was originally given this land they weren't making deeds yet. So, I'm going to the local tax office tomorrow to see if they have any records that show Sir Benjamin owned the land. I'll never forgive myself if after two hundred years of Sweetwaters owning this place, I'm the one who loses it."

"Hey," Roberto put a hand on Will's shoulder, "don't be so hard on yourself. This isn't your fault. Listen, I'd better get to lunch, but remember, we're all in this together." He called back as he crossed through the bushes. "We'll find those papers."

Will sat down on the picnic table bench and looked around the yard. His eye caught something yellow underneath the bushes and he lowered his head to the ground to see what it was.

"Sully, is that you under there?" The big dog froze.

Will clapped his hands. "Sully, come here, boy."

"Spencer, what do I do? I can't disobey him."

"Okay, go to him--but don't say anything about me."

"Spencer, how many times do I have to tell you, no one can hear me but you. You're the one who has to stay quiet."

"Oh, yeah, I keep forgetting."

Sully crawled out from under the bushes and jogged over to Will. He rubbed his face on Will's pant leg and jumped up, putting his huge paws on Will's chest and licking his face.

"Good, boy," Will said, laughing. Sully jumped back to the ground and sat in front of him. "I don't know what I'm going to do, Sully. This farm is all we have. I don't know what Spencer and Emily would do if we had to leave it—not to mention Roberto, Sofia and Anna." He rubbed

Sully's head. "You know it's times like this when I miss Jenny the most. She always knew how to make me feel better. I can just hear her now, she'd say 'Will, you worry too much. As long as we have each other, we'll be just fine.'"

Sully laid down in the grass and a tear rolled down his face.

"You got something in your eye, boy?" Will reached out to wipe the tear. "Well anyway, I'd better go in and keep looking for those papers. You're a great listener, Sully." And with that Will went into the house.

"Spencer...Spencer?" Sully heard the faint sound of crying. **"Are you okay?"**

"Yeah, I'm okay. I just miss my mom."

Sully didn't say anything else. He waited until Spencer was ready to talk.

"Sully," Spencer finally said, "we've got to help Dad. It's not his fault we might lose Sweetwater Farms. And," Spencer thought for a moment, "I think I know just who to ask about that deed!"

✻ ✻ ✻ ✻ ✻ ✻ ✻ ✻ ✻ ✻ ✻

The Spring Valley Mall was located right in the middle of town. It was really just a little collection of shops and a lot smaller than one of the mega-malls down in Charlotte. Kate took Spencer and Emily there every August to get new clothes before the school year began. They would shop all day at Whitaker's Department Store and get ice cream at Sally's Sweet Shop. There was also a hardware store, a shop that sold kitchen accessories and a jewelry store—and at the end of the row of stores was the Town and Country Hobby Shop. Emily had never been there but had always been curious about exactly what they sold.

Mr. Walker pulled the van into a handicapped parking space at the front of the parking lot. "You need any help, son?"

"No, sir, I got it," Jonas replied. "We'll be back in a minute."

Jonas pushed the button on the wall of the van. The door slid open and the platform lowered Jonas to the ground.

"Come on, Emily," he said, pushing the lever forward on his chair.

They passed by the different store fronts and as they went by the hardware store Emily looked through the window and ducked behind Jonas's chair.

"Emily, what are you doing?" he asked, looking over his shoulder in an attempt to see her.

"In the store," she said in a whisper as she pointed to the glass window, "it's that man I was telling you about. The man who wants to take our farm—Billy Wynn!"

"Well, why are you hiding?"

"I don't really know."

"Hey, there are a couple of other men in there with him. It looks like they're getting some shovels and—oh, no!"

"What!" Emily asked. "What else do they have?"

"It's an axe! You know the kind with the long handle like firemen use to bust down doors."

He began laughing over the story he was making up to frighten her.

"Ha ha!" she said. "I don't scare that easy, Jonas Walker—but I sure would like to know what they're saying."

"Well, I'll just go and find out," and he reached for the handle on the front door of the store.

"Not without me!" Emily said as she grabbed the door handle from Jonas and held it open for him.

Jonas rolled through and Emily went in after him. She hid behind the first row of shelves she saw. Jonas made his way to where he had seen Billy Wynn, staying one aisle over from the three men, pretending he was shopping for batteries. Emily moved from one aisle to another like a secret-agent spy. She crouched behind a barrel of miscellaneous screwdrivers and took a giant step forward—landing her right behind a huge, cardboard flashlight that was twice her size.

CHAPTER NINE

"All right, boys, this should be enough equipment to get you going," Billy said. "Remember, the journal Sir Angus left says that one of the maps in Sir Benjamin's trunk will show what we're looking for. And I have a feeling I'll find the deed to the land in there, too. So, all we have to do is find that trunk!"

Emily let out a gasp before she clapped her hand over her mouth.

"What was that?" Billy asked as he started to walk over toward the large flashlight.

Jonas jumped in. "Excuse me! Um—do you think you could reach those batteries for me?" He pointed to the top shelf.

Billy turned toward Jonas and noticed his wheelchair.

"Sure, son," he said. "Which ones do you need?"

Emily saw her chance and headed for the door at the front of the store. Right before she grabbed for the handle one of Billy's men stepped in front of her, stopping her in her tracks. Her heart started to pound.

"Let me get the door fer yeh, lassie." He smiled as he reached out to open it for her.

Emily didn't even look up at his face, but on his arm she could see a tattoo. It had two crossed swords with a snake winding between them, just like the one Spencer had seen on Billy Wynn's alligator boots—and he was speaking with a Scottish accent, like Sir Benjamin!

"Thank you, sir," she said and ran out the open door.

Jonas caught up with her a few minutes later at the hobby shop.

"I wasn't sure where you'd gone."

"Well, I had to get out of there while I could. Did you hear what he said?"

"Yeah, but I don't really understand everything. Like, I know who Sir Benjamin is but who's Sir Angus and what's Billy Wynn looking for?"

❊ ❊ ❊ ❊ ❊ ❊ ❊ ❊ ❊ ❊ ❊

WHO'S THE BOSS?

Sully and Spencer went back under the bushes to wait for Anna. Kate came out the back door of the house and sat at the picnic table to put on her riding boots. Spencer tried to get her attention.

"Psst—hey, Gram," he whispered.

Kate looked around but continued to put on her boots when she didn't see anything.

"Hey, Gram, I'm over here—in the bushes."

Kate stopped what she was doing and looked around.

"Spencer, where are you?"

He crept out from under the bushes.

"Well, hello, Sully. Where's Spencer?"

The dog came over and sat in front of her.

"I'm right here, Gram. It's me, Spencer. I found out how to join with Sully."

Kate stared at the big dog for a moment, trying to believe what her ears were hearing. She saw the dog's mouth moving and heard Spencer's voice but she was having trouble putting the picture together.

"Gram, did you hear me?"

She cleared her throat and swallowed hard. "Spencer—how did you do it?"

"Just like you said, Gram. Anna helped me figure it out. I built up energy by running side by side with Sully. He jumped and I believed—and we did it! It was just like you said."

"Oh, Spencer! Look at you!" She jumped up from the table. "You're actually in there with Sully! Can he talk to you? Can you talk to him? Oh my goodness, I can't believe this!" She gave the dog a big hug.

"Hey, Gram," Spencer said in a muffled voice, "I can't breath, you're hugging us too tight."

"I'm sorry, Spencer—um, Sully, oh, well—Spencer and Sully!" she cried out and laughed.

"But, Gram, now there's a problem."

"What's the problem?" she asked, calming herself down.

CHAPTER NINE

"I don't know how to reverse it. I don't know how to turn back into me! Anna had to go in for lunch and me and Sully were supposed to wait for her here in the backyard. But I'm getting a little scared now and I thought maybe you could help us."

"Of course I'll help you," Kate said with a hug. "It's easy to reverse. It's probably easier than actually joining. All you have to do is relax and believe in yourself again."

"What do you mean relax?" he questioned. "Like go to sleep or something?"

"Well, I guess it's a little like sleeping. But more like thinking really peaceful thoughts so your body will relax. Okay, let's try this--how do you feel right now?"

"Okay, I guess. A little nervous. Maybe a little scared."

"There's nothing wrong with being nervous or scared, Spencer, but when you feel that way it creates energy. What we need now is—no energy. So, I want you to think about something relaxing—how about your mother? You have nice peaceful memories about her, don't you?"

"Yeah, but that also makes me nervous, so maybe I should think of something else."

Kate looked at Spencer and wondered why thinking about his mother would make him nervous.

"Okay, then, what else is peaceful to you?"

Sully's big head tilted back and forth as Spencer was trying to think of something peaceful.

"I know!" he said. "But do I have to tell you?"

"No, you don't have to tell me, you can keep it to yourself."

Spencer thought of the dream he had the other night when he and Nicole were walking near the hayfield. He was lost in his thoughts when his father came out the screen door.

"Hey, Mom," he said, "have you seen Emily or Spencer? I wanted to have lunch with them." Kate looked down at the dog sitting in front of her and winked.

"Well, Emily called and she's with Jonas—and you know Spencer, he could be anywhere."

"Yeah, you're right about that," he said as he picked up Sully's ball and tossed it in the air.

The big dog jumped and tried to get the ball. Kate knew Spencer had no control over what Sully was doing. She stood up and tried to take the ball from Will but it was too late. He threw it as hard as he could and it cleared the bushes. Sully barked and took off after the ball.

Anna had finished her lunch and was on her way back when she saw what was happening. She yelled out Spencer's name and Will and Kate looked back to see her running over the bridge just as Sully leaped over the bushes. While he was in the air, Spencer separated from Sully and landed right in the middle of the bushes. He was covered in leaves and twigs but stayed hidden hoping his father hadn't seen what happened.

"Did you just yell for Spencer?" Will asked Anna as she came into the backyard.

She saw Spencer out of the corner of her eye. "Yes, sir, I thought he was here with you."

"No, I haven't seen him," Will said. "I'm gonna go and look in the barn. If you two see him tell him I want him to come in for lunch."

"Yes, sir," Anna said.

"Okay, son," Kate replied as she watched Will walk down the gravel road toward the barn.

"Now, where's that dog?" Kate said, looking over the bushes by the driveway.

"I don't know."

"It's okay, Anna," Kate said, "I know about Spencer joining with Sully."

"Oh, you do? Well in that case, I don't know where Sully is but Spencer's under the bushes."

Kate bent down and could see Spencer hiding. "Spencer, you got un-joined!"

Spencer looked down at his jeans and his shoes and held his hands in front of his face to make sure it was true. He crawled out from under the bushes.

"I did it, I did it!" he yelled. "I've never been so happy to be—me!"

"That's great, Spencer. You see, you relaxed for just a moment and that's all it took," Kate said.

Sully came running from around the side of the house with the ball in his mouth. He laid it down on the grass like nothing had happened and barked at Spencer.

Spencer laughed. "Okay, Sully, we really have to have a talk about what the word boss means."

❊ ❊ ❊ ❊ ❊ ❊ ❊ ❊ ❊ ❊ ❊

When Jonas and Emily got back to his house they went right to work on Sully's DNA.

"Well, there's nothing special here," Jonas said. "It looks like any other dog. So, everything is because of Spencer's DNA just like you said, Emily, and now we have proof. Good work!"

Emily gave Jonas a huge smile.

"Now if I could just figure out why Mr. Wynn and his men want our farm. I'd better get home for lunch, Jonas. I'll see you tomorrow at school and we can talk about this some more."

"Oh, yeah, sure." He paused for a second. "Hey, Emily, do you think you could take me to see the vortex?"

"Sure, Jonas, but how..." she stopped and chose her words carefully, "um—how could you walk there? We have to hike from our house and there's a stream and the mountain."

"Well, I've already been thinking about that," he said. "My uncle, you know the engineer, he and I have been working on a project together and it's almost finished. I think it would get me to the cave."

"Great! Just let me know when you're ready. I'll see you tomorrow."

❊ ❊ ❊ ❊ ❊ ❊ ❊ ❊ ❊ ❊ ❊

Spencer heard Emily's bike tires in the gravel driveway of the house. He ran out the front door and met her as she came walking up the sidewalk.

"Em, you'll never guess what me and Anna did while you were gone!" he exclaimed with his mouth half-full of salami sandwich.

"Can it wait 'til I get a sandwich too?" she asked as she walked to the house.

"Sure, but you won't believe it!" he said.

"Well, I'm not so sure that you'll believe my news either."

Spencer went out to the backyard and sat at the picnic table with Anna. Emily fixed her lunch and met them there.

"So, tell me what you guys did today that was so important," Emily said as she took a bite from her sandwich.

Spencer and Anna looked at each other, about to burst with their news.

"Well, it was nothing really." He was trying to sound humble. "We just did a little experiment where I joined with Sully, that's all."

Emily was taking a drink from her cup, choked and spit it out on the ground. "You joined with Sully? You did? You really joined with Sully?"

"Yeah, it was so cool! You should have seen us. It was all Anna's idea. She figured out that we needed to get *my* energy up, not Sully's. But then we couldn't figure out how to get un-joined so Gram helped us and here we are, back to normal again."

"Oh, you think you're normal!" She giggled. "I'm only kidding, Spencer, I'm really very proud of both of you." She took another bite of her sandwich. "Now, let me tell you my news. First, Jonas and I saw your DNA in the hair sample, and we also saw a lot of other things too."

"Like what?" Spencer asked.

"Like DNA from a lizard and a mouse. And one more thing that we were fascinated by."

"What was it, what's inside of me? As if a lizard and a mouse aren't bad enough!" Spencer felt a little creepy.

She popped the last bite of sandwich into her mouth. "A tree."

"A tree?" Anna gasped.

"Yep—an oak tree."

Spencer shuttered. "Wh-what's an oak tree doing inside of me?"

"I don't know. We haven't figured that one out yet. But there's more." She finished her drink. "We had to go to the hobby store for some supplies and we saw Mr. Wynn in the hardware store with some other men. They were buying shovels and other stuff and they said they had Sir Angus's journal—and they think the deed to Sweetwater Farms might be in Sir Benjamin's trunk."

"Wasn't Sir Angus the man who stole Sir Benjamin's work?" Anna asked.

"Yeah," Spencer confirmed. "The man he followed here from Scotland."

"Anyway," Emily said, still trying to tell her story, "I heard one of the men speak and he sounded like Sir Benjamin. He had a Scottish accent and he had a tattoo of the two crossed swords and the snake on his arm!"

"Like the alligator boots Mr. Wynn was wearing!" Anna exclaimed.

"This is all starting to sound pretty weird to me," Spencer said. "Anna, when you left for lunch, my dad and your dad came here to the backyard. They were talking about Mr. Wynn. My dad said he couldn't find the deed for Sweetwater Farms, but whoever had it would be the owner. So, I got the idea to go and ask him--Sir Benjamin, that is--where it could be. If those men think the deed is in the trunk maybe we can beat them to it. I think we need to go back to the cave."

Emily nodded. "I think you're right."

"Hey, kids, where have you been?" Will asked as he came from around the side of the house. "Don't tell me you've already had lunch."

"Oh, yeah, sorry, Dad," Emily said as she got up from the table.

"Well, *now* where are you going?" he asked as they began to walk off.

"Um—to see Rosebud and Peaches, and maybe to the orchard to play," Emily hollered as she went through the bushes.

"Okay, but don't be gone long. Spencer, maybe when you get back we can throw some ball. Don't you have the Red and Blue Baseball Game tomorrow at school?"

"Oh, man, I almost forgot."

He was just past the bushes when he went running back. He wrapped his arms around his father's waist and gave him a hug. "Hey, Dad, don't worry about anything. Remember, everything will be fine as long as we're together."

Will stood still looking a little confused at what his son had just said. He watched Spencer run back to Emily and Anna and looked at Sully asleep under the bushes. He stayed there for a moment and thought, "That's exactly what Jenny would say." He looked up at the sky and closed his eyes. He felt the warmth of the sun and a slight breeze that blew the wind chimes hanging by the screen door. When he opened his eyes he took a deep breath and went back into the house.

CHAPTER TEN

INSIDE OUT

"Do you remember which way to go?" Emily asked Spencer as she and Anna followed him down the path that led past the hay field.

"Sure! We go past the cemetery and lower pasture. Then we follow the stream until we see the forest."

"Hey, Emily, why did you bring your school backpack?" Anna asked.

"Well, I took all of my books out so I could pack some things we'll need in the cave. First are the goggles. We'll need them to see Suri Lakena and the animals. Next, I packed some snacks and a bottle of water. It's very important to be prepared on a hike."

Spencer looked back at Anna and rolled his eyes at how organized his sister always was.

"Hey, guys, look at that!" Emily pointed out toward the hayfield.

All three children stopped walking when they saw something moving briskly through the hay, trampling it down as it went.

Anna moved closer to Spencer. "What is that?"

Emily began to back away from the field. She was about to run away when she spotted the tip of a yellow tail bobbing up and down in the tall hay.

"Sully!" she yelled out.

The dog ran toward the children and jumped on Spencer. Relieved, the girls laughed and bent over to pet him.

"Sully, we're real happy to see you but I think it's best you stay home," Spencer said as he rubbed Sully's ears.

"Oh, why can't he come?" Emily asked. "Maybe Suri Lakena and Sir Benjamin would like to meet him."

"Well—all right," Spencer said, "but don't get into any trouble, Sully. You just follow us."

The children set off again, walking past the cemetery until they found the stream that ran through the grove of laurel bushes. As they started into the forest Sully ran ahead of them and jumped into the stream. Spencer found the same place where he and Emily had crossed when they were with their grandmother. He stepped on the same two rocks and jumped to the bank on the other side. Anna slowly made her way over the rocks and Spencer held his hand out for her to grab. Emily was next and just as she took his hand her foot slipped off the last rock. He reached down with both hands and pulled her onto the bank.

"Wow, that was close! Thanks, Spencer, you saved my life!" Emily exclaimed as she looked at Anna and giggled.

"Maybe next time I'll let you fall in the water."

Spencer called to Sully and he came running. He splashed through the stream and leaped onto the bank shaking the excess water from his coat. They continued walking and finally reached the maze of pine trees.

"Remember when we were here last time?" Emily asked Spencer. "Gram said that she didn't know which way to go."

"Yeah, until she saw the mountain!" Spencer exclaimed.

"Well, where *is* the mountain?" Anna asked.

CHAPTER TEN

"Just keep looking. Gram said it would reveal itself," Emily replied, turning in a complete circle, looking at the trees.

"Well, I hope we find it soon 'cause these trees are a little spooky," Anna said feeling frightened.

Sully began to bark at a rock and tried to scratch at whatever was hiding under it. Spencer lifted the rock and a spider crawled out.

"Look at that spider!" Emily pointed. "It only has four legs. I thought all spiders had eight legs."

"You're the one in the science club, you tell us," Spencer said as he looked down at the spider. It crept over a leaf and continued walking out of the pine forest.

All three children looked through the tall canopy of pine trees. Sully found a soft spot on the pine needles and lay down to watch them continue to turn in circles.

"There it is!" Spencer exclaimed as he pointed through the pines.

"Wow!" Anna yelled out as she looked at the mountain that had just appeared in front of her.

Sully jumped up at the children's excitement and began to bark.

"Let's go!" Spencer called, leading the way.

The pine needles began to disappear and the ground was soon covered in moss. The distinct aroma of the pines had given way to the pungent odor of the wet forest floor. They had reached the base of the mountain and Spencer stopped.

"Something's wrong," he said as he studied the path. "Remember, Em? Last time, when we started up the mountain, we could see the stream. It was coming down the side of the mountain. I remember it going over huge boulders and then there was that calm pool of water before it headed over to Sweetwater Farms. Just look at it now!"

Anna and Emily moved closer to Spencer as Sully sniffed the moss and leaves on the ground.

"Where is it?" Emily asked. "It was here a few minutes ago 'cause we stepped on the stones to cross it."

"I know—I see the boulders it ran over but now it's all dried up," Spencer reached down and picked up a handful of sand. "Where's all the water gone?"

Anna began to wander around, taking a closer look at the forest. "Something's not right," she thought to herself. She looked back at Spencer, Emily and Sully standing on the bank of the dry streambed and noticed that even though they were in the forest, nothing was green. She looked down at the moss and ferns that grew on either side of the path and they were a weird, brownish-gray color. The eerie sight of the forest sent a chill through her and she ran back over to Spencer and Emily.

"Hey, guys, there's something really strange going on here. Look at the trees."

Spencer and Emily looked up at the trees and around at the other vegetation.

"Where did all the color go?" Emily asked. "Everything looks—dead!"

Spencer reached down and picked up some moss and watched it crumble in his hand. "I think everything *is* dead."

"Maybe we should turn around and go home," Anna said, uneasy.

"That's probably a good idea," Spencer agreed.

"Wait a minute, guys," Emily said. "What if there *is* something wrong? What if Suri Lakena and Sir Benjamin need our help? We should at least go on to the cave and make sure they're okay."

Spencer sighed. "I was afraid you'd say that."

"What do you say, Anna, do you want to keep going?" Emily asked.

"Well, I might regret it, but okay. I'm right behind you."

When they reached the top of the mountain the lifeless trees and bushes were overgrown with creeping vines. The stones that had been placed in a circle were just barely visible because of the rope-like web that covered them. The huge square rocks were still stacked on top of one another, but the window was now covered over by a curtain of dead vines. Spencer and Emily began pulling the climbing plants away.

"What are you looking for?" Anna asked as she watched what they were doing.

"There's a window in these rocks, and if we can just get these old vines off we can look through and see Sweetwater Farms," Spencer said.

"You know, Spencer, these vines weren't here before," Emily said as she cleared away the last of them.

"I know. It's weird. It's like everything *is* the same but then again it isn't. It's inside out or backwards or something!" Spencer exclaimed.

"So, when you guys were here before everything was normal? I mean the trees were green and spiders had eight legs?" Anna asked.

"Well, I don't remember seeing any spiders but, yes, everything was normal," Emily said. "The trees *were* green and these rocks were just like they are now but they weren't covered in these dead vines. Remember, Spencer? We just walked right up, looked out the window and saw Sweetwater Farms."

Emily stared out the window for what seemed like forever, to Spencer and Anna.

"Emily? Emily?" Spencer asked. "What do you see?"

"Well, it's a little hard to say," she said, wrinkling up her face. "I see Sweetwater all right but, boy, does it look different!"

"Let me look," Spencer said as he made room for himself next to Emily. "Oh, my gosh! Is that really Sweetwater?"

"What is it?" Anna yelled. "What's wrong with the farm?"

Anna pushed her way in between Spencer and Emily. Even though they had only left Sweetwater a few minutes ago, there was definitely something wrong. It looked old, very old. The barn was missing part of its roof and the hay in the field was brown and looked like it hadn't been cut in years. There were no horses in the pastures and part of the split-rail fence was falling down. The gravel road leading from the barn to the house was covered over with dead grass. The oak tree in the cemetery looked hollow and lifeless, and the headstones were draped with the same type of creeping vines they had just pulled away from the window. The paint on the farmhouse was peeling off and the front screen door was standing open held on by only one hinge. There were shingles missing from the roof and the birdbath in the front yard was broken and laying in pieces.

"What happened?" Anna asked. "We just left there."

"I don't know," Emily said, "but we better get to the cave so we can talk to Suri Lakena. Maybe she can tell us what's going on."

"I sure hope so," Spencer said. "This whole thing is giving me the creeps!"

Just as before, the children found the trail on the other side of the window. They came to the rock steps and Sully jumped down them with ease. Anna clung to the side of the mountain as she followed Spencer. Emily was close behind, trying to step exactly where Anna had been. She was concentrating so hard that when she finally looked up to see if they were almost to the cave, she became dizzy. Her right foot misjudged the edge of the next step and she slipped. Emily screamed as she fell and slid down the last few steps, landing at the open area in front of the cave. Spencer and Anna laughed as Emily came to a stop right below Ayasha, the falcon.

"Sorry, Emily," Anna said, still laughing, "but the look on your face was hilarious."

"Yeah, you looked like me when I un-joined with Sully and flew into the bushes!" Spencer exclaimed.

"Well, I'm glad I could give you guys something to laugh about." Emily stood up and brushed the dirt from her clothes. "Oh, no! Look at Ayasha!"

The carving of the falcon was cracked and missing one of her wings. The rock she perched on was covered over in a web-like entanglement of creeping vines. Spencer found the wing lying on the ground and gently tried to put it back in place.

"Is this the bird you were telling me about, Spencer?" Anna asked.

"Yeah, I wonder what happened to her."

"I don't know," Emily added. "But look! The medallion's gone!"

They heard the sound of falling rocks. There were huge boulders coming down the side of the mountain heading right for them!

"A landslide!" Spencer yelled.

They ran to the opening of the cave and just missed being hit by a huge boulder that smashed to the ground.

Spencer looked around at all of the rocks lying on the ground. "Boy, Em, when you fall, you really fall. You about brought the whole mountain down!"

"You think I did all this?" she questioned. "I think it was another one of those earthquakes."

"What earthquakes?" Anna asked. "You guys didn't tell me anything about earthquakes."

"When we were here before there were just a few of them and they were very small—almost like tremors instead of earthquakes," Spencer said trying not to scare her.

"I would think that tremors or earthquakes or whatever they are would be the kind of thing you would tell a person," Anna said as she headed for the rock steps.

"Where are you going?" Emily asked.

She started back up the steps. "I think I'll be going home now. Oh, and thanks for the hike."

"Anna, you can't leave," Emily yelled to her. "What about Sweetwater Farms?"

Anna stopped on the second step and looked down. She turned around and took a deep breath. "Okay, I'll go in the cave with you guys--but I want you to know it's under protest that I'm going and I'm not very happy about this situation, at all!"

"What does it mean that it's under protest?" Spencer asked as he took off his belt to make a leash for Sully.

"I don't really know," Anna said. "It's just what I hear my mother say to my father when she doesn't want to do something."

"Well, guys, I don't think we're going to find any of the answers we need out here. I think we have to go in there," Emily said as she pointed to the cave. "Are you ready?"

"Ah—well—sure," Spencer said as he looked at the vines covering the entrance. "But I think it should be ladies first."

"I say we put it to a vote. And I vote for Spencer and Sully to go first," Anna said raising her hand.

"And I second that vote," Emily said as she held up her hand too.

"Oh, man," Spencer said. "I never win when we vote for stuff. I say we let Sully vote too. That would make it fair." He pushed the long vines out of the way.

Emily and Anna got in line after Spencer and Sully. Once in the cave they could feel the same coldness as before. They started their descent and Emily kept one hand on the rock wall and one hand on Spencer's shoulder. Anna had grabbed onto a belt loop on Emily's jeans and was so close to her that Emily could barely take a step.

"Anna, just hold on to my shirt. You're pulling my pants up to my neck and giving me a wedgie!" Emily squealed.

"Oh, sorry, Emily," Anna shifted her grasp from the belt loop to her shirt. "I'm just a little nervous."

Sully barked and Anna let out a scream!

"What's wrong?" Spencer yelled out. "Why are you screaming?"

"I don't know," Anna exclaimed, flustered. "Sully just scared me."

"Look, I can see light up ahead," Emily said.

"Thank goodness," Anna relaxed a bit.

They came to the big open area and Emily took a torch from the wall. As the light shown on the different parts of the cave, they could see that everything was covered in spider webs and the same decayed roots and creeping vines were running everywhere.

CHAPTER TEN

"Let's see if Sir Benjamin's trunk is still here," Emily said, running over to the side wall of the cave.

"Oh, yeah, I almost forgot. It's the real reason we came to the cave in the first place," Spencer said as he let Sully pull him over to Emily.

Emily ran from one huge boulder to another looking for the trunk.

"It's gone! It was right here before."

"Are you sure?" Anna asked. "Maybe it got moved somewhere."

"Who would move it?" Emily asked and realized what she had just said. "BILLY WYNN!"

"You don't think he beat us here, do you?" Spencer asked. "He couldn't have."

Emily held the torch up to look at the rest of the cave. Her eyes became huge, she dropped the torch and screamed.

"Emily!" Anna yelled. "What's wrong?"

Spencer ran over to Emily and picked up the torch. Emily was frozen, looking at the wall on the other side of the cave.

"Emily, you look like you've seen a ghost." Spencer held out the torch to the wall.

Instead of the animal drawings that were there before, there was another drawing that was becoming all too familiar to Spencer and Emily. It was a huge brightly colored painting of the two crossed swords with the snake winding between them. The light from the torch danced along the cave wall and reflected off the snake making it seem like it was alive. It was big and black with reddish-orange coloring along the edges of its shiny scales. It seemed as if it was on fire as it wound its way around the blades. Its eyes were bright yellow and cat-like with solid black slits and its mouth was open, exposing large fangs. It had a dark red tongue that seemed to strike out, piercing the air, and on top of its head were two horns that looked sharp and ready for battle.

"What is that?" Anna asked.

"It's just like the tattoo I saw on that man in the store!" Emily exclaimed.

"Yeah, and I saw it on the boots Mr. Wynn had on the day he came to our house," Spencer added.

Emily walked up closer to the painting. The swords looked so real she reached out and touched one of the blades.

"Ouch!" she cried as she pulled back her hand.

"What happened, Em?" Spencer asked.

"I think the sword cut my finger!"

Spencer examined her hand. "I don't see anything. Maybe the rock was just sharp where you touched it."

"That was weird," Emily said. "I don't recommend anyone else touch the painting. It bites!"

"Hey, there's something different about this painting," Spencer said as he lifted the torch to the snake. "I didn't see that on Mr. Wynn's boots. Look, between the snake's eyes—there's a diamond or something."

"Hey, you're right, Spencer. Look how it shines when you hold the light to it." Emily pushed Spencer's hand holding the torch closer to the wall. "And there's something else. The tattoo didn't have those horns either!"

"That's really strange," Anna said. "Why do you think this one has a diamond and horns, and the tattoo and Mr. Wynn's boots don't?"

"Don't ask me," Spencer said. "I'm about as good with mysteries as I am with science—and we all know how good that is."

"Hey, there's something else weird in here," Emily said. "Remember how there wasn't any water in the stream? Well, look at the fountain. It's all dried up."

"Oh, yeah, I totally forgot about the fountain and the vortex!" Spencer exclaimed.

"You mean the fountain came out of this big hole in the ground?" Anna asked as she walked over to the middle of the cave and looked into the hole. "Whoa, it's dark and deep like a bottomless pit!"

"Yeah and--"

Just as Spencer was about to tell Anna about the fountain, the ground began to shake. Sully started to bark and Spencer wrapped the end of the homemade leash tighter around his hand. Emily moved closer to Spencer and they both grabbed onto a boulder. Anna let out a scream! The ground beneath her gave way and she slipped into the opening where the fountain had been. Spencer and Emily yelled out Anna's name over and over again and when the earthquake stopped, Emily ran over to look into the hole. "Anna! Anna! Can you hear me?"

Sully dragged Spencer over to Emily and both children lay on the ground looking over the edge into the darkness.

"I'm here!" Anna yelled back. "Can you see my hand?"

Through the dust Emily could just barely make out Anna's hand. She was gripping what looked like one of the vines from the cave floor that must have crept its way into the hole.

"Hold on, Anna, we'll try and pull you up!" Emily yelled down into the hole as she grabbed onto the vine. "Spencer, I'm going to reach down for her and you hold onto me, okay?"

"Okay, Em—me and Sully will hold you!"

Spencer held onto Emily's legs and Sully grabbed onto her jeans with his teeth.

"That's it, boy, hold on tight!" Spencer said.

"Hurry up, guys, I don't know how much longer I can hold on!" Anna hollered.

Sully let out a growl and Spencer could feel the slight vibration of another tremor.

"Emily, maybe you should hurry up, I think there's another earthqu--"

The whole cave began to shake again. Emily had just grabbed onto Anna's hand, but instead of pulling Anna out, Anna was pulling her in. Spencer and Sully tried to hold onto Emily but they were being pulled in too. Spencer grabbed onto a rock but it didn't help. He heard a loud crashing sound and saw a big boulder had broken loose from the ceiling of the cave. It hit the floor and broke into smaller rocks that were heading straight for him and Sully.

Spencer had a hold of Emily's left foot and Sully had her right. When her shoe came off into Sully's mouth all of her weight shifted to Spencer and he couldn't hold on any longer. Emily slipped over the edge just as Sully jumped away, narrowly escaping a huge rock. Spencer rolled to the left just out of the path of another rock. When the cave stopped shaking a terrible feeling came over Spencer. He couldn't believe what had just happened. He called Sully over to him.

"Sully, are you okay? Did that rock get your paw?" Spencer felt Sully's leg.

"I'm okay, Spencer, it just hurts a little."

"Oh, boy! I can hear you! We must have joined during the earthquake."

"Yeah, I guess you got your energy up when all of the rocks came at us!"

"You're right, Sully! Hey, we need to find the girls!"

Spencer ran back over to the edge of the hole. He lay on his stomach and looked into the blackness. "Emily! Anna! Can you hear me?"

There was no reply.

"Emily! Anna! Can you hear me?"

Sully walked over and sniffed around the hole.

"Be careful, boy, I don't want you to fall in too."

"But, Spencer, I still smell them. They're still close to the top of the hole. Only there's another smell--something weird."

"Yeah," Spencer said, "I smell it too. Hey cool, I can smell what you smell. I get the smell of Anna. It's a mix of flowery shampoo and--what is that other thing? Oh, yeah, bubble gum!" He grinned. "And Emily is—I know, don't tell me—peanut-butter-and-jelly sandwich!"

"Yep!"

"But what's that other smell? It's like something really old and musty. Like when we had that terrarium in my class at school where we kept the frogs and salamanders. Well, we'll have to worry about that later. Right now we need to get Emily and Anna out of this hole!"

CHAPTER TEN

Spencer lay down on his stomach and looked into the hole again.

"Emily! Anna!"

"Spencer! I hear you!" Emily called back.

"Me too!" Anna hollered.

"We didn't fall down to the bottom of the hole. We're on some kind of ledge. Can you throw down a torch?" Emily yelled up to Spencer.

"Sure! But are you both okay?"

"Yeah, I'm fine," Emily yelled.

"And I just have a couple of scrapes," Anna added.

"Okay, I'm going to throw down the torch. What side of the hole is the ledge on?"

"Just throw it to the right side," Emily answered.

"Okay, here goes!"

Spencer held the torch down into the hole. He stayed as close to the right side as he could, opened his hand and let the torch drop. It traveled down the hole and landed on the rock floor of the ledge. Emily picked it up, and by the light it gave off, Spencer could see both of them.

"It's great to see you guys! Now, how are we going to get you out?"

Anna sat down on a rock. "Maybe you could find a really long vine and pull us out."

"That's a good idea!" Spencer said. "Sully, go and find a long vine so we can pull the girls up."

"Okay, Spencer."

"Who are you talking to, Spencer?" Emily asked.

"Sully. During the last earthquake we joined."

"Good, maybe he can help you pull us out," Anna said. "I think you'll need all the help you can get."

Spencer peered down into the hole. "Hey, from what I can see that ledge is pretty big."

"Yeah, it is," Emily replied. "The hole up there is pretty small, but when you get down here it opens up a lot bigger." She held up the torch to look around.

"Look, there's an opening in the wall on the other side of the ledge," Spencer said.

Emily was intrigued. "Hey, I wonder where it goes?"

"Well, let me just say that I really don't care where it goes," Anna said. "I'm very comfortable sitting right here until Spencer and Sully get us out. Hey, what's that noise? Did you hear that, Emily?"

"Yeah, it sounded like it came from the opening in the wall."

"Um, Spencer—I think you might want to hurry up with that vine." Emily moved toward Anna. "Spencer did you hear me?"

"What?" Spencer hollered.

"Hurry up with that vine—there's something down here with us!"

The girls could definitely hear a noise coming from the opening in the wall. It sounded like something was being dragged across the floor. Anna screamed and Sully dropped the vine he'd been trying to free from the wall of the cave and went running back over to Spencer.

"What's wrong, Spencer, are they in trouble?"

"I don't know, Sully. They say there's something down there with them."

Both of the girls were calling out frantically and Spencer looked into the hole to see what was happening. He couldn't believe his eyes! Coming from the opening in the wall was a huge snake. Its body was as big around as the oak tree in the cemetery. Its tongue was whipping in the air and it was moving slowly toward the girls. It had scales that were shiny and black with little flashes of red and orange on the edges. When it looked up at Spencer's torch he could see the glimmer of the diamond between its eyes.

"Spencer, what is it? We don't see anything!" Emily cried.

"It's the snake in the painting on the wall! And it's heading right for you!"

Emily pulled off her backpack and reached in for the goggles. She held them up to her face; the huge snake came into focus.

"What is it, Emily?" Anna exclaimed. "Let me see!"

CHAPTER TEN

"Here, put your head next to mine and I'll put them on both of us," Emily said, working to make the headband bigger.

The girls peeked out from behind the boulder with their two heads stuck together, each looking through one of the eyepieces.

Anna screamed and Emily covered Anna's mouth with her hand.

"Anna, get a grip!" Emily whispered as they ducked back behind the boulder.

"Spencer? What are we going to do?" Sully asked as he ran around the hole barking.

"I don't know, Sully! I don't know what to do!"

Spencer's arm began to throb with pain. He heard them yelling out his name but he was paralyzed and couldn't help them.

"I know, Spencer. Let's join! We'll jump down on the ledge and we'll fight off the snake. We can take him, Spencer, I know we can!"

Spencer knew it was the only thing to do but he was scared.

"Come on, Spencer! He's getting closer to the girls!"

Sully ran to the far corner of the cave. He turned around and started running toward the hole. As he got closer, Spencer could hear him yell ***"ONE, TWO, THREE,"*** and before Spencer knew what was happening Sully had jumped into the air, landing on him and knocking them both into the hole. The two of them tumbled through the air, and by the time they landed on the ledge they had joined.

"How did you do that, Sully? I thought I had to be the one to believe we could do it!"

"Well, let's just say I called in special forces." Sully backed up against the boulder where Emily and Anna were and began to bark at the snake.

Spencer could feel Sully's strength. Sully wasn't scared at all. Because they were in the same body Spencer could feel Sully's blood flowing through his veins. The big dog was in fighting mode and Spencer was amazed at his courage. The snake was hissing louder and louder and looked massive now that they were on the ledge with him.

He was moving his head from side to side making strikes toward Sully and Spencer.

Emily looked up and could see there was someone else in the cave. She saw torch lights moving back and forth around the hole, and a rope dropped down and almost fell right on the snake. She tried to make out who was coming down the rope but was blinded by a flash of light from the torch.

"It looks like yeh could use a wee bit o' help, lasses!" Sir Benjamin announced as he landed on the ledge and drew his sword.

"Look, Anna! It's Sir Benjamin!" Emily exclaimed.

Anna had her eyes closed but got up the courage to look out from behind the big rock. The giant man with flaming red hair had jumped onto a boulder and was fighting off the snake. Sir Benjamin's sword was slashing at the air, the snake's long fangs were fully exposed as his head thrashed back and forth, waiting for the perfect opportunity to strike.

"Emily!" Sir Benjamin called, "grab onto the rope. Amadeus will pull yeh up!"

"Come on, Anna!" Emily yelled. "You go first!"

Emily pulled the goggles off of Anna's head and tied the end of the rope around her waist.

"Okay, Amadeus!" she cried. "PULL!"

Anna began to rise up from the ledge. She was amazed once she made it to the top that she couldn't see anything tied to the other end of the rope, although she was sure the horse must be there. Once safe on the floor of the cave, she untied herself and threw the rope back down to Emily. Sully was still barking and running around the snake trying to divert him so Sir Benjamin could get a clear shot. Emily had tied the rope around her waist and was just beginning to rise up from the ledge when the snake, his powerful jaws open wide, lunged out through the air at her. Suspended from the rope, Emily screamed, feeling completely exposed and helpless.

Sir Benjamin jumped from the boulder, and, in mid-air, delivered a staggering blow to the gigantic serpent, cutting off one of its horns. Emily swung back and forth from the end of the rope as she watched the snake retreat. Before Sir Benjamin was able to finish his task, the snake quickly made its way out through the opening in the wall.

Emily had reached the top and was safely back in the cave, and she gave Anna a big hug.

"I swear, Anna, I'll never insist that we go into another cave as long as I live! And Amadeus, you beautiful horse! I'm so happy to see you!"

"I'd like to see him too!" Anna said while Emily was still hugging her.

"Oh sorry, Anna—here, look." Emily put the goggles back over their heads.

Anna gasped when she saw the mighty, white stallion with the other end of the rope tied to his elegant black-and-silver saddle.

"Hey, how about throwing the rope back down so we can get out of here, too?" Spencer yelled up to the girls.

"Spencer, lad, are yeh en there with the dog?" Sir Benjamin asked as he put his sword back through the leather belt on his side and walked over to Sully.

"Yes, sir," Spencer replied. "I learned how to join with Sully, my dog."

"Aye, an' join yeh have. An' by the looks of things today, yer gonna make a fine Gatekeeper. Big an' brave yeh are, laddie!" He gave Sully a pat on the head.

Spencer didn't say anything. He just let Sir Benjamin tie the rope around him and Sully. They were almost up to the top when Spencer felt himself relax. By the time Amadeus pulled them over the edge, the two had un-joined and Spencer had the rope around his waist and was holding Sully in his arms. Once they were on solid ground the big dog leaped from Spencer and ran over to the girls.

"Oh, Sully, you're such a fearless dog!" Anna said rubbing his head. "You and Spencer really scared that horrible snake!"

"Yeah, Spencer," Emily added. "You and Sully are heroes! I can't believe how you jumped in the hole to save us. I guess you do care after all!" She gave him a little pinch on the arm.

Spencer looked down at the floor. He knew the truth about what happened. He wasn't fearless; he wasn't a hero. What was he going to do? The vortex needed a Gatekeeper that was brave. Someone who could make quick decisions and be a protector like Suri Lakena and Sir Benjamin. He couldn't even help his own sister and friend when they needed him the most.

Amadeus backed away from the hole and pulled Sir Benjamin safely back into the cave.

"Aye lasses, it felt good to raise me sword again after all these years!" Sir Benjamin exclaimed. "Amadeus—a fine job yeh've done, my friend!"

The white stallion whinnied and pawed at the rock floor.

"Sir Benjamin, this is our friend, Anna," Emily said.

"Ah, a beautiful name fer a beautiful lassie!" he said as he bowed to her. "Now, children, tell me what brings yeh here to this dungeon. An' how did yeh ever find it?"

"Well, we were trying to find *your* cave. We wanted to ask you some questions but maybe we took a wrong turn or something and we found this cave instead," Emily answered.

"Aye, so yeh did," Sir Benjamin replied. "An' do yeh think yeh took the wrong turn en the pine trees?"

"Yes," Emily answered. "Everything started to change right after we left the trees."

"Well, which Guardian brought yeh to the mountain?"

"You mean like Ayasha or Takoda?" Spencer asked.

"Yes, lad, a Guardian should always meet yeh en the pine trees an' lead yeh to the mountain."

"We didn't see a Guardian!" Anna exclaimed. "We only saw a spider with four legs!"

"Very interestin'." Sir Benjamin stroked his long red beard. "Perhaps the spider was a Guardian of the reverse vortex."

"Reverse vortex!" Spencer exclaimed. "What do you mean?"

"Well, children, I've been working on Lakena's vortex, tryin' to figure out what's creatin' the earthquakes an' where all the power es goin'. With the keen eye of Ayasha, an' along with Takoda an' Kuma's help, we found this cave an' the reverse vortex. But instead of givin' life to everythin', like Lakena's vortex, this one es stealin' life from everythin'! An' I got a feelin' that filthy, smelly serpent down there es its Gatekeeper!" He looked back down in the hole. "But listen, children, I don't want yeh to worry a wee bit, yeh hear? Amadeus an' the other animals will help me figure this out. We'll have things back to normal en no time!"

"But what if you can't," Spencer said. "What if--"

"Don't worry, laddie." Sir Benjamin mounted Amadeus. "We will!"

"Wait! Sir Benjamin, before you go we have a question for you," Emily said.

"What is it, lassie?"

"Do you know where the deed to Sweetwater Farms is? There's a very bad man named Billy Wynn who wants to take the farm and our dad can't find the deed. I overheard Mr. Wynn say that maybe it's in your trunk in the cave. That's why we tried to come to the cave today. To see if it's in your trunk."

"Did yeh say the name of Wynn?" Sir Benjamin spun around on the big white stallion. "That's the name of the man I followed here from Scotland! The man that stole me work. Sir Angus Wynn of Kilkardy!"

"It couldn't be the same Mr. Wynn, could it?" Anna asked.

"Well, maybe not the same. Still, it seems very strange," Emily replied. "Sir Benjamin, what was your work, anyway, and why did Sir Angus steal it?"

Amadeus stood easy and rested one of his back legs. Sir Benjamin let go of the reins and relaxed his posture.

"Well, children, at one time me an' Sir Angus was partners—friends, en fact. We were scientists together en the Royal Society of

Edinburgh an' we were workin' fer the King. Yeh see, it was a beautiful time fer scientists an' intellectual thinkers alike. Scotland was the most widely respected country en the world an' me an' Sir Angus were makin' some wonderful scientific discoveries. Our instruction from the King was to try an' figure out how to communicate with animals. Yeh see, he believed the animals held all the secrets of life. But most importantly, he wanted the people of his kingdom to be happy an' he thought that the animals knew how to be happy all the time."

"He sounds like a very nice man," Anna said.

"Aye, lassie, he was a great King indeed."

"So, do you mean you were trying to talk to animals?" Emily asked.

"Aye, lassie, but there was more."

The children clung to his every word as Amadeus shifted his weight and came to rest on his other back leg.

"One day, I arrived at the laboratory early an' overheard Sir Angus an' another man discussin' our work. The man offered Sir Angus a substantial amount of money en return fer our discoveries. Yeh see, he not only wanted to talk to animals he also wanted to train them to do bad things."

"That's not very nice," Anna said.

"Well, the man belonged to a secret organization. They were a greedy group of men who disliked the royal family very much. He wanted to train animals to help en their plot to overthrow the King! Anyway, it wasn't until Mr. Franklin came over from America to a meetin' of the Royal Society in Edinburgh that we--"

"Wait a minute, do you mean Benjamin Franklin?" Emily asked.

"Aye, lass, Ben was a good friend of mine."

"Wait, wait, wait," Emily insisted. "You mean to tell me *you* were friends with *the* Benjamin Franklin?! The man who discovered electricity?! One of the founding fathers of our country?!"

"Aye, lass, he lived en England fer a few years before the big war an' he came to Edinburgh to visit. I remember one day when we were working on that electricity thing—but, that's another story fer another time."

The children stood stunned at the thought of Sir Benjamin and Benjamin Franklin being friends and working on electricity together.

"Anyway," he continued, "when Ben found out what me an' Sir Angus was workin' on, he told us he heard there was a Native American girl who lived en America way up en the mountains of the Carolinas. He said there was a legend the local people spoke of that said she could not only talk to animals but she could also turn into them. Well, before I knew it, Sir Angus stole our work an' left on the next ship to America! So, I followed him here an' I found Lakena before he did."

"So, Sir Benjamin—was Suri Lakena the Native American girl you heard about all the way in Scotland?" Spencer asked.

"Tha's right, laddie. An' as soon as I met her I knew I would never return to Scotland."

"Because you fell in love?" Anna asked, blushing.

"Tha's right an' we were married by her father."

"And that's when you changed your name from Howell to Sweetwater!" Emily exclaimed.

"Aye, lassie—an' it was the happiest day of me life."

"So, Sir Benjamin, do you think the deed for Sweetwater Farms could be in your trunk?" Emily asked.

"No—the only thing en me trunk es me work an' some maps. But I'll ask Lakena. Perhaps she'll know where 'tis. Now, you children should be goin' home. I don't want Katherine worried about yeh."

Sir Benjamin backed Amadeus away from the children, grabbed a torch off the wall and threw it to Spencer.

"Lead the girls out of the cave, Gatekeeper!" he cried out as Amadeus galloped up the corridor to the cave opening. "I'll see yeh again soon!"

The three of them headed toward the cave entrance, looking forward to getting back home.

CHAPTER ELEVEN

FLY BALL

The Red and Blue Baseball Game was a yearly tradition at Spring Valley Elementary. It was held during the last week of school and the teams were made up of girls and boys from the sixth grade. Each of the teams wore red, white and blue tee-shirts with their school mascot, a roaring tiger, on the back. The game started at ten o'clock and all of the other grades were dismissed from class to cheer on the teams.

Spencer couldn't wait to take the field; he thought for sure he was going to play shortstop. He and his father had practiced yesterday afternoon. They worked on double-plays, grounders and pop-ups, and he was ready to show Dwight Fitch and the Pitsner twins a thing or two. He also knew Nicole Darling would be on the sidelines cheerleading and that boosted his confidence even more. It was going to be a great day and he needed it. Yesterday's events were weighing heavily on his mind and he needed something to lift his spirits. He thought for sure the Red and Blue Game was just the thing to do it.

"Okay, when I call your name, I'll tell you if you're on the red or the blue team," the coach announced as he stood in front of the children with his clipboard.

CHAPTER ELEVEN

The baseball field was located directly behind the school. There was a four-foot high chain-link fence around the outfield and only once had anyone at Spring Valley ever hit the ball over it. It happened three years ago when Ricky Fitch, Dwight's older brother, used a wooden bat and pounded the ball directly over the leftfielder's head. It cleared the fence and went sailing into the woods and to this day no one has ever found the ball.

Spencer waited patiently in line for his name to be called. They went in alphabetical order so he knew he'd be last or close to it. There were only two things he wanted. The first was *not* to be on the same team as Dwight, Shawn and Todd. And the second was to play shortstop.

"DWIGHT FITCH," the coach yelled out. "RED TEAM—FIRST BASE."

Spencer looked up from the infield and watched as the other classes filed into the bleachers. He saw Emily and Anna sit down and Jonas in his wheelchair by the third base dugout. Nicole was by first base, practicing cheers with some of the other sixth graders who didn't want to play in the game.

"SHAWN PITSNER—SECOND BASE. TODD PITSNER—THIRD BASE, RED TEAM."

Spencer watched as the three boys jumped in the air, slapping their hands in high-fives. He looked up and closed his eyes, praying that the coach would say his name for the blue team. He watched Nicole again as her long, blond hair swirled and danced in the air. She was laughing and her smile made her whole face light up. He forgot everything when he was around Nicole—including the baseball game.

"SWEETWATER!" the coach yelled. "SWEETWATER!"

Spencer had his back to the coach, still watching Nicole. One of the other students nudged him and he turned around to see the coach's angry, red face.

"Sweetwater, I asked you a question!" the coach said.

"Ah, I'm sorry, sir. What was the question?"

"Do you want to play baseball or would you rather be a cheerleader?"

Spencer looked around. Everyone was snickering and laughing—and out of the corner of his eye he saw Dwight trying to do a flip like a cheerleader. "I want to play baseball, sir."

"All right then, son, let me see what team you're on." He looked back at his clipboard and Spencer took a deep breath.

"RED TEAM!" Spencer cowered. "RIGHT FIELD!" Spencer closed his eyes and felt like the wind had been knocked out of him.

As Shawn ran by him, he slapped his head. "Come on, sapsucker, let's take the field!"

Spencer walked toward Jonas to get his glove from the dugout. Emily and Anna waved from the bleachers and he waved back halfheartedly. All of his hopes had been ruined. Right field never saw any action. How could he show Nicole how good he was if no balls were ever hit there?

"Hey, tough break," Jonas said as he pushed the lever forward on his wheelchair.

"Yeah, I really wanted shortstop," Spencer replied.

"Well, at least you're playing." Jonas reached for the stats book, lying on the bench. "I got stuck having to keep the stats for the game and also writing an article for the *Spring Valley News*."

"Looks like this might be a bad day for both of us," Spencer said, grabbing his glove and heading to the outfield.

He watched Nicole and the other cheerleaders jumping around in front of the bleachers. When he reached right field he turned around to face the other players on his team. Dwight and the infielders were throwing the ball around and Spencer didn't realize, until he heard the thump of the ball hitting the ground, that Shawn had just thrown the ball to him.

"Well, pick it up, sapsucker!" Shawn yelled from second base.

When Spencer bent over to pick up the ball he noticed something strange about the dandelions it was lying next to. He picked the ball up and looked at the weedy flowers that seemed to be arranged in some sort of pattern.

"Throw it back, Sweetwater!" Dwight shouted from first base.

Spencer threw the ball so hard it cleared Dwight's head and went sailing through the air toward the cheerleaders. Spencer watched in horror as the ball hit one of the posts that held up the sign for the blue team and knocked it to the ground. He let out a sigh of relief as the cheerleaders looked in the direction of the infield players to see who had thrown the ball.

"OKAY, RED TEAM—LOOK ALIVE!" the coach yelled as the first batter came to the plate.

Spencer tried to focus on the game and watched as one ball after the other was hit to the infield players. He watched the Pitsner twins make a double-play and he knew if he was playing shortstop he would have been right in the middle of the action. Again his attention was drawn to the dandelions on the ground. The yellow flowers were definitely arranged in some sort of pattern but he couldn't make it out.

He heard the crack of a bat and his attention turned toward the infield as he watched one of the players make an unbelievable catch to make the third out. Everyone ran to the dugout and he followed knowing he hadn't done a thing to help win the inning. He went over to Jonas to check the batting order and saw his name in the eighth slot.

"Oh, man," he said, "I probably won't get to hit 'til the third inning."

He sat at the end of the bench next to Jonas and watched as Todd got up to bat. He hit a grounder to third and was thrown out at first. The next batter hit a pop-up and in an instant there were two outs. Again, his eyes went to Nicole. He thought there was something magical about her. She always seemed bright and cheerful and he felt the same way when he was around her.

"She's pretty, isn't she?" Jonas said.

"What? Who?" Spencer asked, knowing he'd been caught.

"Nicole. And don't act like you weren't staring at her 'cause I saw you."

"So what if you did?" Spencer said, trying to blow it off.

"Why don't you go talk to her? You're not batting for a while."

"Well, 'cause, um, now's not a real good time for me," Spencer said, turning red in the face.

"STRIKE THREE!" the umpire screamed as the batter swung so hard she almost fell over.

"See, I can't talk to her anyway, I have to take the field." Spencer grabbed his glove and headed toward the outfield.

The first batter for the blue team stepped up to the plate and the very first hit was a line drive right into the glove of the shortstop. Spencer grabbed his head in anguish and spun around in a circle, knowing he should have been the one who made the catch. He kicked at the dirt and his focus once again turned toward the dandelions. Now he could see the pattern clearly: They were spelling words.

"R-E-M," he said to himself as he spelled out the letters. "R-E-M-E-M-B-E-R!"

He made out the first word! "W-H-O," he spelled out again. "REMEMBER WHO...." He tilted his head to one side. "Y-O-U A-R-E!"

He looked at the little weedy flowers and could clearly make out the words: REMEMBER WHO YOU ARE! "How cool is that?" he thought to himself. "But what does it mean—remember who I am?"

He was staring at the ground, studying the weeds, when he heard someone yelling his name. He looked up and saw Dwight jumping up and down and pointing to the sky. Spencer looked up and watched as the baseball sailed through the air and over his head. He ran to pick it up and threw it to Shawn at second base. It went right over Shawn's head to Todd at third base.

"SWEETWATER!" Dwight threw his glove down on the ground. "You're a total loser!"

CHAPTER ELEVEN

Spencer could see everybody in the bleachers laughing and he could hear the rest of his teammates complaining, "Get in the game, Spencer! Look alive, Sweetwater!"

When things quieted down and another player stepped up to the plate he looked over at Nicole. "Maybe she didn't notice," he thought.

But she had. She was looking right at him—but smiling!

"Okay," he thought, "maybe this wasn't so bad. Maybe she thought it was cute or something."

He started to feel better and looked down at the dandelions again. The pattern was no longer there and he couldn't make out any words at all.

"Now I'm really losing it," he thought as he watched Todd catch a pop fly for the third out.

He ran back to the dugout and found his seat next to Jonas.

"Tough inning," Jonas said still looking down at his stat sheet. "Don't worry, Spencer, I won't put that in the newspaper."

"Yeah, I didn't see the ball. Hey, Jonas, can I ask you a question?"

"Sure."

"You know when you and Emily looked at my DNA and you saw I had an oak tree inside of me," Spencer whispered so no one else would hear.

"Well, not really an oak tree but the DNA of an oak tree—and a lizard and a mouse," Jonas replied.

"Yeah, yeah." Spencer looked around. "Well, do you think it means they can talk to me—just like animals?"

"What can talk to you? A tree?"

"Shhh! Not so loud! Not just a tree, but maybe—um—nature. Like flowers and maybe even weeds."

"Well, Spencer, I believe in your case anything's possible. You're very rare. A unique individual. A real-- "

"I know, a scientific oddball," Spencer said, hanging his head.

"Well, I wasn't going to say you were an oddball. But to answer your question, yes, I believe you *could* communicate with them—providing you could figure out their language."

"I think they figured out mine."

"What?" Jonas asked, not paying attention to the game.

Spencer explained what happened in the outfield and what the weeds spelled.

"Very interesting," Jonas said. "What do you think it means, *Remember who you are?*"

"Well, I've been feeling a little weird lately and I think they might be talking about that."

"What do you mean?" Jonas asked.

Spencer went on to tell Jonas what happened in the cave the day before and how Sully was the one who actually joined with him to save Emily and Anna. He explained how he wanted to be a Gatekeeper but that he was scared and didn't know if he could do it.

"SWEETWATER, ON DECK!" the coach yelled.

"Hey, I'm up!" Spencer stood up and grabbed a bat.

He put on a batting helmet and started swinging the bat back and forth in the air. He tapped the bat on each shoe to knock off the dirt and looked over at the bleachers to make sure Nicole was watching. He felt like a professional baseball player as he stood on deck, waiting for his turn at bat. The batter hit a grounder to third base and safely ran to first. He yelled at Spencer to get a hit and bring him home. Spencer approached the batter's box. The umpire called him to the plate. He ground his feet securely into the dirt and held the bat high in the air over his right shoulder.

"STRIKE ONE!" the umpire yelled out.

"But I wasn't ready!" Spencer protested, standing back from the plate and looking at the umpire.

"You stepped into the box, son. Come on, get in the game!"

Spencer was getting nervous. This was his chance to make an impression on Nicole. He stepped up to the plate again and held the bat steady in the air. He ground his feet into the dirt and slightly bent his knees. The pitcher released the ball and it came in fast, right over the plate. Spencer swung hard and felt the bat make contact with the ball. He was about to drop the bat and run to first base when he heard the umpire yell:

"FOUL BALL! STRIKE TWO!"

"Oh, man!" He already had two strikes.

He took a minute and swung the bat a few extra times. He stared at the pitcher and moved to the plate with renewed confidence. He tapped the bat on each of his shoes again and took his stance, the bat high in the air. The pitcher threw the ball and Spencer could feel his body tense. He stood with his feet firmly planted in the dirt and he knew this was it. This was his chance, his moment to shine in front of everybody. Dwight and the twins would have to respect him now. He felt his power as his weight shifted toward his right side and then to his left as the bat glided through the air. "A perfect swing," he thought to himself before he heard the dreaded words:

"STRIKE THREE! YOU'RE OUT!"

He pounded home plate with the bat and headed back to the dugout.

"You'll get one next time, son!" the umpire shouted out as Spencer dragged the bat through the dirt. Dwight and Shawn were standing in front of the dugout and when Spencer walked by Dwight grabbed his shoulder.

"Don't worry about it, Spencer," he said.

Spencer thought he was hearing things. Was Dwight finely being nice to him? Did he really feel bad for him?

"Sapsuckers can't play baseball anyway!" Dwight said and gave Shawn a high-five.

Spencer walked into the dugout, threw the bat in the corner with the others and sat down on the bench beside Jonas.

"Don't worry, Spencer, I won't put that in the paper either." Jonas laughed.

"That's okay, Jonas, it really doesn't matter anymore. This whole day was supposed to go so much better than this."

Spencer picked up his glove and played with the leather stitching. He felt beaten down, by Dwight and the twins always picking on him and about what had happened in the cave the day before.

"Spencer," Jonas said.

"Yeah?"

"Can you get my backpack off my chair for me?"

Spencer reached around to the back of the wheelchair.

"Gosh, this is heavy. What do you have in here?"

"It's a little experiment I've been working on."

Jonas placed the backpack in his lap and pulled out what looked like a pair of hiking boots with some wires attached to them.

"What are they?" Spencer asked.

"Well, they're special boots that my uncle helped me make. He works at NASA. We put hydraulic platform lifts on the bottom of each boot. Just like the one I use to lift my wheelchair into my van, only these are a lot smaller. Then we used magnetic induction to interface with the neurotransmitters in my brain." Jonas looked at Spencer and knew he didn't understand a word he was saying. "Basically, they can help me walk. I just put them on and attach these wires and pads to my legs. Then I get my brain to tell the boots to walk and my legs start moving. The only problem is my muscles won't allow me to stand for very long. So, until I solve that problem I just practice with them in my lab."

"That's the coolest idea ever! Does your uncle fly rockets for NASA?"

"No, he mostly builds them."

"Cool," Spencer said as he studied the boots.

"So, Spencer, I have an idea."

"What?"

"Maybe you could wear the boots when you go back to the outfield. You wouldn't miss any balls then. All you have to do is *think* you can jump high and the boots will make sure you do."

"Really? You'd let me wear them?"

"Sure, but just remember, you also have to *think* about how high you want to go. You could jump to outer space if you're not careful."

"Huh—what?" Spencer put the boots on. "Sure, Jonas, outer space—I got it."

Spencer finished lacing up the boots and Jonas connected the pads and wires to his legs.

"Now, the boots won't activate until you *think* about them," Jonas explained. "So, if you don't need them, don't use them."

"Okay," Spencer stood up from the bench and walked around. "These feel pretty good. So, let me get this straight. All I have to do is *think?*"

"That's right," Jonas replied. "Just think about what you want the boots to do."

"LET'S GO, SWEETWATER!" the coach yelled. "TAKE THE FIELD!"

Spencer grabbed his glove and headed back to right field. He looked at the dandelions and thought about the words, *"Remember who you are."* Now he knew the weeds were telling him he was born to be a Gatekeeper—and finally, he was beginning to feel like one. He felt strong with the boots on and he was ready to catch anything that came his way. He pounded his glove with his fist and watched as the pitcher struck out the first two batters.

Then, Michael Green came to the plate. If anyone could break Ricky Fitch's homerun record it was Big Mike. He towered over the other students and the junior-high football coach had already outfitted him with a team jersey. The other outfielders backed up to the fence and Spencer did the same. He stood ready for the ball to come his way as Big Mike swung hard at the first pitch.

"STRIKE ONE!" the umpire called out.

The second pitch was a fastball down the middle. Big Mike swung the bat, just tipping the ball, sending it backwards over the umpire's head.

"STRIKE TWO!" the umpire yelled.

Spencer could feel the blood pumping through his veins and it felt like his heart was going to jump out of his chest. He had forgotten all about the boots and was just concerned with Big Mike and the next pitch. The pitcher stood on the mound and looked back at the outfield players to make sure they were ready. The students in the bleachers were silent. The pitcher looked at the catcher and wound up for the pitch. As the ball whizzed through the air Spencer could tell it was outside and he couldn't help feeling relieved. Then he saw Big Mike shift his body over to the right. When he did, it lined him up perfectly with the ball and the next thing Spencer heard was the *crack* of the bat as it made contact with the ball.

It was a fly ball climbing higher and higher in the air and coming straight for him. He couldn't judge the distance of it at first and thought for sure he was out too far. He started running in the direction of Dwight at first base but stopped as he watched it sail over Dwight's head. He started backing up and could see the outfield fence out of the corner of his eye.

"It's going over!" he thought, turning around and running faster.

Suddenly, one of the bootlaces came undone and he stumbled. Then he remembered:

"The boots!"

When he said the word *boots* he could feel something move under his feet. He stopped running and planted them flat on the ground. He could feel himself being lifted into the air.

"AS HIGH AS THE BALL!" he yelled out as he flew above the fence.

Spencer stretched out his arm and watched as the ball fell from the sky and into his glove. When he came back down to the ground he checked to make sure the ball was still there—and it was! And that's when he realized he was on the other side of the fence!

"Awesome!" he yelled as the other players ran over to congratulate him and help him climb back over.

"Great catch, Sweetwater! That was the third out! We won the game!" Shawn said, grabbing Spencer's shirt to help pull him over.

"Yeah, sapsucker. I didn't know you had it in ya!" Todd said, patting Spencer on the back.

When Spencer climbed back over the fence he came face to face with Dwight. He looked Spencer up and down.

"How'd you do it, Sweetwater?" Dwight demanded. "You jumped straight up in the air about ten feet."

"So what, Dwight? He made the catch." Shawn ran back to the infield.

"Come on, Dwight!" Todd yelled. "We won the game. What's the big deal?"

"You're still a sapsucker, Sweetwater!" Dwight yelled as he followed the twins.

Spencer paid no attention to Dwight's comment and headed for the infield to shake hands with the blue team. When he finished he walked over to Jonas near the dugout.

"Jonas, these boots are awesome! Did you see me? Did you see how high I jumped?"

"Yeah, Spencer, you did great!" Jonas said as he watched Spencer take off the boots. "Now, I'll put that in my article for the paper."

Emily and Anna came running over from the bleachers.

"Great catch, Spencer!" Emily exclaimed.

"Yeah!" Anna agreed. "I'll bet Dwight Fitch never caught a ball like that."

Spencer looked at Jonas as he finished tying his shoes. "No, I'll bet he hasn't. Come on, guys, let's go eat lunch."

Spencer helped Jonas put the backpack on his wheelchair and they all started across the field toward the back of the school.

"Um, Spencer—I think someone's coming to talk to you." Jonas was watching Nicole walk across the infield, heading right for them.

"Come on, Emily and Anna, let's go. Spencer, we'll see you at the picnic tables."

Spencer was in a state of shock as he watched Nicole walk toward him. As scared as he was in the cave yesterday, nothing was as bad as this. What would he say to her? What would she say to him?

"Hi, Spencer," she said. "That was a great catch!"

"Thanks," he said, looking down at the ground.

"Are you going to lunch now?" she asked.

"Yeah, but then my dad's coming to get us 'cause we have to take my dog to the vet." Spencer finally looked up. "Are you going to lunch?"

"Yeah, my mom isn't coming to pick me up until later."

"Well, if you want you could eat with me, my sister and my other friends," Spencer said.

"Okay, I'll go and get my lunch and meet you at the picnic tables."

"Okay, that sounds like a plan," he said.

He watched her walk across the field and up the hill that led to the school. He hit his forehead with the palm of his hand.

"Spencer, you idiot, *that sounds like a plan* is the dumbest thing you've ever said." He started walking toward the picnic tables and a big smile came over his face.

"I can't believe it! I'm having lunch with Nicole Darling!"

CHAPTER TWELVE

DOCTOR SWEETWATER

The Miles Veterinary Clinic was located on Route 3 just a few miles past Ennis Tucker's store. Harry Miles opened the clinic after graduating from veterinary school more than thirty years ago. He restored an old barn on his property and turned it into offices and exam rooms. It was equipped with the latest technology and machines to do all kinds of tests on animals. He was exceptionally pleased when his niece, Jessie, wanted to become a vet and work with him at the clinic. They specialized in dogs and cats but could also take care of large animals like horses and cows. Somehow Sully always knew when they were getting close to the clinic because he would hang his head out the car window and bark.

Will pulled into the parking lot. "Hold on to his leash, Spencer. Don't let him jump out of the car."

"I got him, Dad."

When Will opened the car door Sully jumped out, pulling Spencer with him, and dragged him over to the grass by the front door of the clinic.

"Walk him around a little bit, Spencer. Emily and I'll go in and fill out the paper work," Will said.

"Okay, Dad. I think he's curious about all the smells around here anyway."

"Hey there, Mr. Sweetwater, how are you today?" the receptionist asked as Will and Emily walked up to the front desk.

"We're doing fine, thank you. We've brought Sully to see Jessie—Dr. Miles, that is."

"And what kind of a problem is Sully having?"

"I think he's a little better now, but he was feeling real bad a few days ago. Like he had a stomach problem or something. He'd lost a lot of weight and didn't want to eat. But, like I said, I think he's doing better now. Anyway, Dr. Miles said that we should bring him in for tests."

Spencer and Sully came busting through the door and Sully began smelling around each chair in the waiting room. He dragged Spencer over to a lady who was sitting against the back wall. She was holding a black-and-white cat and Sully stopped directly in front of her. He stretched his neck out so he could get a better whiff of the cat.

The cat stood up on the lady's lap and hissed. It raised one paw in the air, and with its claws fully exposed, took a swipe at Sully.

"Watch it, buster!" the cat said. **"You're getting a little too close!"**

"Hey, I heard that!" Spencer thought as Sully backed away from the cat. "But how did I hear that?" He knelt down on the floor and whispered into Sully's ear. "Can you hear me, boy?"

"Yep!"

"How did that happen?" Spencer wondered.

"Sully Sweetwater!" the vet's assistant called from a door down the hall.

"Come on, Spencer, bring Sully over here," Will and Emily got up from their chairs.

They walked through the main office area and down a hallway to a large room that held various-sized wire kennels with dogs in them. On the opposite side of the room was a big scale. The vet's assistant tried to get Sully to sit down on it so she could get his weight. Every time she got him in place he stood up and walked off.

"Sully, what are you doing?" Spencer asked with his thoughts.

"This thing wobbles and it scares me!"

"Well you have to sit still—the lady has to see how much you weigh."

Sully sat on the scale, tail tucked under and ears lowered and didn't take his eyes off Spencer. The vet's assistant then led them to an exam room just off the big room.

Emily looked down at the last kennel they passed and saw a shy, yellow dog sitting in the corner watching them as they walked by. "What's wrong with that dog?" she asked the assistant.

"I'm not exactly sure. I do know someone found her over on Elk Creek Road. They didn't know who she belonged to so they brought her here. They thought she was going to get hit by a car and as it turns out she might have 'cause she can't hear in one ear."

Emily sighed. "Poor thing."

Spencer was following his father into the room when Sully stopped him to look in the kennel with Emily.

"Whoa, check her out! She's cute!"

"What? Who?" Spencer said to Sully as he tried to see the dog in the kennel. "Take it easy, boy, it's just another dog."

"This is not just another dog—she's beautiful!" Sully pulled on the leash to get closer.

"So, she doesn't belong to anyone?" Emily asked.

"I don't think so. But here's Dr. Miles, she can tell you more about her."

"Hi, everybody," she said as she reached out to shake Will's hand. "It's great to see you again."

Will smiled. "Hello, Jessie."

"Wow, it looks like Sully really likes this dog," she said.

"What's her name?" Emily asked.

"We're not sure," Jessie said. "When she was dropped off last week she didn't have a collar so we don't know much about her."

"She sure is pretty," Will said, watching Emily with the dog.

"If you think she's pretty now, just wait until she puts on some weight," Jessie said. "She must have been on her own for a while. She's a little on the thin side. She's also deaf in one ear and I don't think surgery is an option for her."

"That means she can't hear in one of her ears, Sully," Spencer said.

"Who cares? She's wonderful!"

"How old do you think she is?" Will asked.

"Maybe three or four," Jessie replied.

Sully looked at Spencer. **"What else are they saying about her?"**

"They're saying she's three or four years old."

"All right! I love an older woman!"

Spencer laughed out loud.

Will raised an eyebrow. "What's so funny, son?"

"Oh nothin', Dad."

"Can we take her home, Dad?" Emily asked. "Since Spencer has Sully, she can be my dog. Please, please, please," she begged, pulling on her father's arm.

"I just finished telling your grandmother no more animals, and you expect us to go home today with a dog? And besides that, how do we know how Sully will be with another dog. Maybe he won't like her."

"Oh, I wouldn't worry about that, Dad," Spencer said. "I have a feeling they'll get along great!"

They all watched as the two dogs smelled each other through the wire kennel.

"I'll tell you what," Jessie said. "How about we go ahead and examine Sully and that'll give your dad a chance to think about it."

Will nodded. "That's a good idea. I forgot something in the truck anyway. I'll be right back."

He headed to the front of the clinic and the children followed Jessie into the exam room.

CHAPTER TWELVE

Jessie had a feeling Will was going to make a phone call to Kate about the new dog. She checked Sully's heartbeat and looked in his eyes and ears. She looked at the chart to verify his weight and pushed on his tummy. Spencer could hear Sully laugh.

"I have to say, Sully seems a lot better than he was the other day," Jessie said as she stood back and looked at him. "I wonder why? Is there anything different with him?"

Emily and Spencer told Jessie about the food experiment. Emily told her about the pot pie and the eggs and toast—and Spencer told her about the corn and Anna's allergies.

"Well, I think you children have done an excellent job with him. I'm still going to run some tests today, so we can make sure he does have food allergies but it looks like you found his problem."

Spencer gave Emily a high-five.

"But," Jessie added, "dogs can't eat people food all the time. They have to eat dog food because it has vitamins and minerals they need to keep them healthy. So, once I do the tests today and we find out exactly what Sully's allergic to we'll put him on some special dog food. Okay?"

"Yes, ma'am," Spencer and Emily said at the same time.

Will came back into the room and told Jessie he'd found what he needed in his car. Jessie knew that was code for: "I talked to Kate and we can take the new dog home." Jessie explained to Will what she thought Sully's problem was and Emily told him about their experiment. Jessie led Sully out of the room to run the tests and Will and the kids started to walk back to the front of the clinic. Emily stopped at the shy dog's kennel again.

She sat on the floor and stuck her fingers through the wire to pet her. "Good-bye, little sweetie. Don't worry, I'll talk to my grandmother and tell her all about you and how much we'd love to have you come and live with us at Sweetwater Farms."

The shy dog made her way over to Emily's fingertips and rolled over on her back.

"Oh, look," Spencer said, "I think she likes you."

Will reached over Emily's shoulder and unlatched the door to the kennel. He pulled it open and the dog got up and slowly walked out.

"What are you doing, Dad?" Emily asked.

"Well, don't you think if you're going to pet your new dog she should be lying in your lap?"

It took Emily a minute to realize what her father had just said, but when she did she jumped up and threw her arms around his neck.

"Really? Really? I thought you said no more animals!"

"Well, I called your grandmother and we both thought it would be okay."

Emily sat down on the floor and her new dog curled up in her lap.

❊ ❊ ❊ ❊ ❊ ❊ ❊ ❊ ❊ ❊ ❊

When they got back to the farm Kate, Sofia and Anna were waiting on the front porch. When the truck pulled up the two dogs jumped out and Emily and Spencer followed.

"That's one pretty dog you have there, Emily." Kate knelt down to pet her. "And I think with a little love and some good food we'll put weight back on her in no time." Kate stood up. "You know, Emily, when we do get that weight on her, I think you're going to find that she's a pretty big dog. She might get about as big as Sully."

"Really! How about that, Spencer? I'll have a big dog too!" Emily exclaimed.

Sofia and Anna sat on the ground so they could pet the new dog.

"Have you picked out a name, Emily?" Sofia asked.

"No, not yet. I have to think about it."

The two dogs sniffed around the bushes together and then the new dog came back over to Emily for more attention.

"She already loves you, Emily," Anna said, watching the dog roll over on her back.

CHAPTER TWELVE

"So, Mom, what do you think of our new addition?" Will asked.

"You were right, son, she's the one you've been looking for."

Emily looked up at the two of them. "What do you mean—the one you've been looking for?"

"Well, we've been looking for a dog for you for a long time. Spencer has Sully and we thought it would be good for you to have a dog too," Will said. "Jessie set the whole thing up. I asked her when she was here the other day to keep an eye out for a dog for you. She called this morning and said she thought she had the perfect one. And I guess she was right. The only thing you have to remember is that she can only hear out of her left ear."

Emily jumped up and hugged her father and grandmother.

"You two are so sneaky," she said, "but I'm glad you are!"

"Now," Will looked at his mother, "can we all agree that this is the last animal for Sweetwater Farms?"

They all laughed and everyone agreed.

"But, Dad," Spencer said, "what if one comes along that really needs our help? We can't just turn our back on it. We have to help it, don't we?"

Will took a deep breath and looked at Kate.

"You want to answer that question, Mom?"

"Well, Spencer, we'll just have to cross that bridge when we come to it." Kate said, half-smiling at Will.

"Anna, where are you going?" Sofia asked as Anna started to run to the other side of the house.

"I've got to go look at something. Miss Kate just gave me an idea for a summer project!"

Everyone watched as the two dogs rolled and played in the grass. They all turned toward the gravel road when they heard the sound of a horn blowing and saw a big, blue truck pulling a horse trailer.

Kate held her hand up to block the sun from her eyes. "Well, speaking of no more animals at Sweetwater Farms, there's Ennis with the new donkey."

"Pee Wee!" Spencer yelled. "I forgot he was coming today! Come on, Emily, let's go to the barn and see Pee Wee!"

Emily called the new dog and Spencer and Sully went running to follow the truck. Ennis backed the trailer up to the barn and dropped the gate. The big-eared donkey was huddled in the corner of the trailer afraid to come out.

Emily looked into the trailer. "Ah, he's scared. And he's also the funniest little animal I've ever seen."

"Don't make fun of him," Spencer said. "He doesn't like it."

Ennis wanted to clip a rope onto the halter of the little donkey, but every time he tried Pee Wee would turn around and try to kick him.

"You want me to do it?" Kate asked. "Maybe he prefers a woman's touch."

Will laughed. "Or, as little as he is maybe I can just pick him up and carry him."

Spencer could hear Pee Wee crying.

"Just wait a minute, everybody!" he yelled.

They all froze at Spencer's outburst.

"Son, what are you yelling for?" Will asked.

"Um—sorry, everybody. Mr. Tucker, could I maybe try and get him out. I think if I explained everything to him he'd be okay."

"Sure, Spencer, it's okay with me if it's okay with your dad."

"I don't know, son. Remember what happened with Peaches?" Will said.

"Please, Dad, just let me try. I promise I'll be careful."

Kate winked at Spencer and handed him the rope. "Something tells me he'll be just fine, Will."

Spencer walked onto the trailer and saw Pee Wee had his head buried deep into the corner of the hay bin. "Hey, little guy, remember me?"

Pee Wee turned around and looked at Spencer. He blinked his eyes.

"MISTER! I thought you forgot about me!"

CHAPTER TWELVE

Spencer clipped the rope onto the halter and knelt down to rub the donkey's ears.

"We'd never forget about you, Pee Wee. This is going to be your new home and I promise this one will be your last!"

The donkey took a few steps back from Spencer and his whole body began to shake. He raised his head in the air, opened his mouth and let out a long, deep bray. Spencer covered his ears as the loud sound echoed off the walls of the trailer.

"Wow! I didn't know that such a little donkey could make such a big sound!"

"I'm sorry, Mister—I can't control it. It happens whenever I'm excited."

"So, I guess that means you'd like to live here at Sweetwater Farms?"

"Sure thing, Mister!"

"Okay, but remember, my name is Spencer."

"Okay, Mister," the donkey said as he followed Spencer off the trailer.

Kate found a stall for Pee Wee and gave him some grain and hay. The little donkey willingly followed Spencer into the stall and everyone watched as he settled into his new home. When Kate was sure Pee Wee was all right she walked Ennis to the truck and Will went to the orchard to find Roberto.

"Did Pee Wee talk to you?" Emily asked as she stood at the stall door with Spencer.

"Yeah. I could hear he was crying, like when we first found him in Mr. Tucker's barn. But when I explained this was his new home and he'd always be at Sweetwater Farms, he understood and was happy."

"Is that when he made that funny noise?"

"Yeah," Spencer laughed. "He said he can't help it. It happens when he's excited."

Emily nodded. "Like Sully wagging his tail when he's happy."

"Hey, you're right. I wonder why people don't have something like that."

"Well, we kinda do. We smile!"

They heard a sneeze from one of the cats up in the loft.

"What was that?" Emily asked.

"I don't know. Let's go up and check."

When they climbed the wooden ladder to the loft they saw Dudley and Gerri sitting by a bale of hay and Dudley sneezed again.

"I wonder if he's got a cold," Spencer said.

"I don't know," Emily said as he sat down on the floor next to them.

"Cold, smold," Gerri said, jumping onto the hay bale. **"If you hadn't stayed out all night chasing that mouse you'd be fine."**

"I don't have a cold," Dudley replied. **"You think you're so smart but you don't know anything."**

Spencer began to laugh at the two bickering cats.

"What's he laughing at?" Gerri asked.

"I don't know," Dudley said. **"He can't hear us—can he?"**

"Spencer, why are you laughing?" Emily asked.

"You should hear these guys, Em, they're a riot. I mean I knew they had personalities but you should hear what they're saying. They sound just like us when we argue. Just like a real brother and sister."

"He CAN hear us!" Gerri yelled, jumping behind the bale of hay.

"Wait for me!" Dudley darted behind the hay after her.

"Hey, guys, don't be scared," Spencer whispered, looking over the hay at the two of them.

Dudley sneezed again and Spencer reached over and picked him up. He placed him in Emily's lap and then got Gerri.

"Okay, you guys—yes, I can hear you talk. I just found out the other day. Isn't it great?"

"I guess so," they both said.

"So, Dudley, how about we find out why you're sneezing?" Spencer said as he gave Gerri to Emily and took Dudley onto his lap. "Would that be okay with you?"

"Sure," Dudley said as he looked up at Spencer.

"So tell me how you feel." Spencer held the cat out in front of him and looked in his eyes.

"Fine, I guess," Dudley replied.

"You don't feel fine," Gerri interrupted. **"You've been sneezing all day. And tell him about the mouse and how you stayed out all night!"** Gerri looked up at Spencer. **"He stayed out all night because he could never find out where the mouse was hiding. Tell him, Dudley—tell him why you couldn't find the mouse."**

Dudley looked at Spencer and hung his head.

"I couldn't find the mouse because I couldn't see him," he said in a low voice.

"That's right!" Gerri added. **"You can't see two feet in front of you and yet you thought you could leave the barn and go mouse-hunting."**

Spencer looked down at the gray cat and Dudley raised his head. **"It's just like she said—I can't see two feet in front of me."**

"That's why we have to do everything together, so I can show him the way," Gerri said looking at Emily. **"Can she hear us talking too?"**

"No—just me," Spencer replied.

"Hmm," Gerri said, licking her paw.

Spencer looked at Dudley again and saw he had a runny nose and he felt a little warm. "Well, my diagnosis would be that Dudley does have a cold. So, when I have a cold my gram tells me to drink lots of fluids and get plenty of rest."

"Excuse me, Doctor Sweetwater," Dudley said looking up at Spencer. **"What's a fluid?"**

Spencer smiled. "Well, I just mean to drink a lot of water. And I'm not really a doctor—not yet anyway."

Spencer explained everything to Emily and they sat in the loft for a while petting the cats.

"Spencer, you're going to be a great vet," Emily said, pulling a piece of hay from the bale to play with Gerri.

"Thanks, Em. It doesn't hurt that they can talk to me. That makes it all a little easier."

"Yeah, but besides that, you also know how to make them feel better and not be scared. That's a very important part of a vet's job."

"I guess you're right. I never thought about that."

"Spencer, do you think you could talk to my new dog and let me know if she's happy at Sweetwater Farms?"

Spencer realized how lucky he was to be able to talk to animals. He felt bad for Emily because she couldn't do it--but he had an idea.

The two of them climbed down from the loft and ran outside the barn with the two dogs. They ran to the backyard of the house and saw Anna looking around the old storage shed behind the driveway.

"What are you doing, Anna?" Emily hollered over to her.

"Oh, nothing," she called back, acting a little suspicious.

"Come over here with us. Spencer's gonna show me how to talk to my new dog."

Anna walked through the bushes to the backyard.

"Can you show me how to talk to Sweetie Pie too?"

"Sure," Spencer replied. "Now, the most important thing to remember is that animals can't speak like we can."

The two girls laughed.

"No, really—it's very important to remember that. You have to think like they think, not like people think."

He called to Sully and the big dog came running over to him. "Now, Sully can't understand words."

"Sure I can, Spencer."

"Shhh," Spencer whispered to Sully. "I'm trying to teach them how to talk to their animals."

"That's easy, Spencer. All they have to do is watch us. Pay attention to us. Play with us. And then they'll know our language. You can always tell how we're feeling because our bodies show it. We're not like people because sometimes people don't show how they're feeling. Sometimes they hide it. Like, remember when you wanted to go to the fair—you'd

waited all year, and when it finally came you had a tummy ache. You didn't tell anyone and while you were there you started feeling even worse. Everyone had to come home early."

"Yeah, I remember," Spencer said, feeling sad all over again.

"Well, we're not like that. You know exactly how we feel all the time. Like when we bark. It means we want something."

"Like when you bark at me to come and play?" Spencer asked.

"Yep."

"But sometimes you just stand in the front yard and bark at nothing."

"It may look like I'm barking at nothing but with my great ears I hear a lot of things and I always want to know what I'm hearing. So, when I'm in the front yard barking, I'm saying—I want to know what that sound is."

"Okay, I got it. So, I should tell the girls if they pay attention to their animals, they'll understand their language?"

"That's right. It's actually pretty easy because we always tell the truth."

Emily pushed. "Anytime now, Spencer."

"Okay, all you have to do is watch your animal. For instance, Anna, when Sweetie Pie is hungry, what does she do?"

Anna thought for a moment. "She walks around her food dish!"

"That's right!" Spencer said. "And what does she do when she wants you to pet her?"

Anna looked at Emily and thought about the question.

"She walks around my legs and purrs!"

Emily was starting to understand and she called her new dog over to her.

"So, when she rolls on her back like this," Emily said, watching the dog roll over, "she wants me to rub her tummy?"

Spencer nodded. "That's right. Animals talk to us all the time but we just don't realize it. Just because they can't speak doesn't mean they're not talking."

The children played with the dogs until it was time for supper, and Anna went home to "talk" to Sweetie Pie and Spencer and Emily took the two dogs into the house. Spencer gave Sully his new dog food. He loved it. Emily showed the new dog where her food dish was and they watched as she ate all of her dinner too. After having their supper the children went upstairs and the two dogs followed. When they finished their homework they got ready for bed and Kate came upstairs to tuck them in.

Kate sat down on Emily's bed with the new dog. "So have you decided on a name for this little angel?"

Emily stuck her head out of the bathroom with a toothbrush hanging out of her mouth.

"No, do you have any ideas?"

Kate stroked the dog. "Just one."

"What?" Emily asked from the bathroom.

Kate waited for a moment until Emily finished in the bathroom and jumped into bed.

"Remember how we named Rosebud after your grandfather's mother, Rose?"

"Uh-huh."

"Well, do you remember that time we went to Charleston to visit my mother?"

"Not really," Emily said.

"Well, her name was Margaret Lee. She was a beautiful woman and I loved her very much. So I was thinking, if you wanted to, you could name her after my mother."

Emily squirmed in the bed and turned her eyes toward her new dog.

"Um, Gram, no offense but I don't know if I want to name my dog Margaret. It's a nice name and all but--"

Kate laughed and hugged Emily.

CHAPTER TWELVE

"No—no, Emily, not Margaret. Everybody called her Maggie—Maggie Lee."

Emily sat up in bed.

"That's a great name! I love it!"

She hugged her grandmother and looked the little dog right in the eyes.

"You can be Maggie Lee of Sweetwater Farms!"

The new dog wagged her tail, jumped up on Emily and licked her in the face.

"She likes it, Gram! Look she's wagging her tail—that means she's happy!"

Kate smiled and settled Emily and Maggie Lee in bed, pulling up the covers and tucking them in. She turned off the light and walked down the hallway to Spencer's room.

"Knock, knock," she said before going in.

"Oh—hey, Gram," Spencer said, "come in."

He was already in bed reading an astronomy book and Sully was sleeping beside him. Kate sat on the edge of the bed and petted Sully's head.

"Gram, can I ask you something?"

"Anything."

"When is the second full moon? I was looking for it in my *Stars and the Universe* book but I can't find it."

"Have you been thinking about Suri Lakena and being a Gatekeeper?" she asked.

"Well, just a little." Actually he had been thinking about it a lot. Kate got up and walked over to Spencer's desk. She looked at the calendar he had on the wall and counted the days between Lakena's moon and the end of the month.

"Here. It's seven days after Lakena's moon."

She crossed back over and sat on the bed. Sully began to snore and they both laughed.

"So, if it's seven days from Lakena's moon then that means..."

Spencer held up his hand and counted on his fingers.

"That's in two days!" He shot straight up in bed.

Sully was startled by Spencer's outburst and jumped to his feet. He looked at Spencer and Kate, and after he was sure everything was all right, he stretched, turned in a circle and plopped back down on the bed.

"Now, Spencer, I don't want you to worry," Kate soothed.

"I know, Gram, but two days is not very long."

"It may not seem like it, but when the time comes you'll know what your decision will be."

"What do you mean?"

"Well, I just mean that you're given information every day to help you make your choice. And I'm sure you don't even realize it."

Spencer thought for a moment and remembered the dandelions on the baseball field.

He told his grandmother about them and what they had spelled out.

"That's what I mean, Spencer. You'll get more and more help every day. You just have to watch for it. It'll also become easier for you to join with Sully and the other animals. I know it seems like being a Gatekeeper is really scary but you'll have the help of the plants and animals and every other living thing."

"Hey, Gram, back up a minute," Spencer said. "You said it'll become easier for me to join with Sully and other animals. Well, it already happened. Today, when we were at Jessie's office, I heard a cat talk and I heard Sully talk and I didn't even have to get my energy up."

"See how quickly it's happening? And it was easy, too, wasn't it?"

"Yeah, it was, Gram," Spencer said, feeling better.

"Now, I want you to get a good night's sleep and think happy thoughts. Maybe you can think about the end-of-school party. It's only a couple of days away." She kissed his forehead.

"Okay, Gram. I'm gonna try and guess what present you'll have for me!"

CHAPTER THIRTEEN

THE LEGEND OF THE UKTAH

Spencer tossed and turned in bed. Sully woke up every time Spencer turned over so he eventually jumped down and curled up on the rug next to the bed. After a while Spencer was able to relax and he fell into a deep sleep.

He dreamt he was in the pine forest and didn't know which way to go. He could smell the pine trees but it turned into an old, musty scent and he remembered the snake in the cave. He heard leaves rustling behind him and started to run. He found the trail that led to the top of the mountain but he felt like he was being chased by someone or something. When he reached the top he hid by the stone window. He looked back at the trail and felt sure whatever was chasing him would show itself.

The wind began to blow and clouds passed by overhead. A dark shadow fell over the entire mountain and he felt a chill. He decided to make a run for the cave, but he stopped to look through the window. Nothing was there: Sweetwater Farms was gone. It was as if it never existed. He saw the hills and trees but there was no barn or house. There was no cemetery or oak tree, no pastures or horses. His heart started to beat faster; he knew he had to find Suri Lakena.

He heard something else behind him so he ran for the trail to the cave. The rock steps were covered in damp vines and his feet slipped out from under him. He slid down the steps, and when he landed in front of the cave—he woke up!

He opened his eyes and his bedroom came into focus. He ran his fingers through his sweaty hair and threw off the covers.

"Sully," he said in a whisper, "where are you?"

The big dog groaned as if he were agitated at being woken up.

"Come here, boy!" Spencer said quietly as he patted the bed.

Reluctantly, Sully jumped up and lay down beside him.

"Hey, boy," Spencer said, putting his arm around Sully's big chest. "I had a bad dream."

Spencer pulled the covers up, and as Sully started to snore Spencer fell back to sleep. This time, as he drifted off, he could hear the sound of bells. He dreamt he was following Suri Lakena down the dark corridor of the cave. Up ahead he could see light from the torches and in this dream he felt safe. He turned around and saw the huge wolf, Takoda, walking behind him. Then Kuma, the jaguar, ran ahead and jumped onto a boulder. Ayasha was already in the cave flying around the fountain. Spencer had the wonderful feeling he was with friends he had known all his life.

"You will be safe here, my grandson," Suri Lakena said as she motioned for Spencer to sit beside Kuma. "It is time we explain everything to you. I have come to you in your dreams because in dreams we see truth."

Spencer sat on the boulder next to Kuma, and Takoda lay down on the rock floor beside him. Ayasha slowed her flight and landed on his shoulder.

"First, Spencer, these animal guides will be Guardians for you—as well as for the mountain. If you choose to become Gatekeeper they will serve you as they have served me all of these years. They possess wisdom from the past and insight into the future." She looked at each animal and said: "Tonawanda!"

"What does that mean?" Spencer asked.

"It is an ancient word for the Guardians which means to unite as one."

Spencer looked at the jaguar and the wolf as he stroked Ayasha's head. He could feel their power as each one joined with him. He looked at Kuma and felt her strength and courage through every muscle in his body. When the power of Takoda pierced his heart, he felt a fierce dedication to serve. Ayasha jumped down on his lap and looked into his eyes. She took flight and Spencer felt like he went with her. Around the cave they flew, and as he began to relax he could feel what it was like to fly. When she landed, Spencer felt himself leave her, and he was sitting on the rock once again.

"You see, my grandson, the Guardians are very powerful. They will serve you well," she said, kneeling in front of him.

"But Suri Lakena, I'm..." Spencer looked down at the ground, ashamed to speak his heart.

His eyes began to fill with tears and she gently lifted his chin with her fingertips.

"Tell me, Spencer, what is troubling you?"

"I'm—afraid to be the Gatekeeper."

"My child, I know this decision is not an easy one to make. Remember, I once had to make it myself."

Feeling a little relieved, Spencer wiped his eyes with the back of his hand.

"I was about your age when my father brought me to this mountain. The Gatekeeper before me was my great-great-great-grandfather—Wonotah. He explained everything to me just as I am telling you now. He told me of my new family, the family of all creation—and he explained how I am a part of every living thing--of every flower and tree, of every bird soaring in the sky and every fish swimming in the great ocean." Spencer looked at Suri Lakena. She wiped his tears and moved his red hair away from his face. "Do you understand this, my child?"

"Sort of. Is it kinda like Jonas finding DNA in me from other things—like animals and trees?"

"That's right, Spencer. Because you are a child of the sun, you have a part of every living thing inside of you. That's why you have been chosen to be the next Gatekeeper—so you can protect all living things and keep them safe."

Spencer was beginning to understand.

"So, if I don't become Gatekeeper, everything will die?" he asked even though he was afraid to hear her answer.

"Well, let me try to explain it like this. The energy that is coming from the positive vortex is love. It is sending out that love in the form of rain, sunshine and positive energy so all things can grow. It is why Katherine gets up in the morning to feed her precious animals. It is why your father takes such good care of you and Emily. Now, my grandson, do you know what the opposite of love is?"

Spencer remembered his feelings for Dwight Fitch.

"Is it hate?" he asked feeling ashamed.

"Well, you would think that would be the answer, but actually, it is fear. You see, Spencer, life will continue in the reverse vortex but it will be very different from what we know now. You saw it when you came to the mountain with Emily and Anna. The spider looked different, the plant life was different and there was no fountain in the cave and, therefore, no water to run down to Sweetwater Farms."

"And like the pond too!" he exclaimed.

"That's right. The vortex also controls temperature and if the reverse vortex is allowed to take over, everything will be affected." Spencer was able to understand. "So, things don't die—they just *live* different?"

"That's right, Spencer. Haven't you felt the energy from the reverse vortex?"

Spencer didn't understand her question.

"You felt it on the day your sweet mother died and every day since when you think of her. You felt it when Emily and Anna were in the hole with the snake and you didn't know what to do."

Spencer was surprised she knew these things about him.

"Don't be surprised, Spencer, I am a part of the Universe and, therefore, a part of you."

"So, how do I stop the fear?"

"The key to removing fear and replacing it with love, is understanding. If you know where the fear comes from and understand how it began you can remove it. You can always choose to live with fear or without it."

"I don't really understand."

"I'll explain further. Let's talk about your mother. Before she died you felt safe, didn't you?"

"Yes."

"And how did you feel after she died?"

Spencer rubbed his arm as the pain began to shoot to his shoulder.

"It's all right, Spencer," she said, calming him by placing her hand on his arm. "Because you feel things so deeply, you are experiencing fear as pain in your body. Now, when your mother died, did you feel scared?"

He nodded his head.

"Did you feel nervous, too, as if you didn't know what would happen next and were afraid it would be something bad?"

Again, he nodded.

"My dear grandson, I know you will always miss your mother, but there is nothing to fear in her death. Just like you, she is and always will be a part of the great Universe, and that means she is everywhere. Your mother will always be with you, but she speaks to you in a new way now. Remember when you taught Emily and Anna how to talk to their animals?"

"Yes," he said, wiping his eyes.

"Well, it's the same thing. Your mother may not be able to take you to school or read books to you, but you can still see her beautiful face—

in Emily. And you can hear her soft voice when the wind blows. And, through your memories, you can remember how she used to tuck you in at night and tell you she loved you. Do you understand, Spencer?"

He was trying to put together everything she had just told him. He stood up from the rock and felt as if a huge weight had been lifted from his shoulders.

"I get it!" he exclaimed. "Mom is still with me—in a way. All I have to do is think different! Right?"

"That's right, Spencer," she said. "And if you think different, as you put it, then you can replace the fearful thoughts you have about your mother's death with loving thoughts of her life. It is your choice to let this fear you have inside live on and grow, or you can replace it with the love that streams from the positive vortex. You have seen both worlds here on the mountain and now you have to choose which one is right for you."

Suri Lakena stood up and held out her hand.

"Come with me, Spencer, there's something I want you to see that might help you make your decision."

He took her hand and they walked to the fountain. She waved her hand in front of it and the vortex began to rise. The deep purple and violet light swirled around the cave and Spencer watched as the huge cone-shaped vortex moved upward.

"Hold on tight!" she said as she held his arm and jumped into the vortex.

Spencer didn't even have a chance to think about what had just happened. He closed his eyes for a second and when he opened them they were standing on the bank of a beautiful stream of water. He could see apple trees in the distance and a small house and a barn.

"Where are we?" he asked.

"We're at Sweetwater Farms," she said. "Two hundred years ago."

"Whoa!" Spencer replied. "How did we get here?"

"The vortex has many wonderful powers. You might even say it's magical," she answered with a smile. "Now, I want to show you something I think you'll find very interesting."

CHAPTER THIRTEEN

They walked past the barn and Spencer saw Sir Benjamin working in the hayfield.

"Hey, Sir Benjamin!" he yelled. "Sir Benjamin!"

"He cannot hear you, Spencer. We're only here to glimpse the past, not become part of it."

When they reached the house they went in and saw a man with a long, black beard dressed in the same type of Scottish clothing that Sir Benjamin wore. He was a tall man with jet-black hair and he had a pistol in his belt. He was looking through Sir Benjamin's trunk and papers and maps were thrown everywhere.

"Who is that?" Spencer asked.

"That, my grandson, is Sir Angus Wynn—Sir Benjamin's partner."

"Oh, yeah, Sir Benjamin said he followed Sir Angus here from Scotland. He said Sir Angus stole his work. So what is he looking for?"

"Me," she answered. "Just watch."

Spencer heard the door open and he couldn't believe his eyes. Coming into the house was Suri Lakena. She looked different though. She was younger and she had on a long dress and he could see that she was going to have a baby. He looked over and she was still standing next to him. He looked back and forth several times before he could believe what he was seeing. She put her finger to her lips to quiet him and pointed for him to watch.

Sir Angus was asking the young Suri Lakena to tell him her secrets. He said he could make them all rich and they would be very powerful. Then Sir Benjamin burst through the door. His red hair looked like it was on fire as he began to argue with Sir Angus.

Spencer couldn't take his eyes off of the two men. He felt like he was watching a movie. The young Suri Lakena stepped between the two angry men to try to calm them down. Sir Angus grabbed her and threw her to the ground. He shoved Sir Benjamin who fell over the trunk and lay on the floor beside her.

Sir Angus stood over the couple and slowly drew his pistol from his belt. He pointed it right at Sir Benjamin and began to squeeze the trigger. Suri Lakena closed her eyes and raised her hands to the sky. She began to say something in her Native American language, and, all of a sudden, as if magic, Sir Angus turned into a snake and fell to the floor. Spencer couldn't believe his eyes. He watched Sir Benjamin help Suri Lakena to her feet. She picked up the snake and placed it in a leather bag and tied the top securely so it couldn't get out.

Sir Benjamin and the young Suri Lakena left the house. Spencer, stunned, looked to the older Suri Lakena standing next to him. She put her arm around his shoulder and before he knew it they were back in the cave with Ayasha and the other animals.

"Wow, did that really happen?" he exclaimed. "Did he really turn into a snake?"

"I'm afraid so, Spencer," she said sadly. "You see, Sir Angus was a very bad man and he let fear control his life."

"What was he afraid of?"

"Well, Sir Angus grew up as a very poor child in Scotland. He lived in an orphanage in Edinburgh because he didn't have a family. It was a terrible place and he had to fight the other children for food and clothes. He was very smart and did very well in school, so when he grew up he was selected to do work for the Royal Society with Sir Benjamin. But he never forgot his difficult childhood and it made him a very fearful man."

"Why did that make him fearful?" Spencer asked.

"Because he thought that everything he had worked for could be taken from him at any time. He believed that he had to acquire more and more money so he would never be poor again."

"So, that's why he stole Sir Benjamin's work and tried to get the secrets from you? Did he want to sell them to that bad man who was trying to overthrow the king?"

"That's right, Spencer."

"So, what happened to him?"

"Well, remember when we were in the past and you saw me on the floor with my hands in the air?"

"Yeah."

"Well, I was asking the Universe for help and that's when Sir Angus was turned into a snake. But not just any snake—he was turned into the Uktah."

"What's a Uk—um...whatever you said?" Spencer asked.

"There was a legend that was told by my people. It was a story of a giant serpent with horns and a large shiny stone between his eyes. They said it roamed these mountains for thousands of years and it was called the Uktah. The legend said that if you were ever bitten by the Uktah you would be under his spell, and you would be forced to roam the mountains with him for all eternity. All of the people in my village were afraid of him and so I believe when I asked for help the Universe breathed life into the legend. The Uktah was the only thing that could hold all of Sir Angus' evil."

"So, what did you do with Sir Angus—I mean the Uktah?"

"We put him in the vortex. We thought the positive stream of energy would hold him there. But now I believe he's found an escape and is existing in the reverse vortex and making it stronger."

"So, he's been in the vortex for two hundred years?"

"Yes, my grandchild. He has been waiting for the time when the vortex is at its weakest. The time when a new Gatekeeper will be put in place." Spencer rubbed his arm again and Suri Lakena could tell he was afraid. "Come, Spencer, there is one more thing I wish to show you."

They stepped into the vortex again and this time when Spencer opened his eyes they were standing on top of the mountain. Everything was green and beautiful just as it had been the day his grandmother had first brought him and Emily there.

"Why are we here?" he asked.

"I want you to look through the window in the rocks," and she led him over to the opening.

"Can I ask a question first?"

"Anything, my grandson."

"Does this window have special powers or something?"

"It is the window of truth," she said without hesitation. "What you see is a true picture but it is based on the energy flowing from the vortex."

"Oh—now I get it! What you see is real, but it depends on if there's energy flowing from the positive vortex or the reverse vortex."

"That's right, Spencer."

He looked through the window. "Hey, look! Everything's back to normal! I see all the animals and there's Gram on the front porch of the house in the rocking chair."

"That's not your grandmother, Spencer."

"It's not?"

"No, that is your daughter."

"What! I don't have a daughter!"

"I have brought you here to see your future, Spencer. I wanted you to see what a wonderful family you have created."

"Hey, who's that working in the hayfield?" he asked.

"That is your son, William. You named him after your father and his father before him. During your lifetime you have done wonderful things, Spencer. You have been a wonderful friend and doctor to all the animals and you have made Sweetwater Farms bigger and better than it ever was. You have given a wonderful gift to your children and they have been able to support and raise beautiful families because of it. Do you see the children playing under the bridge in the stream?"

"Yeah."

"Those are your son's children. Your grandchildren." She kissed his head.

"Cool, I have grandchildren! But, hey, who'd I marry?"

"Well, we have to save a few surprises, don't we?"

Spencer stepped away from the rock window. "So, why did you want me to see my future?"

"I wanted you to see your possible future." She placed her hand on his shoulder. "This is the future you will have if you choose to live in the energy of the positive vortex. But if the reverse vortex takes control—well, I think you have already seen what life will be like then. Haven't you, my grandson?"

"I sure have," Spencer said, looking back at the window. "So, if I choose the positive vortex what do I have to do? Do I just have to love everything?"

"Oh, no." Suri Lakena smiled. "You only have to love yourself."

"What do you mean—myself?"

"Well, remember I said you can turn fear into love by understanding where your fears come from?"

"Yes, ma'am."

"Well, you just have to be brave and find the courage to confront them. You find that courage by loving yourself and wanting good things for yourself. Remember how we talked earlier about your mother? Didn't it make you feel better just to talk about it?"

"Hey, yeah!"

"As you confront your fears they will go away and in the place of them will be love."

"So," he said, "does this mean I have to confront Sir Angus—I mean the Uktah to get rid of it?"

"If you decide to become the Gatekeeper, I'm afraid the answer is yes. Sir Angus is spreading fear and you're the only one who can stop him and return the positive power to the vortex."

"You can't help me?" he asked becoming scared again.

"As you saw when you first came to the cave with your grandmother my power is tied to the vortex and I am growing weaker. I am sorry, my grandson, but I cannot help you. But you must remember, you are a part of all creation and, therefore, you will always have the power of the Universe with you."

Spencer could hear his name being called and gradually Suri

Lakena started to fade away.

"Spencer, Spencer," Emily said as she tried to wake him. "Come on! Get up! It's the last day of school!"

She trotted out of the room with Maggie Lee following and Spencer sat up in bed and rubbed his eyes.

"Was that all a dream?" he thought as he looked around the room. "It seemed so real."

He lay in bed and thought back to what Suri Lakena had told him about the snake and Sir Angus. He thought about seeing Sweetwater Farms two hundred years ago and his grandchildren. When he remembered what she had told him about his mother he jumped out of bed. He threw on some clothes and ran downstairs and out the back door. He made it to the cemetery in record time and swung open the iron gate.

His mother's grave site was covered with acorns and leaves so he knelt down in the dirt and brushed them to the side. He reached out for her headstone and for the first time since she died, his arm didn't hurt. He felt as if the fear of her death had covered over all the love he had for her. And now, with the fear gone, the love was free to live again. Memories of her began to flood in and he closed his eyes and stayed in the moment. He could feel her arms around him and her voice softly in his ear:

"Spencer...you are my heart, you are my little boy. We will always be together. For as long as you live and then after you depart this world, our souls will be joined. I will always love you, my son."

He thought of how she used to wake him in the morning before school. She would brush his hair back from his eyes and kiss his forehead—and tell him that today would be the best day ever. He thought about everything Suri Lakena had told him in his dream. About his choice of living in fear or living in the love of the positive vortex and now he knew what she meant. He could feel love all around him, and it was something worth fighting for. Now he knew what his decision would be.

CHAPTER FOURTEEN

THE KNIGHTS OF THE SWORD

"Where have you been?" Emily asked as Spencer reached the top of the staircase.

"I went to see Mom."

"You went to the cemetery this early?"

He walked into his bedroom. "Yeah, I needed to talk to her."

Emily followed him and sat down on his bed.

"You'll never guess what I found out on the computer last night," she said as he picked out his clothes for school.

"Well, you'll never guess what I did last night either. Well, not what I did—but what I dreamed."

"Let me go first—I think mine's more important."

"I wouldn't be so sure," he answered.

"Well, I stayed up past my bedtime, and Gram and Dad don't know, so don't say anything. Anyway, I tried to find out what the crossed swords and snake symbol mean and I traced it all the way back to England in the 1700s. It was a secret group of men that wanted to overthrow the king and they were called Knights of the Sword—First Degree."

Spencer was about to walk into the bathroom but stopped and came over to the bed instead.

"Why were they called First Degree?" he asked.

"Well, I think, First Degree was the first group of them that tried to overthrow the king, because there was a Second and a Third Degree too."

"Spencer! Emily!" Kate called from downstairs. "Come on and get breakfast before school."

"Yes, ma'am," Emily yelled back.

"So, do you think the man that Sir Benjamin overheard Sir Angus talking to that day in their lab was a member of the Knights of the Sword?" Spencer asked as he ran through the possibilities in his mind.

"I think he must have been—and maybe Sir Angus was, too."

"Hey," Spencer asked, putting the pieces together, "do you think Mr. Wynn and his men are part of that group too?"

"Yep! But I couldn't find any more information on them after the Third Degree. The website I found said that after the Knights of the Sword failed in their attempts to take over the throne they just kind of disappeared."

"Emily and Spencer! I'm not going to call you again!"

"Okay, Gram. We're coming," Emily answered.

"So, why do you think Billy Wynn wants our land? What's he looking for?" Spencer asked putting on the clean shirt he had pulled out of his dresser.

"Well, when Jonas and I were in the hardware store we heard him say they needed to find something on our property. They said they needed the map of Sweetwater Farms and they thought it and the deed were in Sir Benjamin's trunk." Emily grabbed her backpack from the floor and headed out the door. "I guess we'll have to talk about this later, Gram's gonna kill us if we don't get downstairs for breakfast."

Spencer sat on the edge of the bed and put on his shoes. He was thinking about Sir Angus being the snake and becoming more and more powerful because of the reverse vortex. He thought about Billy Wynn and how he needed to find a map of Sweetwater Farms because he was looking for something—and it hit him!

He stood up and ran to the hallway. Emily was just starting down the stairs.

"I got it! I know what Billy Wynn is looking for!"

❊ ❊ ❊ ❊ ❊ ❊ ❊ ❊ ❊ ❊ ❊

"What are you two whispering about?" Kate asked as she peeked around from the kitchen and saw Spencer and Emily sitting on the top step of the staircase.

"Oh, nothing, Gram," Emily answered as she and Spencer popped up and headed down the stairs.

Kate was pouring cake batter into a pan.

"Emily, when you finish your breakfast could you go down to the barn and tell Roberto to leave Peaches and Rosebud in their stalls? After I take you children to school I've got to brush them."

"Can Spencer do it?" she asked, picking up an apple and heading to the living room. "I've got to get my library books together to take back to school so I don't get fined."

"Well, shouldn't you have done that last night instead of staying up late on the computer?" Kate called as she winked at Spencer. "When will you kids learn that I know everything that goes on with you two?" She put the cake in the oven. "Spencer, would you mind telling Roberto for me?"

"No, ma'am. I want to check on Dudley anyway."

"Why, what's wrong with Dudley?"

"He's got a cold."

"How do you know that?"

"Well," he said, slurping up a spoonful of milk from his cereal bowl, "when I talked to Gerri and Dudley yesterday, we kinda figured it out.

He was sneezing and he had a temperature and his eyes were watery. So, I told him to do what you tell us to do, get lots of rest and drink plenty of fluids."

Kate walked over to Spencer and knelt down in front of him.

"It's like you were born to take care of animals. Do you like helping them and making them feel better?"

"I *love* making them feel better!" He thought about his dream last night and remembered what Suri Lakena had told him about the positive energy from the vortex being love.

Kate hugged him and then he put his bowl in the sink and headed out the backdoor to go to the barn. It was a warm spring morning and he looked across the pasture and saw Roberto feeding Rio and Blue. He climbed to the top rail of the fence, sat down and waited for him to finish. Abbey was making her way over to Roberto and the other horses, but stopped by the fence where Spencer was sitting.

"Hi, Abbey!"

"Good morning, Spencer," she stretched out one of her long back legs, **"how are you on this glorious day?"**

"I'm fine. How are you?"

"I'm old is how I am."

Spencer grinned. "You're only as old as Gram, and that's not so old."

"Well, for a horse it is." She lifted her huge head in the air and opened her mouth wide to yawn. Spencer could see all of her teeth and her long tongue and laughed. **"Oh, excuse me, my boy, but I didn't sleep a wink last night."**

"Abbey!" Roberto yelled. "Breakfast!"

Spencer could see Roberto putting grain in Abbey's feed pan.

"Come on, Miss Abbey—come and get it!"

"You'd better go and get your grain before Rio and Blue eat it," Spencer said.

"They better not if they know what's good for them." She started to walk away, but stopped and turned back toward Spencer. **"Remember**

my boy—you have the power of the Universe with you at all times. That includes me and the other animals at Sweetwater Farms too."

Spencer looked into her soft brown eyes and had the same feeling he had in the cave with Takoda and the other Guardians. He wasn't sure exactly what it was, but he knew he liked it.

❊ ❊ ❊ ❊ ❊ ❊ ❊ ❊ ❊ ❊ ❊

"Good morning!" Emily called through the screen door of the farmhouse. "Is anybody home?"

"Good morning, Emily," Sofia said as she came out onto the porch.

"We were going to leave for school and Anna never came to the house. Is she still here?"

"No, she left early this morning to work on her project. I bet I know exactly where to find her. You go back to your grandmother's car and I'll go get her."

"Okay. Thanks, Sofia. Bye!"

"Good-bye, Emily. Enjoy your last day of school!" And, with that, Sofia headed toward the workshed behind the house.

In a few moments Anna came up the driveway from the back of the house and jumped in the car.

"Where were you?" Emily asked.

"It's a secret. But I'll be ready to show you tomorrow at the party," she said proudly.

❊ ❊ ❊ ❊ ❊ ❊ ❊ ❊ ❊ ❊ ❊

Spencer, Anna and Emily piled out of the car. They said their goodbyes to Kate and walked to the flagpole. There was a new energy swirling around the children as they hurried to get to their classes. It was the last day of school and there was definitely a feeling of excitement in the air.

"I say we all have lunch together to plan our strategy," Emily said as she leaned against the flagpole.

"Plan our strategy about what?" Anna asked, slipping one of the straps from her backpack onto her shoulder.

"About Billy Wynn and Sir Angus and everything. It seems while you were working on your *secret project*," Emily rolled her eyes, "we figured out what Billy Wynn is looking for and why he wants Sweetwater Farms."

"Well tell me," Anna said.

The bell rang and Spencer was relieved. He hadn't told Emily the whole story this morning about his dream and Suri Lakena. He told her about seeing the past and about Sir Angus being the Uktah but he didn't tell her about his decision to become Gatekeeper. He didn't tell her that he had to get rid of the Uktah so it would stop pulling power from the vortex. He didn't know why—but he didn't tell Emily or Anna.

"Okay, so the plan is to get together at lunch." Emily looked at each of them. "Right, Spencer?"

"Oh, yeah, right," he said turning away to go to class.

"I'll tell Jonas too," Emily yelled as he walked away. She watched him as he went through the front door of the school and then turned to Anna. "I think there's something wrong with Spencer."

"Maybe he's just thinking about it being the last day of school or maybe he's worried about his grades. Wasn't he supposed to turn his project in today?"

"Hey, that's right—maybe that's all it is," Emily said only half believing that was it.

✲ ✲ ✲ ✲ ✲ ✲ ✲ ✲ ✲ ✲ ✲

The bell rang for lunch and all the students converged on the cafeteria. Spencer sat down with Emily and Anna and Jonas pulled his wheelchair up to the end of the table.

"Hey, guys. I was just telling Anna what I learned about the Knights of the Sword," Emily said, pulling her sandwich out of her lunch bag.

"What are the Knights of the Sword?" Jonas asked.

"They were a group of very bad men in England that tried to overthrow the king. We think that Sir Angus was one of them and now we believe that Billy Wynn is one of them too." Emily said as she took a bite of her peanut-butter-and-jelly sandwich. "We think that's why Mr. Wynn wants Sweetwater Farms."

Jonas and Anna looked at each other not really understanding what Emily meant.

"Because he's looking for Sir Angus and the reverse vortex!" she blurted out.

"But if they're both Knights of the Sword, why does the snake picture on the wall of the cave look different from Mr. Wynn's boots and that man's tattoo?" Anna asked.

"Huh, good question," Emily answered.

Jonas looked at Spencer, who was opening his milk carton.

"Do you think that's why Billy Wynn wants your property?" Jonas asked, noticing Spencer's silence.

"Huh, yeah. It's just like Emily said. We think Billy Wynn must be related to Sir Angus somehow. We think he's trying to find the reverse vortex because he knows it's gaining power and he wants to use it to do bad things."

"So, now what do we do?" Anna asked, peeling her orange.

"We still have to find the deed to the property. That's the only way we can keep Billy Wynn from getting Sweetwater Farms," Emily answered.

Jonas still watched Spencer and knew his mind wasn't on the deed or the Knights of the Sword. Something else was bothering him but he wasn't sure what it was. He grabbed Spencer's sandwich hoping to turn his attention to something else and when he held it up in the air Dwight Fitch walked by and snatched it.

"So, what did your granny fix you today, sapsucker?" he scoffed as he ran around to the other side of the table throwing the sandwich to Shawn.

Emily jumped up from her chair and tried to get the sandwich as Shawn threw it to Todd.

Spencer looked down at his lunch tray and closed his eyes. "When will this ever end?" he thought.

"*When you end it,*" a voice in his head replied.

"What? Who said that?" he asked as he looked at Jonas.

"Awww, our little sapsucker talks to himself now," Dwight said as he reached down and stole Spencer's milk from his tray.

Spencer could feel the blood pumping through his body. He remembered how it felt to be in Sully's body that day in the cave when they were fighting the snake. It was a new feeling to him—courage. He watched as Shawn pulled the ribbon from Anna's hair and that did it. Something in him snapped. He stood up from the table and walked around to the other side so he was face to face with Dwight. A silence fell over the cafeteria and Spencer became aware that everyone had stopped eating and was now watching them. He looked past Dwight and saw Nicole standing by the drink machine. He held his ground and returned his gaze to Shawn.

"How about giving Anna back her ribbon," he said, his voice shaking slightly. "And, Todd, I'll take my sandwich."

"Oh, well, since you asked so nice," Dwight said as he laughed, "we won't do it!"

Out of the corner of his eye, Spencer could see some of the other students laughing. He felt like he was shrinking lower and lower to the floor as the sound of laugher was rising higher and higher. He felt afraid again and defeated—and then he heard the voice in his head.

"*You must confront your fear. It is the only way to be rid of it—forever!*"

Now Spencer recognized the voice. It was Suri Lakena. As soon as he realized it was her, he felt a rush of heat go through his body. Just like when he was in the cave, he felt the Guardians inside of him. Kuma's strength and courage pumped through his veins and he could hear the howl of Takoda. His heart began pounding in his chest and he felt as light as a feather and remembered flying with Ayasha. He could hear Suri Lakena's voice again...*"the power of the Universe is always with you"*... and once again his courage returned. Dwight and the Pitsner twins had their attention on Anna and Emily, so he turned around and whispered something to Jonas. Jonas nodded his head and rolled his wheelchair away from the table. Spencer told the three boys to turn around.

"Okay, you guys have had your fun and I think we've had enough. I want my milk and sandwich, and please give the ribbon back to Anna. I've asked you twice and there won't be a third time."

He stood in the aisle between the tables and held his position. Jonas was behind him holding a lunch tray, and Dwight and the twins couldn't see Jonas from where they were standing.

"Come on, Dwight," Todd said. "It's the last day of school and this isn't fun anymore. Let's just give them their stuff back." He handed Anna her ribbon and Anna gave him a nasty look in return.

"Yeah," Shawn said as he tossed the sandwich on the table. "I'm tired of this, too."

"Oh, you two are just little chickens, aren't you?" Dwight said to the twins as they shook their heads and walked away.

"Dwight, I've got a question," Spencer said. "Why is it that you give everybody a bird name, like sapsucker and chicken? Oh, but wait, my mistake—what is it you call me? Oh yeah, red-headed sapsucker. Hmm," he scratched his head, "that's interesting because I think there's a red-headed woodpecker and there's a yellow-bellied sapsucker, so which one am I? 'Cause I don't think I can be both!"

Everyone in the cafeteria roared with laughter. Dwight was so mad his face turned red and he started to shake. He threw down the milk and started running for Spencer with his arms straight out in front of him. Just before he reached him, Spencer stepped aside. There wasn't enough time to stop and Dwight tripped over Jonas's wheelchair and fell face first into the tray that Jonas had layered with chocolate pudding.

Laughter filled the cafeteria and Spencer gave Jonas a high-five. Dwight lay on the floor, his face covered in sticky chocolate. Even the Pitsner twins were doubled over laughing as he tried to scrape the pudding from his eyes. Someone started to clap and soon the whole lunchroom was filled with applause for Spencer and Jonas. Spencer was beginning to understand what it was like to confront his fears. It made him feel good.

He walked over to Dwight and held out his hand to help him up. "What do you say we leave all this behind us here in the sixth grade?"

"Yeah, whatever," Dwight mumbled, ignoring Spencer's hand.

Spencer watched Dwight walk carefully to the boy's bathroom trying not to slip.

"Hey, we make a pretty good team!" Jonas exclaimed.

"Yeah, guys, that was really something!" Anna patted Spencer on the back.

"And I can't believe what I heard, Spencer. You know the difference between a red-headed woodpecker and a yellow-bellied sapsucker!" Emily exclaimed.

"See, Em, I do study—sometimes."

❊ ❊ ❊ ❊ ❊ ❊ ❊ ❊ ❊ ❊ ❊

"Anna! Anna!" Emily called out from the back door of the house. "Gram, did you see where she went?"

"I think I saw her go out to the workshed. But you just leave her be! She's working hard on something out there and she wants it to be a surprise for tomorrow," Kate answered as she iced the cake she had baked earlier.

Emily walked to the counter and dipped her finger in the icing when her grandmother wasn't looking.

CHAPTER FOURTEEN

"I've got eyes in the back of my head, Emily, so don't think I can't see what you're doing," Kate said as she turned around from the refrigerator.

"Then can I lick the bowl when you're finished icing the cake?"

"Yes, just go over and sit at the table. I'll be finished with it in a minute. Hey, where's Maggie Lee?" Kate asked as she put the last bit of icing on the cake.

"Oh, she went to the barn with Spencer and Sully to see Pee Wee. I was supposed to get Anna and meet them there, but that didn't really work out. So, I'll go after I lick the bowl."

Kate sat in a chair and set the bowl down in front of Emily. "Why don't you tell me what's on you're mind?"

"Why do you think there's something on my mind?" Emily answered as she scooped up some icing with her finger.

"I reminded you just this morning that I know everything that goes on with you children," Kate said as she wiped some icing off of Emily's cheek.

"I'm just thinking about some things."

"Like what?"

"Well, you have to promise that you won't get mad," Emily said looking sheepishly at Kate. "We know about Billy Wynn and the deed—and that you and Dad don't know where it is."

"And just how do you know that?"

"Remember the day that Mr. Wynn came here to the house?"

"Yes."

"Well, I didn't really mean to—but I kinda overheard you and Dad talking when he left."

"Emily Sweetwater! Were you eavesdropping?"

Emily squirmed a little in her seat. "Yes, ma'am—just a little."

"I'd like to know how you eavesdrop just a little," Kate said as she got up from the table and took the bowl to the sink. "Emily, this is nothing for you and Spencer to worry about. Your father and I are handling it."

"But, Gram," Emily said, "what are we gonna do if Billy Wynn finds the deed before we do?"

"I just told you it's nothing for you to worry about. Now, don't you think you should be getting outside on such a beautiful day? Your new dog is going to think you don't want to play with her. And I need to finish getting ready for the party tomorrow."

"Yes, ma'am." She rose reluctantly from the table. "Gram, can I ask you something else?"

"Of course."

"When is the next Lakena's moon?"

Kate wondered about Emily's question and walked over to the table and sat in a chair.

"Why do you ask?"

"Well, I thought that since I have Maggie Lee, maybe we'll join together like Spencer and Sully and you and Abbey. So, do I have to wait until next spring? Didn't you say that it happens every spring?"

Kate reached out for Emily's hand and pulled her over to stand in front of her.

"I said it happens in springtime—but I'm afraid it's not every springtime. Lakena's moon is tied into the energy of all of the vortexes in the world. There's really no way of knowing when the next one is going to happen—it has something to do with how much energy the whole planet is pulling at one time. That night, when Spencer made his wish for Sully, was the first time I'd seen one since I joined with Abbey."

Emily was lost in her thoughts for a moment. She stared at her grandmother.

"That was thirty years ago!"

"I'm afraid it was, Emily. I'm sorry, honey," Kate said, patting her hand.

"Oh, man. I just thought that Maggie Lee and I," she choked on her words as her eyes filled with tears, "I thought we could be like you guys and be together, forever."

"Well, I'll tell you what, Em. You're together now and she can still be your best friend. You can love her and take care of her just the same as if you had joined—right?" Kate held Emily in her arms.

"Right, Gram," Emily wiped her eyes, "it'll be fine. We'll still be best friends and I'll take care of her just the same."

Kate brushed the hair away from Emily's face.

"Now, how about you go and find that new dog of yours and give her a hug from her Grandma Kate. And later, if you want, we can make the dogs some special treats for the party tomorrow—something that Sully can eat too."

❊❊❊❊❊❊❊❊❊❊❊

"That's it, little guy. Go on over and introduce yourself," Spencer said to Pee Wee.

"But what if they don't like me, Mister?"

"Who wouldn't like you, Pee Wee? You're a very handsome donkey and you've got a great personality."

"Really? I do?"

"Sure you do. And I just know that Peaches and Rosebud are gonna think so, too. Now, just go on out there and meet them. They're real nice."

Pee Wee looked out into the distance and could see the two little horses grazing by the trees. He started to walk toward them but soon turned back to Spencer.

"One thing, Mister."

"What's that Pee Wee?"

"I'm not gonna tell them my name is Pee Wee. It's kind of a funny name and I don't want them to laugh at me. Is that okay?"

"Sure—but what are you going to tell them to call you?"

"I'm not really sure. I'll think about that later."

Spencer sat on the top rail of the fence and watched Pee Wee walk over to Peaches and Rosebud. The two dogs were lying on the grass by the bottom rail until Sully jumped up and ran to the barn, yelling something about a mole he had been trying to corner. Spencer jumped down from the fence once he was sure Pee Wee and the little horses were acquainted. He sat next to Maggie Lee and put his arm around her.

"So, Maggie Lee, how do you like your new home?"

Maggie Lee looked into his eyes and cocked her head back and forth as if she didn't understand this new language she was hearing.

"It's okay, girl. I can talk to animals," Spencer said with a big smile.

She continued to look into his eyes. **"You can hear what I'm saying now?"**

"I sure can, Maggie Lee. Pretty cool, huh?"

"Yeah. And I can hear you a lot better than I can hear other things."

"That's because I'm talking to you with my thoughts—kinda like how you and Sully talk to each other," Spencer said remembering her hearing problem. "When you try to hear other things like the sound of Dad's tractor or when Emily calls you for dinner, it might be hard for you. Dr. Miles told us that you can only hear out of your left ear. Do you understand?"

"Yes, I understand. It's okay, I just have to turn my head a little to hear them better—but can I ask you a question?"

"Sure you can."

"Did Emily know I couldn't hear in one ear?"

"Yeah, she did."

"And she wanted me anyway?"

"That's right, Maggie Lee. And Sully said it didn't matter to him either because he thought you were wonderful. And I agree—you're a very special dog."

"How do you know I'm special? I don't feel like I'm special. I'm not trained very well and I'm real skinny—and my last owners, the family I lived with before, moved away and left me. They just left and didn't take

me with them." She looked up at Spencer. **"Why do you think they did that?"**

"I don't know, but if you'd like to stay with us here at Sweetwater Farms, we'd love it."

"Thank you—but I don't really know who I am or where I belong," she said hanging her head.

"What do you mean you don't know who you are?"

"Well, you have lots of animals here—like Sully for one. He says he's a purebred Labrador ...or something. He even has papers to prove it. I don't know what papers are but they sound like they're very important. And the horses—Miss Abbey says she's a Tennessee Walking Horse and even Rosebud says she's a registered Miniature Horse—and she was only born last week! I don't have any papers, so I'm not really sure who I am or even if I belong here at Sweetwater Farms. The only thing I have is the name my owners gave me—mutt. Should I have papers for that? Is that who I am?"

"I'm sorry you're not sure who you are, but we all love you very much and we think you belong here at Sweetwater Farms with us. The only thing you need to remember is that you're an animal and we love *all* animals here—papers or not!" Spencer hoped his pep talk was helping her feel better about herself.

Emily came running down the gravel road to the grass where Spencer and Maggie Lee were sitting. She plopped down and began to rub Maggie Lee's head.

"I couldn't find Anna. Gram said she's working on her project again." Emily could tell there was something wrong with Spencer. "What is it, Spencer? Why are you so quiet?"

"Maggie Lee and I were just talking."

"You were?" Emily's eyes lit up. "Did you ask her if she liked it here at Sweetwater Farms? Does she like me and Sully and all the other animals?"

Spencer told Emily what was bothering Maggie Lee. He told her about her old owners calling her a mutt and about how they left her. He told her about the other animals at Sweetwater Farms having papers and being registered or purebred animals.

"So what?" Emily responded. "So what if the other animals have papers and stuff. Maggie Lee is the most special of all! Tell her that, Spencer! Tell her that's why I love her. That's why when I saw her at Dr. Miles's office I knew we were meant to be together—because I'm different too. You know how you're always telling me that I don't fit in with regular kids because of how I love science and other weird stuff. Well, tell her that's why we're perfect for each other!"

Spencer looked at his sister and a smile came to his face. Her words were perfect. They were exactly what a scared dog needed to hear to make her feel better. Although, it seemed like Emily only cared about facts and figures and science books and experiments, when it came right down to it, she had a big heart and she was pretty special too.

CHAPTER FIFTEEN

SIR SPENCER

Emily was almost asleep, but she could see a light somewhere in the hallway. She pulled back the covers and eased out of bed, trying not to wake Maggie Lee. Tiptoeing out of her room, she saw light glowing from underneath Spencer's bedroom door.

"What are you doing?" she asked as she pushed the door open.

He quickly ran across the room and covered her mouth with his hand.

"SHHH!"

As soon as he was sure she would stay quiet he released his grip, pulled her into the room and closed the door.

"Why are you dressed like that?" she asked as she looked him up and down.

"Okay, you can't tell Gram or Dad—but I didn't tell you all of what Suri Lakena told me in my dream last night."

Emily continued to look at Spencer's crazy outfit. He was wearing his hiking pants, the ones he wore when their father took them camping in the Linville Gorge every summer, and a hooded red sweatshirt. Both the pants and the sweatshirt were stuffed with something that made him look huge. But the strangest part of all was the football helmet on his head. It was his father's helmet from college and Spencer had the hood of the sweatshirt pulled over it so you could barely see his face.

Emily sat down on his bed. "Why are you wearing that ridiculous outfit?"

Spencer began to shed the clothes and Emily could see he had wrapped his arms and legs in toilet paper before he put on the pants and sweatshirt.

"Oh, my gosh," she giggled as he unraveled himself, "did you use all the toilet paper in the house? Gram's gonna kill you!" She began to rub Sully's head, bent over him and whispered in his ear. "Uh-huh, oh yes, I agree completely, Sully. He's totally lost his mind."

He finished taking off all of the toilet paper. "Ha, ha, you are so funny."

"So, what else did Suri Lakena tell you last night?"

"Well, remember how I told you Sir Angus was the snake and he was stealing power from the positive vortex?"

"Yeah."

"Suri Lakena told me the only way to stop him was to confront him and get rid of him—forever! And she said that only the new Gatekeeper could do it."

She was glued to Spencer's every word and forgot she was supposed to be quiet. "You've decided to be the new Gatekeeper!"

"SHHH," Spencer said in a whisper.

Emily's thoughts carried her into the future and she knew what this meant for Spencer.

"Do you have to help Suri Lakena...um," she gulped, "kill the snake?"

Spencer sat down on the bed beside Emily and looked at Sully, who was falling asleep. "She said she can't help me. She said her power is tied to the positive vortex and she's growing weaker."

"So how," Emily thought for a moment, "how are you going to do it?"

"I don't really know. I've been thinking about it all day and I haven't come up with a good plan yet—except making up this outfit for protection."

"You need a shield and a sword and stuff like that," Emily said, remembering how Sir Benjamin fought off the snake before.

"But I don't have anything like that. And even if I did—I don't know how to use a sword," he said, his enthusiasm deflated. "I don't really think I've thought this through very well."

Emily brightened. "I have an idea. First thing in the morning I'll call Jonas. I'll bet he can help us."

"Help...us?" Spencer questioned.

"Spencer," Emily said as she got up from the bed, "we'll do this together. If the reverse vortex gets bigger, it might take over everything and that would be bad for all of us."

"I guess it would be," he answered, relieved she wanted to help.

She opened the door and looked both ways before starting for her bedroom.

"Hey, Emily," Spencer whispered.

"Yeah?"

"Thanks," he said giving her a smile.

Spencer got ready for bed and turned off the light. He settled in under the covers and put his arm around Sully. The big dog sighed and took a deep breath. Spencer rolled over and noticed a bright light shining through the window. He got out of bed and went over to the window to look outside. The moon was full and hung in the sky like a huge, white pearl. It was different from Lakena's moon and he knew it. It had the same sort of energy coming from it, but he knew it was here for one thing— his answer.

****

He only slept for a few hours before he rolled over and looked at the clock. He laid there thinking about the task that loomed before him.

Ever since he saw the full moon last night he knew he had to confront the Uktah—alone. He couldn't ask Emily and Jonas to help him and his stomach flip-flopped at the thought of going to the cave by himself. Sully grumbled as Spencer pushed back the covers and he put his hand on the big dog to quiet him.

"Go back to sleep, Sully," he said as he stumbled in the dark to get to the bathroom.

"But, Spencer, where are you going?" Sully yawned. **"It's still dark outside."**

"Don't worry, boy." Spencer rubbed Sully's head. "It'll all be over before you even wake up."

Sully seemed satisfied with Spencer's explanation and rolled over, burying his head in the covers. Spencer took a piece of paper and a pencil into the bathroom and turned on the light. He wrote Emily a quick note and put it on his desk next to the lamp.

Emily,

I know you said you wanted to help me, but I think this is something I'm supposed to do by myself. If I don't come back—please take care of Sully and tell Gram and Dad I said goodbye.

Your brother,

Spencer

P.S. Thanks for being a great sister!

✻✻✻✻✻✻✻✻✻✻✻

He put on his outfit—football helmet and all—before leaving the house. As he started down the gravel road he could see a faint light in the sky where the sun would be rising. He turned back to look at the house for what he thought could be the last time.

"Psst."

A voice from out of the darkness. Spencer turned toward the pasture and saw Abbey and Blue standing by the fence.

"Hey, guys. What are you doing up so early?" Spencer whispered.

"The question is, my dear boy, why are you up so early and where are you going?" Abbey questioned.

"Well, there's just--" Spencer was stumbling over his words because he wanted to keep it a secret.

"Never mind, my boy. We already know where you're going."

"You do? But how do you know?"

"The moon told us," Blue said.

Spencer looked confused. "I'm not sure I understand."

"The moon told us that you had made your decision to become the Gatekeeper. And by the way—congratulations! We're all very proud of you," Abbey said as she bowed her head to him.

"We are here to serve you," Blue said as he bowed down to him as well.

"But how did the moon tell you?" Spencer asked.

"The same way it told you that you had to go to the cave by yourself," Abbey said.

"Oh," Spencer said only half-understanding what she meant. "Well, I'd better get going."

"Wait, my boy. There's one more thing," Abbey said as she came closer to the fence. **"Now that you're the Gatekeeper you'll need a mount."**

"What?" Spencer asked. "What's a mount?"

"Well, I'm Katherine's mount and Blue's your father's mount and Rio was your grandfather's mount. And now, if you allow him, Rio shall be your mount. Your horse, Sir Spencer!"

"Sir Spencer?" he questioned.

Spencer heard the sound of hoof beats. He looked out in the pasture and could see Rio running at a full gallop. His silvery-yellow mane and tail were blowing in the crisp morning air. He stopped on the hill in the middle of the pasture and reared up. As the new morning sun reflected off his sleek golden body he let out a loud whinny and Spencer could see the blaze of white that ran from the top of his forehead down the middle of his nose. He had never seen Rio this way. He thought of him as his grandfather's horse. A nice horse. A beautiful horse. But never like what he was seeing now! A powerful, majestic horse like Amadeus. Spencer thought for sure he must be seeing things, so he went to the fence and climbed to the top rail to get a better look. Rio took off again at full speed, and he was coming right at Spencer. Just before he reached the fence he leapt into the air, clearing it easily. As he soared across, Spencer could see what a truly magnificent animal he was. He jumped down from the fence as Rio trotted over to him and he couldn't believe it: Rio had on his full set of tack which Spencer hadn't seen on him since his grandfather died. His saddle and bridle were smooth tan-and-black leather and were trimmed in engraved silver with red stones. His breast collar had his grandfather's initials etched on a plate right in the middle of his chest. When he reached Spencer he stretched out one leg and bowed.

"I am at your service, Sir Spencer," he said in a deep voice. **"I will assist you on your first mission as our new Gatekeeper. And, if you allow me, I will serve you always as your trusted mount."**

Spencer ran his hand along Rio's long neck.

"I would be honored to have you as my mount." Spencer put his foot in the stirrup and swung his leg over the saddle. "But I don't know if you should call me Sir Spencer. I haven't even done anything yet."

"Oh, you will, Sir Spencer!" Rio exclaimed as he reared up again.

Spencer held onto the saddle and waved his hand in the air at Abbey and Blue.

He gave them a solemn salute. "Wish me luck!"

"You won't need luck, my boy. You have the power of the Universe behind you!" Abbey declared proudly.

Spencer and Rio started down the gravel road and Abbey and Blue watched as the little boy in the football helmet, wrapped in toilet paper padding, rode out of sight.

❋❋❋❋❋❋❋❋❋❋❋

"It sure seems dark in here," Spencer's voice quivered.

Rio glanced at the pine trees overhead. **"The trees are blocking out the light."**

Spencer jumped off Rio and tied the reins to the saddle.

"This is as far as you can go, Rio. I have to go up the mountain by myself," Spencer said sounding a little uneasy.

"Are you certain, Sir Spencer? I would go with you anywhere."

"I know you would, boy." Spencer rubbed his neck. "But I want you to go home now. I need to do this alone."

Spencer watched as the golden horse turned and walked away into the pine trees. As he stood there, all alone, he started to feel weird and his stomach began to flip-flop again.

"Okay," he thought, "Sir Benjamin said you have to be taken to the mountain by a Guardian."

He started to look around but he didn't see anything. There were a few streaks of sunlight that broke through the trees and the shadows that fell played tricks with his eyes. He turned to the left and looked over his shoulder—thinking he saw something. He looked the other way thinking he saw something else. He sat down on the soft floor of pine needles and felt a strong gust of air against his cheek as something flew by.

"Ayasha!" he yelled out as he looked up at the canopy of trees overhead.

"Shall I guide you to the cave, Sir Spencer?" she said in a soft voice as she swooped down and landed on his shoulder.

"I'd like nothing better, Ayasha, but I'm afraid I need to go to the reverse vortex. Can you tell me how to get there?"

"No, I cannot—but the other Guardian can."

"Where do I find the other Guardian?"

"He is there." She spread out her wing and pointed. **"Under that rock."**

Spencer walked over to a large rock sitting at the base of one of the trees. Ayasha jumped to the ground as Spencer bent over to get a better look.

"Under here?" He pointed, looking at Ayasha.

"Yes, he is the Guardian of the reverse vortex," she said hopping around on the pine needles.

Spencer tried to lift the rock. He had it turned over half way when the same four-legged spider he had seen before crawled out. Spencer jumped back as soon as he saw it, and the rock went crashing back to the ground. Spencer stared at the spider that only days ago looked normal—except for having four legs. Today, though, there was a noticeable difference in the spider. He had grown ten times, no, one hundred times his size and was almost as big as the rock itself.

Ayasha jumped onto Spencer's shoulder, and Spencer took a few steps back.

"Um, hello there, Mr. Spider," he said, not really sure how to converse with a spider. "Can you take me to the mountain where the reverse vortex is?"

"And why should I take you there? What business do you have?"

His voice was high-pitched and the sound of it made Spencer cover his ears. He knew he had to think fast and come up with an excuse.

"I, I need to tell Sir Angus, I mean the Uktah, something about Sweetwater Farms."

"Hmm. I'll take you there but what will you pay me in return?"

Spencer thought for a moment about what a spider would like. He couldn't remember anything he had learned in science class about spiders.

"Well, I have this sandwich I made for my lunch," Spencer said remembering the salami sandwich in his pocket.

"What is a sandwich?" the spider asked in a squeaky voice. Spencer looked at the sandwich and tried to think of how to describe it. **"Never mind! Just leave it on the rock and I'll see to it later."**

The spider turned around and started walking through the trees.

"So, does that mean you'll take me to the Uktah?" Spencer asked, unsure of whether to follow him or not.

The spider raised a leg in the air and motioned to follow him, so Spencer and Ayasha did, trailing slightly behind him. When they reached the edge of the pine forest, as if by magic, the huge mountain appeared. It was just as before, the stream was dried up and everything looked dead.

"I've done what you have requested and now I must return to my sandwich." He turned and headed back to his rock.

"Okay. Well, thank you, Mr. Spider," Spencer said as the spider again raised one leg in the air, this time as if to say, "No problem."

"Ayasha, I want you to return to Suri Lakena," Spencer said as he lifted the falcon from his shoulder.

"But, Sir Spencer, I serve you, also. I will help you with the Uktah."

"No, I would rather know that you, Kuma and Takoda are safe. I'll be fine." His stomach flipped over as he spoke.

The little bird spread her wings and Spencer could feel a rush of air as she took flight.

****

"Sully," Emily whispered. "Sully? Where's Spencer?"

Sully stretched, jumped to the floor and looked around the room. He wondered what Emily was doing there, but when he saw Spencer was gone he remembered what Spencer had said when he left earlier that morning:

"It'll all be over before you wake up."

He began to bark and turn in circles. Emily tried to quiet him and as she grabbed his collar her eyes caught sight of the note with her name on it. She read what Spencer had written.

"Oh, man, he's gone crazy, Sully!"

Sully barked again and ran out of the room. Emily went to the computer room and picked up the phone. When Jonas answered, Emily told him the whole story.

"Okay, I'll meet you at the cemetery in fifteen minutes," he said.

"Okay, but how--"

Emily heard Jonas hang up before she had a chance to ask him about walking to the mountain. She ran back to her bedroom and got her backpack. Maggie Lee was playing with her new chew toy on the floor and Emily kissed her head, told her to stay and raced out of the room. Maggie Lee could hear Sully barking, so she jumped onto the bed and looked out the window. She saw Sully running through the backyard and, not long after, she saw Emily running after him. She dropped her toy on the bed and ran down the stairs. When she came to the closed screen door she began to bark until she got Kate's attention.

"Well, for goodness' sake. Where's everybody going in such a hurry?" Kate asked as she opened the door. Maggie Lee ran out and went as fast as she could to catch up with Emily. "I just hope everybody's back in time for the party." She headed back to the kitchen.

When Emily came to the stream, she crossed the bridge and followed the path that led to Anna's house. She knocked lightly on the screen door and hoped Anna would answer so she wouldn't have to explain anything to Sofia or Roberto.

"Anna!" she said in a whisper through the screen door. "Anna!"

"Hi, Emily!" Anna appeared from around the side of the house.

"You nearly scared me to death! Where did you come from?" Emily exclaimed.

"I was just putting the finishing touches on my project before the party this afternoon. What's going on? Why are you so excited?"

Emily told Anna all about Spencer being the new Gatekeeper and the letter he left for her. "So, come on. We have to help him with the Uktah!"

Anna stared into Emily's eyes, trying to take in the story she had just heard.

"I don't think I'm really the right person to--"

Emily grabbed onto Anna's shirt and pulled her down the path. They went over the bridge and as soon as Anna was finally able to think about what was happening, she yelled:

"STOP!"

CHAPTER FIFTEEN

Emily stopped and looked back at Anna.

"What? Why are we stopping?"

"I don't think—I don't think I can go back to that cave, Emily. It was dark and scary and I especially don't want to see that *snaky* thing again. And besides that, you promised we would never go in another cave—ever again!"

Emily understood that Anna was scared. She was too.

"But, Anna, Spencer's there by himself. We have to help him. He's my brother—and your friend. Come on, we've got to hurry!" she yelled as she started running again.

Anna thought about out her choices. She thought about being in Mr. Tucker's barn and how Spencer made Pee Wee feel better when he was crying. And she thought about Sweetie Pie and how Spencer had taught them how to "talk" to each other. She knew she had to help her friend.

She started to run down the gravel road after Emily. "Emily Sweetwater! You get me into more trouble!"

✻✻✻✻✻✻✻✻✻✻✻✻

The girls went past the hayfield and followed the footpath that went alongside the stream. They started up the hill that led to the cemetery, and as they rounded the bend Emily couldn't believe her eyes. There, standing by the black wrought-iron fence, was Jonas. When he saw the girls he began to take very robotic steps toward them. It was as if his legs were being given commands to lift up and come back down to the ground. He had two metal poles, one on the outside of each leg, that were fastened to his hiking boots. Each pole had a hinge at the knee so he could bend his legs when he walked. The poles came up to his waist and were fastened to a thick belt. The whole apparatus held him upright and that allowed him to walk.

"Well, if I didn't see it for myself I would never have believed it."

Emily stood frozen at the sight of him coming down the hill.

"Jonas, you can walk!" Anna exclaimed. "How did you do it?"

"Well, I have an uncle that works at NASA. Remember, Emily? I told you about him. Anyway, he helped me make these boots. They have hydraulic lifts in them that can help me lift my feet—and these metal poles keep me from falling over."

"That's amazing!" Anna exclaimed. "So can you walk all the way to the cave?"

"I think so. I'm sure gonna try."

Emily noticed Jonas was wearing his backpack. "What's in the pack?"

"Goggles! I was able to duplicate the ones your mother made. I made two extra pairs. I guess they'll come in handy today."

"I'm not so sure," Anna said. "The last thing I want to do is see that snake again."

"Well, we should get going if we're going to help Spencer," Emily announced and headed back down the hill. "Hey, Jonas, did you see Sully run by here?"

"Yeah, and another dog was following him."

"Another dog?" Emily looked at Anna. "Oh, my gosh—Maggie Lee must have gotten out of the house. If Maggie Lee is at the cave with Spencer she could get hurt. She can only hear out of one ear! Jonas, can you run in those boots?"

"Sure!" Jonas picked up the pace to keep up with the girls.

****

Spencer stood on the top of the mountain and looked around. It seemed creepier than it had before. The sun was gone, the sky was cloudy and the wind began to blow. Spencer thought he heard dogs barking but decided it must be his imagination. He started for the trail that led to the rock steps and just as he was about to begin his descent he heard a rustling in the bushes. He turned around to see what it was and a ball of yellow fur leapt out and landed on top of him.

"Sully! And Maggie Lee! What are you two doing here!" he yelled as the two dogs jumped up and licked his face.

"We're here to help you, Spencer," Sully said as Spencer knelt in front of him. **"We do everything together!"**

"Yeah!" Maggie Lee exclaimed. **"Remember you said I was part of the family at Sweetwater Farms? That means we do everything together, like Sully said, right?"**

"Yeah, Maggie Lee, I did say that. But this could be dangerous and Emily would never forgive me if I let anything happen to you. I'm very happy to see you guys but you have to go home. Please, Sully, take Maggie Lee home."

"But, Spencer," Sully hung his head, **"you helped me when I was sick. You made me feel better. Can't I help you like you helped me?"**

"I'll be fine, Sully, don't worry. Suri Lakena says I have all the power of the Universe with me."

"You mean you have special forces too? Just like us animals?"

"I guess so. At least that's what she told me."

"Okay, Spencer, we'll go. But be careful!"

The two dogs turned around and headed back down the mountain. When they were out of sight he walked down the rock steps. Once in front of the cave he stopped for a moment as thoughts of Sweetwater Farms ran through his mind. He was thinking of when he was a little boy playing in the stream while his mother sat on the bank holding Emily. He remembered being with Suri Lakena and seeing his own grandchildren playing in the same stream. "There's only one way that will happen."

He took a deep breath and went into the cave.

❊❊❊❊❊❊❊❊❊❊❊❊

"Why are you stopping, Sully?" Maggie Lee asked.

"This isn't right. I can't let Spencer go into that cave and face that snake all by himself. I'm his dog! We're partners!"

"But he told you to go back to Sweetwater Farms. And you can't disobey him—can you?"

"Well, he did just ask me to take you back home. So, if you go back by yourself I can stay here."

"Sully, I think you're pushing it a little. And besides that, you guys are my new family. If you're staying, so am I."

"Okay, so we'll get in trouble together!"

****

"Keep going, I'm right behind you!" Jonas yelled to the girls as they ran into the forest and came to the stream.

"Okay, Jonas, just be careful. Gram says this is bottom land and there could be sinkholes," Emily called back.

"Yeah, it is kinda soft and squishy around here," Anna added as Emily found a place in the stream to cross.

"Oh, I see what you mean," Jonas said as his foot fell into a hole.

Emily looked back at him from the other side of the stream. "Are you okay?"

"I'm fine. I just found one of those holes."

The girls waited for Jonas to cross the stream and they all ran to the pine trees.

Jonas looked around at the trees and was amazed at how many there were. "I can't believe these trees! There are hundreds of them!"

"It's weird, huh?" Anna said as she sat down on the rock where the spider lived.

"So, now what do we do?" Jonas asked looking at the two girls.

"Well, now we have to get a Guardian to take us to the mountain," Emily said.

"Like Ayasha or Kuma?" Jonas asked.

CHAPTER FIFTEEN

"Unfortunately, I think it has to be the other one."

As Emily was talking the spider slipped one leg out from under the rock and wrapped it around Anna's leg. Emily saw the spider out of the corner of her eye. She stopped talking to Jonas.

"Um, Anna—don't move," she said quietly.

"Now, you know if you say that to me, I'll have to start running and screaming at the top of my lungs, don't you?" Anna asked getting excited.

"But I'm serious, Anna, don't move," Emily said, acting as normal as possible.

Anna sat perfectly still on the rock and turned her head ever so slightly to look down at the ground where Emily and Jonas were looking.

"Oh, my gosh!" she said in a low voice and closed her eyes. "Is that what I think it is?"

"Yes." Jonas came closer to Anna. "It's the appendage of an arthropod of the class Arachnida—and by the colorization of the appendage I would say it is a non-venomous variety."

"Oh, why did I ask?" Anna moaned, her eyes still closed.

The spider slowly released its hold on Anna's leg and she jumped up from the rock. Emily walked over to the rock and began to lift it.

"Emily!" Anna shouted. "What are you doing?"

"It's the Guardian," she said. "Come and help me."

Jonas fell to his knees and helped Emily lift the rock.

"There's no way I'm coming anywhere near that thing," Anna said.

Just as Emily and Jonas turned over the rock the spider crawled out. Anna gasped at the size of it and Emily jumped back. Jonas held onto the tree and pulled himself back up.

"Why is it so big?" Anna asked as she hid behind one of the trees and peeked out from around it.

"I'll bet it's because the reverse vortex is gaining power," Emily said.

"Fascinating!" Jonas exclaimed, watching the spider walk through the trees.

"Look, he's waving at us to follow him!" Emily exclaimed. "Come on, guys! That means you, too, Anna!"

"I'm coming."

❋❋❋❋❋❋❋❋❋❋❋

The spider returned to his rock and had just finished settling back in when he heard footsteps again. There was a gap between the rock and the ground, and from his hiding place he could see anyone who came into the pine forest. Three men stopped to look around and he tried to understand the language they spoke.

"Do yeh think we're goin' en the right direction, Billy?" one of the men asked.

"I'm not sure, but we've got to be close. We're supposed to wait here fer a Guardian to take us to the mountain."

Just then Ayasha landed on the shoulder of the biggest man. He petted her soft feathers and when she flew off the men followed her. The spider went deeper into his hiding place happy he didn't have to show anyone else to the reverse vortex.

❋❋❋❋❋❋❋❋❋❋❋

"Maybe I should have asked Sully and Maggie Lee to stay here with me," Spencer thought as he made his way down the dark passageway of the cave. "It seems darker than I remember."

Once he made it to the main area, there was some kind of fog hanging in the air. The faint light of the torches created shadows that moved like ghosts along the cave walls. A shiver ran through him as he walked over the roots and vines that covered the cave floor. He looked at the hole in the ground where the snake had once been. The fog was coming from there. The reverse vortex was rising, but, instead of the purple and silvery sparkles of the positive vortex, it was a swirling thick cloud of gray fog.

Spencer walked over to it, and, as the mist surrounded him he noticed the same funny smell as the last time he was there. He looked around the cave. He heard the sound of something being dragged across the floor just like before. He began to take a few steps back from the vortex and his feet became entangled in the vines. Spencer fell to the ground, and as he lay there the sound became louder and louder. He tried to free himself by pulling at the vines but had no luck.

The reflection of a diamond appeared on the cave wall right in front of him. He turned around and could see the Uktah slithering down one of the corridors. It looked like it had grown ten times its size since the last time he saw it. Its tongue was slicing through the air, and as it entered the cave its yellow eyes were glued on Spencer. It moved around the outside wall of the cave as if it were sizing up its prey. Spencer watched it move in and out of the fog as he struggled to break free of the vines.

"Okay, Spencer—think! What would Suri Lakena do?" Just as he said those words he heard Sully's familiar bark. He felt relieved and afraid at the same time. The two dogs came running over to him and began to bite and chew on the vines. "Sully! Maggie Lee! What are you doing here? I mean I'm glad to see you but I told you to go home!"

"I know, Spencer, but we just had to see if we could help you. And from the look of it, I'm glad we came back," Sully said, vines and roots hanging from his mouth.

They freed Spencer and the three of them ran to hide behind some boulders in the corner of the cave.

"Should we join again, Spencer, like we did before?" Sully asked as he ran in circles.

"Not this time, Sully. I'm afraid he's gotten way too big for that." Spencer peeked out over the boulders at the snake. He was on the other side of the vortex and through the fog Spencer could see that the horn Sir Benjamin cut off had grown back! "Oh, man, I can't catch a break," he said as he slid back down behind the boulders. "Well, guys, I think it's time to call in the special forces!"

CHAPTER SIXTEEN

TONAWANDA!

Spencer pulled off the football helmet. "So, how do I do it Sully? How do I call in special forces? And what are special forces anyway?"

"I don't know exactly. I guess I never really thought about who they are. I just know when I need help all I have to do is ask and I always get it."

Spencer sighed. "Oh, great."

"I think I know," Maggie Lee said. **"Is it like when I was on my own and I made a wish that someone would come to help me—like you and Emily?"**

Spencer thought about what she said, and, Sully cocked his head back and forth trying to figure it out, too.

"That's it!" they said together.

"I just have to make a wish. Like Lakena's moon!" Spencer exclaimed.

"Or like when we join!" Sully added.

"Yeah. I just have to make a wish and believe it will happen!"

Spencer put on his helmet and peeked out from one side of the boulders. The snake looked like it was sleeping but Spencer could see its eyes were open still staring at him and the dogs. He closed his eyes tight and whispered:

"Okay, I'm not really sure who I'm talking to...but could I please have some help with the snake. Please...I don't know what to do. I know I said I'd be the new Gatekeeper but—well, maybe you could show me how I do it. I learn new things real easy so maybe if you could just show me or just give me some ideas. Anything, anything at all would help. Thanks, um...Universe."

The sound of hoof beats echoed from one of the corridors. Spencer strained his eyes trying to see through the fog, and, just like before, Amadeus jumped through the swirl of the vortex and came to a stop in front of Spencer.

"Sir Benjamin!" Spencer exclaimed. "I'm so glad you're here! Look at the snake—look how big he's gotten!"

"Aye, laddie, he's grown to be a huge beast hasn't he?"

"Can you help me like you did before?" Spencer asked, already feeling relieved.

"I'm afraid not, laddie. I've lost too much power jus' like Suri Lakena. But I've brought the Guardians an' they can help yeh."

Spencer looked around the cave but couldn't find them. He turned back to Sir Benjamin but he had vanished!

"Oh, great—he's gone! Now, what do I do?"

He looked at the snake as it was slowly making its way toward them. He bent down and put his arms around the dogs.

"I'm afraid this could be it guys. Unless I think of something..." He remembered when he joined with the Guardians—Suri Lakena used a special word. "Now, what was that word?"

The dogs stared at him, not knowing what he was talking about.

"Tanawon? Tonawondo?" He peeked over the top of the boulders just as the snake was lifting his huge head to strike.

"I've got it! TONAWANDA!"

He felt a surge of power blast through his body. Sully began to bark.

Maggie Lee started to growl, the hair on her back standing straight up.

"What's wrong, guys?" Spencer asked, unaware of what was happening to him.

His blue eyes had turned a yellowish-gold color and fangs were beginning to stick out from his mouth. He was getting taller and taller, and, all at once, he fell forward onto all fours. His sweatshirt began to rip open and a thick coat of fur sprang out from his chest and back. He raised his head in the air, showed his fangs and let out a powerful howl.

He ran out from behind the boulders to the other side of the cave. The snake quickly picked up the scent of the wolf and went in for the kill. Takoda and Spencer, now joined as one, narrowly escaped the strike and ran around to the back of the snake. The wolf jumped onto a boulder, leapt into the air and landed right behind its huge head. The snake thrashed and flailed in the air to shake off Takoda, but the wolf sank his fangs deeply into his thick scales.

Again, Spencer shouted out: "TONAWANDA!"

His paws began to grow ten times their size and huge claws sprang out. The wolf was suddenly gone and Kuma was in his place. The gold-and-black jaguar held onto the Uktah with one of her massive paws and used the other as a weapon. She raised it high in the air and swung it down with all her might. The razor-sharp claws came down on the Uktah's enormous head, sinking deeply into one of its cat-like eyes.

The snake let out a tremendous shriek and swung his head to the cave floor, thrashing about from left to right. Kuma lost her grip and was thrown to the ground. She landed at the base of the boulders where the two dogs were hiding. Sully and Maggie Lee were terrified at the sight of her lifeless body. Slowly she began to shrink in size. In a few seconds she was gone and Spencer appeared.

"Spencer, are you all right?" Sully whispered, nudging him with his nose. **"Spencer, please answer me."**

A bit shaky, Spencer sat up and took off the football helmet. He blinked his eyes a few times and looked around. Once he realized where he was he quickly stood up. He eyed the snake.

"Whoa, that was awesome!"

"He's okay, Sully!" Maggie Lee said as she danced around.

"Yeah. I'm okay. But I think we made him really mad!"

The snake continued to thrash his head from side to side, but soon stopped and retreated to the other side of the cave.

Spencer saw a light coming from one of the corridors. He was shocked but relieved to see Jonas, Emily and Anna. He was afraid to yell to them, so, instead, he threw a rock to get their attention. When they saw him behind the boulders, he waved his hands in the air and held a finger to his lips to signal them to be quiet. He pointed to the snake in the corner and they all put on their goggles. When Anna adjusted hers and looked at the snake she started to scream, but Jonas put his hand over her mouth.

The three children lay on the ground and began to crawl over to Spencer and the dogs. Jonas kept an eye on the snake as he pulled himself along the dirt floor. They all eventually made it to the boulders and were relieved to be together again.

"So, what's the plan?" Jonas asked as he put his backpack on the ground and looked over at the snake.

"I was hoping you had one," Spencer answered.

"The only thing I have is what's in my backpack," he said, and, began to empty it on the ground. "I have an energy bar that I've had since school started back in September—and a pack of tissues that my mother makes me carry for my allergies."

"I don't really think either of those will help us," Anna commented.

"Hey, what about this?" Jonas exclaimed, reaching down deep into the pack and pulling out a bottle of clear liquid.

"Um...Jonas," Spencer said as he reached out for the bottle, "this is hand sanitizer. What can we do with that?"

"Well, if I could get close enough I could pour it into his eyes. It would at least buy us some time until we think of something else."

"Great idea!" Emily exclaimed.

Spencer and Anna looked at each other as they tried to understand.

"It's got alcohol in it!" Jonas and Emily cried out at the same time.

"Oh, cool!" Spencer exclaimed.

"I don't know, guys," Anna said. "That sounds like a pretty dangerous plan."

"Do you have a better idea?" Jonas questioned.

"No—but how are you going to get close enough to do it?"

Spencer and Jonas both looked down at the hiking boots Jonas was wearing.

"Sweet!" Spencer exclaimed.

"What?" Emily questioned. "Why are you looking at his boots?"

"The boots have hydraulic lifts in them," Jonas answered.

"Yeah, so?" Emily questioned.

"That means they can go really high," Spencer explained. "Like you can jump really high—say like if you wanted to jump on the back of a snake or something."

"You're going to jump on his back?" Anna gasped.

"She's got a point, Jonas. Why don't you let me do it?" Spencer asked, not wanting to point out how dangerous it might be for Jonas.

"Or maybe I should do it," Emily said. "I'm smaller and lighter than the two of you. Maybe he won't even know I'm there."

"Yeah--until it's too late," Spencer added.

"Hmm, you're right," Emily said, feeling the lump in her throat.

"It's okay, guys. I'll be fine. It'll be the first time in my life I'll feel like I'm actually helping instead of feeling like I'm a burden."

Spencer gave Jonas a smile and understood this was something he had to do. They all looked over the boulders to see where the snake was. He had made his way to the vortex and his one good eye was fixed on the children.

CHAPTER SIXTEEN

"Hey, what happened to his eye?" Jonas asked.

"Let's just say that jumping on his back is no piece of cake," Spencer said. "I've tried it and as you can see I didn't accomplish much."

"Sure you did, Spencer," Jonas said. "Now I only have to get the sanitizer into one eye. Good work!"

Spencer felt proud. He smiled and handed him the bottle of sanitizer.

"Okay, wish me luck." Jonas stepped out from behind the boulders.

"Hey, Jonas, you can wear my helmet," Spencer whispered as he held it out.

"Thanks. That could come in handy."

Jonas put on the helmet and looked at the snake. Their eyes met and he felt a chill. The snake's eye blinked and his tongue whipped out, testing the air. As a swirl of dense fog rolled past Jonas made his move: Staying close to the cave wall, he got into position directly behind the snake.

He studied the snake's massive body and tried to figure out how he was going to hold onto him once he was on his back. He hadn't planned very well. He looked over at his friends, who were soon to be easy prey, and he realized he had no choice.

"AS HIGH AS THE SNAKE!" he yelled.

Within seconds he could feel the boots rumble under his feet. He took off like a rocket and flew through the air, landing on the back of the snake.

"WHOA!" he cried as he struggled to hold on.

"Uncap the bottle!" Emily shouted.

Jonas pulled the bottle from his pocket and tried to hold on to the snake with one hand while uncapping the sanitizer with the other. He dug harder into the sides of the thick body of the serpent with his boots. With the bottle uncapped he began pouring the sanitizer down the front of the snake's head.

The serpent let out a monstrous screech and lifted his head further into the air, bringing it down with a crash to the cave floor and flinging it back and forth. The bottle slipped from Jonas's hand and fell to the boulders below. Then, as if tired of dealing with Jonas, the snake flung his head and body from side to side, harder and harder.

Jonas lost his grip and fell from the snake, landing near the corridor in the cave wall. The serpent reared in the air and let out an horrific roar that echoed throughout the cave.

"Yeh dare anger the Gatekeeper of the vortex!" he bellowed as the two girls and Spencer looked out from the boulders.

They couldn't believe their eyes: The head of the snake was slowly fading away, and, in its place, was the face of a man. Spencer knew it was the same man he had seen in Suri Lakena's house two hundred years ago. He remembered the jet-black hair and long beard.

"Who is that, Spencer?" Emily asked as she watched the man's face morph in and out with the head of the snake.

"It's Sir Angus!" he whispered.

Jonas, on the other side of the cave, held his hand up in the air, waving it back and forth so Spencer and the girls could see he was all right.

Relieved about Jonas, they turned back to the disappearing snake. Not only could they see the man's face but his head, shoulders and chest. He was dressed like Sir Benjamin, but he had on a metal chestplate embossed with the two crossed swords and the snake. They heard loud, forceful snorts and the head of a coal black horse emerged. As he came into view the children could see he was adorned with a full set of silver armor.

The snake was totally gone and in its place was Sir Angus, sitting upon the huge black horse with fire in his eyes.

"I am the Gatekeeper—Sir Angus Wynn of Kilkardy!" he roared at the children. "What business do yeh 'ave here?"

"You're not the Gatekeeper," Spencer said. "Suri Lakena was the

Gatekeeper and now I'm it—I mean it's me," he said, shrinking at his words.

Sir Angus roared with laughter. "What? Why, yer jus' a child—a wee lad. My steed, Maximus, would be a better Gatekeeper than yeh. An' Suri Lakena es a fool if she's thinkin' I would never escape from the vortex. Well, I found a way! An' now I'm more powerful than she ever was!"

"No!" Spencer yelled. "She's not a fool! And Sir Benjamin said--

"Benjamin? Yeh mean Sir Benjamin Howell? He's the biggest fool of 'em all!" He tore a piece of red cloth from his swath. "Sir Benjamin an' I were partners. I gave 'em both the opportunity to be rich an' powerful and they turned me down! An' now they're nothin'—an' I am the new Gatekeeper!" He tied the cloth around his head covering his injured eye.

"I'm afraid I can't let that happen," Spencer said, stepping out from behind the boulders. He heard Suri Lakena's words in his head: *"Fear isn't real unless you give it power."*

Spencer looked into the fiery eyes of Maximus and up at Sir Angus sitting high in the saddle staring down at him. He stood his ground and put his hands on his hips like he was protecting the girls and the dogs.

Sir Angus let out a roar of laughter at the sight of the little boy standing there.

"Am I to fear yeh then, lad? Yeh can't stop me now tha' I've finished me transformation! I now 'ave enough power to leave the cave! So, yeh can say goodbye to yer little farm an' yer nice little life. Now that I'm takin' over, everyone will be under my control. I will rule with fire and fear! An' then I will 'ave power over all things!"

He galloped around the cave and jumped through the vortex, landing near the boulders. A heavy wave of fog rolled past and he seemed to vanish. No one could see him, but they could still hear the sound of hoof beats on the rock floor of the cave.

Maggie Lee couldn't understand where he had gone, and she kept turning her head back and forth to catch a spark of sound. In her confusion, she stepped out from behind the boulders, and by the time Emily saw her, it was too late. Sir Angus rode out of the fog, and, with one hand, he bent down and picked her up. Emily screamed and Maggie Lee squirmed and wiggled as he lifted her onto the saddle. He came to a stop in front of the vortex and Maximus reared up while Sir Angus cackled with joy.

"Yeh see, yer all fools! All it takes es a little doubt an' yeh forget yer heads. Yer terrified tha' the dog will get hurt! Yer so full of fear tha' yeh can't think straight—too paralyzed to take action! The world es full of fools an' before long I'll 'ave all of yeh under my control!"

Emily was pleading with Sir Angus not to hurt Maggie Lee and Anna was crying. Sully was running around in circles not really knowing what to do and Spencer knew this was exactly what Sir Angus wanted. He did have control over them and Spencer had to figure out how to get it back.

Sir Angus was holding Maggie Lee up in the air when, out of nowhere, a lasso cut through the fog and went around the shoulders of the giant man.

"Jonas?" Spencer wondered silently.

Shocked, Sir Angus struggled to free himself. He let go of Maggie Lee and she fell through the air. Emily screamed and Spencer reached out just in time to catch her.

Two men appeared in the fog. One of them threw another rope over Maximus, and together they held on tight as Sir Angus and the horse struggled to break free. And then, coming through the fog, a third man appeared. He looked like Sir Angus and was just as large. He had the same black hair—but he looked a lot younger. All three men were dressed in maroon and gold. They had on black boots with the emblem of the two crossed swords and the snake. Spencer thought they looked like the Three Musketeers. As the two men struggled to hold the ropes the third man jumped onto a boulder to get a closer look at their captive. Spencer noticed there was something familiar about the third man: he knew he had seen him before.

"Ah, my dear old grandfather—what trouble 'ave yeh made this time?"

"What do yeh mean grandfather?" Sir Angus bellowed as he squirmed in the ropes.

"My name es Billy Wynn! Yer my great-great-great grandfather!"

Spencer couldn't believe what he was hearing. It was all coming together now. They both had the same last name and Billy wanted a map of Sweetwater Farms...to find his grandfather!

"They are related!" Emily whispered as she moved closer to Spencer.

Anna moved closer too. "Yeah—and they look just like each other!"

Sir Angus pulled and tugged at the rope.

"Well, if yeh are indeed my grandson, then take the ropes off, lad!"

"I didn't come here to help yeh, Sir Angus. I'm here to take yer power an' to make sure yer plans never succeed!"

Billy jumped from the boulder and walked toward the children. They huddled together as he approached them.

"There's nothin' to be afraid of, children. Let me properly introduce myself. I am Billy Wynn, Knight of the Sword—Twelfth Degree," he said, removing his hat and bowing to them.

"Twelfth Degree?" Emily questioned. "We didn't know they went up that high."

"Well, back when my great-great-great grandfather, Sir Angus, was a member of the Knights they were a very bad group of men. They even tried to overthrow the King of England!"

"We know," Emily said, "I looked them up on the computer."

"Then yeh must also know tha' through the years the original Knights fell out of existence."

"Yeah, I read that too!"

"Well, Sir Angus's son, Sir Robert of Kilkardy, grew up to become a soldier en the King's army. After many years of service to the King he asked fer the opportunity to clear the tarnished name of Wynn. He wanted to command a new group of Knights—this time, however, they would *serve* the King an' be protectors of the Kingdom. Sir Robert wanted to prove tha' Sir Angus an' all his evil were gone forever. He led the new Knights of the Sword an' brought them back to power."

"Oh, so that explains why you have the same crossed swords and snake as Sir Angus," Emily said.

"Tha's right lassie. It was important to Sir Robert to keep the same emblem, but fer the new Knights, the crossed swords meant allegiance to the King and the snake symbolized rebirth."

"Cool!" Spencer said.

"Through the years our numbers 'ave grown an' there are Knights all over the world. The Knights of the Sword are now protectors of all of the vortexes on the planet an' we came here because Suri Lakena called fer us."

"Suri Lakena?" Spencer questioned. "But you came to our farm and wanted to buy it."

"Hey, yeah," Emily said. "And what about your accent? You didn't talk like that before."

"Aye, yer right, Emily—an' yeh can bet those weren't real alligator boots either," he said with a smile. "I do apologize if I caused yer family any concern. I'm afraid I had to use any means necessary to find Suri Lakena an' the vortex. Yeh see, we are Knights—not Guardians--we don't have special powers. We have to use regular means to achieve our goals. We're like--

"Calling in special forces?" Spencer asked.

"Tha's it exactly lad! We're special forces!"

Sir Angus began to squirm and pull at the ropes.

"Yer all fools!" Sir Angus roared as he stretched out his arms breaking free of the ropes. He pulled out his sword and cut the rope that was around the neck of Maximus. Once he was free, he galloped toward the two men who had been holding him captive. He pinned one of the men against the wall of the cave. Maximus reared up and came down hard, delivering a firm blow and knocking the man out.

Sir Angus then charged toward the other man, grabbing the back of his shirt and lifting him in the air. He turned Maximus and galloped back toward the vortex, jumped through it and dropped the man into the bottomless pit.

He turned his attention to Billy. "If yeh are indeed my grandson, yeh will follow me to take over the world!" The giant horse reared up and Sir Angus waved his sword in the air. "Yeh cannot hold me with mere ropes! Yeh fools! I am Sir Angus Wynn of Kilkardy!"

He spun the horse around and headed toward one of the corridors. He let out a tremendous laugh that seemed to shake the whole cave, and began to morph back into the huge snake. He slithered up the corridor as Jonas grabbed onto one of the ropes that was still attached to his neck. Billy ran toward the snake, jumped onto a boulder and leapt into the air. He grabbed onto the other rope and Sir Angus dragged both Jonas and Billy up the corridor. Spencer and the girls ran after the snake with the two dogs close behind.

When they reached the opening of the cave Jonas let go of the rope and watched as the snake went over the edge of the cliff. He yelled at Billy to let go but Billy held fast and went over the cliff with Sir Angus.

When Spencer and the girls reached Jonas they helped him to his feet.

"Jonas! Are you all right?" Anna asked.

"Yeah, I'm fine. Just a couple of bruises here and there." He walked over to Spencer who was looking over the edge of the cliff. "Can you see him down there?"

"I can't see anything," Spencer answered fearing for Billy's life. "But I have this weird feeling he's heading for Sweetwater Farms."

"We have to stop him!" Emily exclaimed.

Spencer turned around and looked at everyone. He knew what he had to do. He was still the only one who could get rid of the Uktah and Sir Angus.

"Anna, could you take off your belt and use it as a leash for Sully?" Spencer asked.

"Sure but why does he need a leash?"

Anna looked into Spencer's eyes then he turned from her and looked back over the cliff.

"He might try to follow me," Spencer said.

"Spencer! You can't go over the cliff," Emily said. "You'll get hurt. Look how high up we are."

"I'm afraid I have to agree, Spencer," Jonas said. "Billy probably does this sort of thing all the time but it's a little different for you."

Spencer looked at each of them. "I'm the Gatekeeper. I gave my word to protect the vortex."

Emily knew Spencer was right.

"Okay, they're heading for the pine forest," she said looking at Jonas. "And just beyond the pine forest are--"

"The sinkholes!" Jonas shouted out. "That's it Spencer! Just get the snake, I mean Sir Angus to the sinkholes. As big as he is I'm sure he'll fall right through. Actually, there's a hole on the other side of the stream that should be perfect."

"That's right, Jonas. Your foot fell into it!" Anna said as she fixed the belt over Sully's head.

"Emily, you hold onto Maggie Lee," Spencer said.

Spencer walked over to Sully and bent down in front of him.

"You know you're the best dog in the world, don't ya, boy?" Spencer said as he rubbed his head.

"But, Spencer, I can go with you, I can help." Sully nuzzled Spencer's hand.

"I know, boy, but I want to make sure you stay safe and I need you to look after the girls. Can you do that for me, Sully?"

"Okay, Spencer, but if you need me all you have to do is--"

CHAPTER SIXTEEN

"I know, Sully, make a wish and call in special forces."

Sully sat down next to Anna. **"Don't forget, Spencer."**

Spencer walked over to the edge of the cliff.

"I've got an idea, Spencer," Jonas said. "You can use the boots to get down the mountain."

"I've got a better idea." Spencer moved closer to the statue of Ayasha. He lifted his head in the air and held his arms out to each side. "TONAWANDA!"

He felt his arms begin to stretch out from his body as long, brown and blue feathers started to grow.

"What's happening to him?" Anna cried, wrapping Sully's leash tighter around her hand.

Emily watched as his head became covered in soft, downy feathers and a short beak began to emerge. "He's turning into Ayasha!"

After the transformation was complete, he looked around at his friends and took flight. The children were stunned! They continued to stare at the sky long after he was gone.

"I can't believe what I just saw!" Jonas exclaimed. "He just turned into a falcon and flew off the mountain. That's not right, that's not normal!"

"Well, I guess we'd better start getting used to it." Emily began to climb up the rock steps. "Because whether we like it or not, that's Spencer!"

* * * * * * * * * * *

The eyesight of the little falcon was incredible. Spencer was able to see everything on the ground. The huge snake was heading right for the sinkholes and he knew he had to act fast. Spencer noticed a man standing near the stream. It was Billy! He must have had the same idea about the sinkholes.

"Come on, Ayasha—we have to go full speed to get to Billy before the snake does!" The little falcon pulled her wings in tight to each side and soared through the air like a missile. When they got to the stream she landed on a rock in front of Billy. Right before his eyes, the little bird began to grow. Her wings spread out again and slowly Spencer's arms emerged through the feathers.

"So, yer the new Gatekeeper," Billy said bowing to Spencer. "The Knights of the Sword vow to stay by yer side to defend the Great Planet."

"Thanks, Billy. Now we have to figure out what to do with that snake," Spencer said while looking around for the hole Jonas told him about.

"There!" Billy took a few steps back from the stream and pointed to the hole.

They could hear a rustling in the trees before they saw the huge black head of the snake coming right for them.

"There's no time to discuss a plan." Billy positioned himself on the other side of the hole. "I'll be the bait. He'll try to come fer me and he'll fall into the hole. Yeh go over there an' hide behind those rocks."

"But, Billy, what if something goes wrong? What if--"

"Don't give into the fear, Spencer. Remember, tha's jus' what Sir Angus wants yeh to do."

Spencer got down behind the rocks and watched as the snake crossed the stream. When Sir Angus saw Billy, his huge head rose in the air and he let out a mighty roar.

"What es this? My grandson has come to stop me again!" he howled as his thick red tongue flicked back and forth in the air.

The ground began to give way underneath the monstrous serpent. The small hole that was once there was becoming a gaping pit of crumbling earth. Spencer watched with terror as the hole began to swallow up the huge snake--and the ground that Billy was standing on!

"Billy!" Spencer shouted. "Look out!"

Spencer ran out from behind the rocks but it was too late, Billy had already tumbled into the hole. The snake's mouth was wide open and one of its fangs was holding onto a large root. When Spencer found Billy, he could see he was holding onto the rope that was still around the snake's neck.

"Billy! Hold on!" Spencer yelled, frantically running around the hole.

He jumped up onto the rocks and could see Billy holding tight to the rope. The snake swung back and forth as it tried to hold on to the root and pull itself up at the same time.

Spencer closed his eyes, "Okay, Sully—I NEED YOU!"

❊ ❊ ❊ ❊ ❊ ❊ ❊ ❊ ❊ ❊ ❊

Jonas and the girls were coming down the trail from the mountain. Anna was still holding onto the leash, and just as Spencer said those words Sully stopped. He had a strange feeling something was wrong. He put his nose in the air and tried to figure out the energy that was now moving through his body.

"Come on, Sully." Anna tried to pull him along.

But Sully didn't budge. His ears were locked forward, trying to pick up any sound from the pine forest. Spencer's words became clear and they ripped through him like a bolt of lightning. He started to bark and pulled back knocking Anna to the ground. She was caught off-guard and lost her grip on the leash.

Sully took off in a flash. He ran to the bottom of the mountain and headed for the stream. As he approached the sinkhole he could see Spencer standing on the rocks.

"Sully! Up here, boy!"

The big dog ran up the rocks and stood next to Spencer.

"What happened? Why is Billy in the hole with the snake?"

"The ground gave way underneath him and he fell in!"

"How can we get him out?"

"Spencer!" Billy yelled. "I'm going to climb up to the head of this thing an' pull it off of the root!" He wrapped the rope tighter around his hand.

"But you can't, Billy! If he let's go you'll both go down into the hole," Spencer shouted back.

"There's no other way, lad. We have to get rid of him! I'll be fine! I'll always 'ave the Universe to look after me!"

Spencer knew he was right. He bent down and put his arm around Sully.

"It was a pleasure to serve with yeh lad! An' keep an eye on my nephew, Dwight. He's a good boy—jus' a little misguided! An' yer goin' to be a great Gatekeeper, Spencer!"

With that Billy pulled himself up the back of the great snake, and with one last effort, jumped to the head and held onto the horns. The serpent swung back and forth, trying to break free of Billy's hold. The dirt started to crumble and the root they were hanging from began to pull away.

"It's the end fer yeh, my grandfather! I'm putting a stop to yer evil once an' fer all!" Billy yelled. He jerked on the horns, and when he did the root finally gave way.

The snake began to fall and Billy let go of the horns. The Uktah hooked one fang back into a thick root. Billy continued to drop deeper into the hole but managed to grab another root and was able to hang onto it with one hand.

"NO!" Spencer screamed. "Billy! Billy!"

"My grandson is weak!" Sir Angus hissed. "He can't even finish the job he came here to do. But yer different, aren't yeh...Gatekeeper? Help me get out of this pit, an' together we can do great things! Jus' help me an' we can become powerful together!"

The root Billy was holding started to break free from the dirt wall.

"Spencer, it's all up to yeh now, lad! Remember who yeh are!"

Billy fell into the darkness of the hole.

"NO!" Spencer jumped to a higher rock to try to see some sign of Billy. Fighting back tears, he looked at the snake still hanging on the thick root.

"I'll never join forces with you!" he yelled at Sir Angus. "I'm going to finish the job that Suri Lakena and Billy set out to do! TO GET RID OF YOU FOREVER!"

Sully let out a bark and ran to Spencer.

"Are you thinking what I'm thinking, boy?" he asked Sully.

"I'm ready when you are, Spencer!"

The two of them stood side by side, high up on the rock. Spencer shouted: "ONE, TWO, THREE—JUMP!"

They both leapt into the air and Spencer disappeared as the big yellow dog fell onto the back of the snake. The root pulled away from the dirt wall and the snake lost its grip and began to fall. Sully ran up its huge back, and when he came to the horns he leapt into the air and grabbed onto another root with his teeth. He swung back and forth and watched the snake fall deeper and deeper into the blackness of the hole.

"Great work, Sully!" Spencer cried.

Sully watched as the root he was hanging from began to pull away from the side of the hole. **"Yeah! But now what do we do?"**

They looked up from the darkness and saw a hand reaching out for them. It grabbed onto the scruff of Sully's neck and pulled him safely out of the hole. Spencer and Sully began to un-join and when Spencer was totally back, he lifted his head and was looking into the eyes of the person who had saved their lives.

"Oh, my gosh!" he exclaimed. "What are *you* doing here?"

CHAPTER SEVENTEEN

SWEETWATER ANIMAL SOCIETY

"Mr. Tucker?"

"At your service, Sir Spencer," he said as he bowed. "I heard you might need some help. Are you and Sully all right?"

"We're fine. But how did you know we were here?"

"Billy told me."

When he heard Billy's name Spencer thought of the last words Billy said to him as he fell into the hole; his eyes began to fill with tears.

"He told me I was going to be a great Gatekeeper," he said, wiping his eyes.

"And he was right," Ennis said. "It's okay, Spencer. Billy knew what he was doing. It was his job to protect the vortex—and he knew it could be dangerous."

"Wait a minute! You called me Sir Spencer! How did you know about Billy and the vortex and me being a Gatekeeper?"

Ennis sat down on one of the rocks. He called Spencer over to him and wiped his dirty face with his handkerchief.

"When Billy came to my farm and wanted to buy it, I saw his boots—they had the two crossed swords with the snake on them."

"Yeah. I saw them too."

"Well, I wasn't sure if he was a Knight so I didn't say anything. The next time I talked to him I noticed he was covering up his Scottish accent and that gave me another clue. I decided to do some research on Mr. Wynn and I found out that he never owned any resorts. But then, besides all that, I just had a feeling about him."

"You just had a feeling he was a Knight?" Spencer asked.

"Yes, because you see, I'm one too."

Spencer couldn't believe his ears. "You are?"

"I sure am, son. I'm a Knight of the Sword—Eleventh Degree. And because of that I kind of knew what to look for."

"Does Gram know?"

"No, she doesn't. And I'd prefer to keep it that way. You see us Knights don't really like a lot of people knowing who we are. We can do our job better if we do it in secret. I've lived in this valley my whole life and have helped to protect the vortex. Sir Benjamin and I have been trying to figure out where all the power was going—but I guess you and Billy figured it out before we did." He looked back at the sinkhole.

Jonas and the girls came running through the forest with Maggie Lee. She went right up to Sully, and Spencer laughed as he listened to her scold Sully for leaving them.

Ennis stood up from the rock and gave each of the girls a hug.

"Mr. Tucker, what are you doing here?" Emily asked.

"Oh, I was just out on a walk and I ran into Spencer and Sully." He gave Spencer a wink.

Emily looked into the big hole and wanted to ask Spencer about the snake but didn't know how with Mr. Tucker standing there. "Um, Spencer, did you take care of that thing we were having a problem with earlier?"

Spencer looked at her for a few seconds before he understood she meant Sir Angus.

"Oh, yeah," he said with a big smile. "It's all taken care of."

"Thank goodness! But how did you--"

"I'll explain everything to you later. Right now we have a party to go to, and Gram's gonna get real mad if we don't get back home right away."

"I agree! And I could really go for a party about now!" Anna exclaimed.

✲ ✲ ✲ ✲ ✲ ✲ ✲ ✲ ✲ ✲ ✲

"Why is it when you need something done you can't find a soul to help you?" Kate said to herself as she spread the tablecloth on the picnic table.

Will came walking into the backyard from the driveway.

"Hey, Mom, where are the kids?"

"I'm not sure. I thought they might be playing out in the orchard. They better get back soon so we can have this party!"

"Well, Sofia and Roberto should be over in a minute. I'll go and get cleaned up so I can help you get things together."

Kate heard the kids coming through the bushes.

"Where in the world have you been?"

"We had to take care of that little power problem at the cave," Emily said as she went into the house.

"Power problem?" Kate questioned as she watched the dogs get a drink of water and lie down under the tree.

"Yeah," Spencer said. "Remember all of the earthquakes when you first took us to the cave? And remember Suri Lakena and Sir Benjamin were fading in and out because they were losing power. Well, we fixed it!"

"And just how did you fix it?"

"It all started with me deciding to become the next Gatekeeper." He sat down at the table. A smile came to Kate's face and she sat down beside him. "You see I got up early this morning-- and oh, yeah, I almost forgot, we're out of toilet paper. Anyway..."

He continued to tell her the story of Sir Angus and the Uktah. He told her about Billy and how he was a Knight and how brave he was.

When he finished she put her arms around him and gave him a hug. "You are one special little boy. No, I take that back. You are one special young man!"

Spencer beamed at his grandmother's words.

"Now, go on inside, Gatekeeper, and get cleaned up for the party!"

✻ ✻ ✻ ✻ ✻ ✻ ✻ ✻ ✻ ✻ ✻

"Kate! Where should I put this?" Ennis called as he came out of the house carrying the chocolate layer cake she made for the party.

"Just put it there on the picnic table," Kate yelled back as she and Sofia finished hanging the *Congratulations* sign.

The backyard was perfectly decorated for a party with colorful balloons and streamers. Roberto brought out the extra tables from the basement and Kate decorated them with blue tablecloths and napkins, and in the middle of each table was a vase of fresh-cut daffodils.

Emily grinned as she came through the screen door. "Wow, everything looks beautiful!"

"Yeah, Gram, this is great!" Spencer agreed. "Hey, but why does the workshed have a tarp over it? I know, I bet you've hidden our presents in there, right?"

"Very funny." Kate walked over to the kids. "That's Anna's project."

"Yeah!" Anna exclaimed as she came through the bushes and into the backyard. "You'll find out soon enough."

"Hey, can I give the treats to the dogs?" Emily asked when she saw the plate of bone-shaped cookies on the picnic table.

"Sure." Kate said. "They worked hard today too!"

Emily gave Sully and Maggie Lee each a cookie and they went back under the tree to enjoy them.

Will was sitting at one of the tables and Roberto noticed he kept looking at his watch.

"Is there somewhere else you need to be?" Roberto asked with a laugh as he pulled a chair out from the table.

"Very funny," Will said, leaning in closer to Roberto. "I invited someone to the party."

"You did? Who?"

"Remember Jessie--I mean, Dr. Miles?"

"Yeah," Roberto answered. Then it hit him that Will actually had a date. "Really? You invited her?"

"Yeah. Well, she did help us with Rosebud and Sully. And she found Maggie Lee for Emily, so, I just thought I should thank her. That's all." Will looked down at the tablecloth.

"Hey, you don't have to sell me. I think she's great!"

Just then Jessie came walking into the backyard.

"Jessie!" the kids yelled when they saw her.

"What are you doing here?" Spencer added.

"I came for the party!"

Will got up from the table when he saw Jessie. Kate watched as he walked over to shake Jessie's hand and a big smile came across her face.

"What are you thinking about?" Ennis asked as he watched Kate looking at Jessie and Will.

"I'm thankful," she said, turning to Ennis and smiling. "It's been a rough couple of years but I think this family is going to be just fine."

Spencer saw Jonas coming up the driveway in his wheelchair and helped him to a table. "Why didn't you wear your boots?"

"I still need to work out a couple of problems with them. I thought I'd better use my wheelchair and give my legs a rest after the day we had."

"Okay, everybody, I have a special announcement to make!" Kate exclaimed, as she stood by the willow tree. "I'd like to say congratulations to all of our students!" Everyone applauded as she held her punch glass in the air. "We're very proud of all of you, and if you'll please come up to the tree I have something special for each one of you." Spencer, Emily and Anna started to walk toward the tree. "Jonas—you too!"

The children gathered around her, and she handed each of them a little white box tied with a red ribbon.

Emily was the first to open her box. "It's a medallion!"

"Yeah, just like the one Ayasha has!" Anna shouted.

Roberto looked at Sofia. "Who's Ayasha?"

"I have no idea."

Beaming, the children put the medallions around their necks. On one side of the medallion was the lion holding the sword with the name Howell underneath. And on the other side was the huge oak tree from the cemetery with the name Sweetwater.

"Now, you can all be honorary Knights of the Sword!" Kate whispered as she hugged each of them.

❊ ❊ ❊ ❊ ❊ ❊ ❊ ❊ ❊ ❊ ❊

Anna saw a girl coming toward the backyard from the driveway.

"What's she doing here?"

They all turned around and saw Nicole Darling. Spencer felt his stomach flip-flop and he could tell his face was turning red.

"Oh, sorry, Spencer, I forgot to tell you," Jonas said. "Your grandmother said to invite whomever I wanted to the party, so I invited Nicole. We'll just say it's my end-of-school gift to you."

"Hi, everybody!"

"Hi, Nicole," they all said.

"I'm glad you could come," Spencer said, at a loss for anything else to say.

"Thanks, me too. Hey, our teacher asked me to give you this." She handed him a paper. "I helped her clean the classroom this morning and she said she forgot to give it to you. Is it your final project? What did you do it on?"

"I did a report on famous people and their animals throughout history. Like George Washington—he had a horse named Nelson. He was riding him when the British surrendered. Also, Abraham Lincoln—he had a cat and two dogs. The cat was named Tabby and the dogs were named Fido and Jip. And, Emily, did you know that Sir Isaac Newton, your hero, invented the cat flap to put in doors? He wanted to make sure his cats could come in and out of his laboratory if they wanted to."

Emily grinned. "That was a great idea for a project, Spencer. I'm sort of impressed."

Spencer took the paper from Nicole.

"I got an A on my project!"

Emily whispered to Anna, "There may be hope for him yet!"

❊ ❊ ❊ ❊ ❊ ❊ ❊ ❊ ❊ ❊ ❊

After everyone ate dinner and had cake and cookies, Spencer asked Kate, "So, is it okay, Gram? Can I go and get Pee Wee and the cats?"

"You sure can, Spencer. I think that's a wonderful idea."

Spencer went back over to the table where the children were sitting.

"Anna, could you get Sweetie Pie and bring her back here?"

"Sure but why?" Anna asked.

"Just go and get her—it's a surprise. And Em, can you go with me to the barn? I'm going to get Pee Wee, and can you get Dudley and Gerri? I have a little surprise for them too."

In a few minutes they all returned with the animals, and they all gathered around the willow tree.

Spencer asked Nicole to hold Pee Wee's halter while he went in the house. When he came back he called Maggie Lee over and he sat down in the middle of the animals with his backpack.

"I just wanted to welcome the new animals to Sweetwater Farms."

"Oh, thank you," Sweetie Pie said as she nuzzled Anna's arm. **"I for one am very happy to be here!"**

Pee Wee pulled a clump of grass out by its roots. **"That goes for me too, Mister!"**

"Yeah!" Maggie Lee shouted as she sat next to Pee Wee and raised her front paws in the air.

"But we're not new animals," Gerri said as she sat on Emily's lap. **"Why are me and Dudley here?"**

"We're thankful for our other animals too!" Spencer said as he petted her head.

"Oh, all right then," she said, lying down on Emily's lap.

"Since we're having this party, I couldn't think of a better time to give you all something." He reached into his backpack and the first thing he pulled out was a little diamond crown. "This is for you, Sweetie Pie. The diamonds aren't real but I thought since you came from royalty you should have a crown."

The little cat sat up straight as an arrow as Spencer placed it on her head.

"I can't believe it," she said keeping her head still so it wouldn't fall off. **"It's perfect! Thank you, Spencer. You have indeed made me feel like a queen!"**

"Spencer! It's great!" Anna said. "Thanks!"

Spencer looked over at Dudley and noticed him squinting his eyes so he could see. He reached into his backpack and pulled out a little pair of glasses.

"These are for you, Dudley." He placed them on his nose. "I thought they would come in handy during those late night mouse hunts."

Dudley sat up in Emily's lap and blinked his eyes a few times.

"I can see! Wow—I can see everything!"

Gerri jumped down to the ground and walked back and forth by Spencer's leg.

"All I can say is that you had better take care of those. They were probably very expensive and you'll never get another pair if those break," she said to Dudley.

Spencer petted Gerri's head. "I gave him those for you too."

"Why, what do you mean?" she questioned.

"Now you don't have to keep an eye on him. You can go and do whatever you want."

"Hey, you're right! Did you hear that, Dudley? You're on your own now!"

Everybody laughed as Dudley lay in Emily's lap with the little glasses on. Spencer reached into his backpack again and this time pulled out a piece of paper rolled up with a purple ribbon tied around it. He pulled off the ribbon, held the paper up and read aloud:

"*The Miniature Donkey Registry hereby certifies that Donkey registration number 28703 has been issued to Sweetwater Farms for the Miniature Sicilian Donkey, Yukon Jack. From this day forward the registered name shall be Yukon Jack of Sweetwater Farms.*"

Spencer put the certificate in front of Pee Wee. The little donkey lifted his head in the air and let out a bray that shook the whole backyard.

"Really, Mister? That's my name? It's not Pee Wee? I have an actual real name and I'm registered and all?"

"That's right Pee--I mean Yukon Jack. I asked Mr. Tucker to check with the people who had you before and they still had your papers. We had them transferred to us to show that we're your new owners."

"Wow, Yukon Jack, that's me!"

Spencer watched as Maggie Lee walked over to the bushes and lay down beside Sully. He reached into his backpack one more time and pulled out another certificate.

"Hey, what's this?" Spencer watched Maggie Lee out of the corner of his eye. "It seems like I have another registration certificate." Maggie Lee raised her head and looked at Spencer. "This one says:

CHAPTER SEVENTEEN

"The Mixed Breed Dog Registry hereby certifies that Mixed Breed registration number 0001 belongs to Maggie Lee of Sweetwater Farms. And it has been determined that she is a mix of Labrador, Hound Dog and Golden Retriever."

As Spencer was reading the certificate Maggie Lee walked over to him.

"Really? I have papers too? And I'm all those dogs?"

"That's right, Maggie Lee. I asked Jonas to check your DNA. I said you were a very special dog and this proves it." Spencer rubbed her head. "So, now, you're no different than any other animal here at Sweetwater Farms."

Maggie Lee jumped on Spencer and licked his face.

"Wow," Nicole said, "it's like she can actually understand what you're saying."

All the children turned around to look at her and they laughed.

"Well, since this seems to be a good time to give gifts--Emily and Spencer, I have something for you," Jessie said as she walked over to the willow tree. "When you left my office the other day, I was so impressed with the experiment you did for Sully that I talked to the company that makes the dog food for our office. I told them how you figured out his problem and it inspired them so much they said they would like to make a special line of dog food."

She pulled her hand from behind her back and held out a can.

"Hey look, Spencer—it's us!" Emily shouted. "You, me and Sully are on the can! We have our own dog food!"

"How cool is that!" Spencer exclaimed. "And look, Gram, this flavor is called Grandma Kate's Pot Pie!"

Everybody laughed. Spencer and Emily hugged Jessie and proudly showed the can to everyone. Sofia looked at Anna and gave her a little nudge. "Show them your project now."

"Okay, but you come and help me." Anna grabbed her mother's hand and pulled her toward the shed.

Anna cleared her throat and everyone turned their attention to her and Sofia.

"Finally," Emily yelled out. "Are we really gonna get to see your project now?"

Anna looked at her mother and seemed nervous about removing the tarp.

"Are you ready, *hija?*" Sofia asked as she grabbed one end of the tarp.

"As ready as I'll ever be," Anna said and grabbed the other end.

And with one pull the tarp floated into the air and everyone at the party let out an "Ohhh."

The shed had been painted red with yellow trim. Above the door hung a beautiful hand-painted sign. It was a family crest like the one on Sir Benjamin's chestplate—only this one had a dog, a cat, a horse and the oak tree from the cemetery with the words *Sweetwater Animal Society.*

Emily walked closer to the shed and looked around.

"Anna, it's beautiful!"

"Yeah, it's great!" Spencer agreed. "But what is it?"

"Well, remember the day Maggie Lee came to Sweetwater Farms?" she asked, smiling at her mother.

"Yeah," Emily said.

"Your father said that maybe it was a good idea she be the last animal we get here. And I just thought that maybe if we started an adoption place, then we could rescue animals and find them good homes. It could be our summer project."

"That's a great idea, Anna!" Spencer said. "That way we can keep saving dogs and cats and donkeys and horses and everything!"

"Hey, and I can do DNA tests on all the animals and we can give them papers like I did for Maggie Lee," Jonas said.

"That's a great idea Jonas," Emily said. "That way they'll all feel as special as Maggie Lee does."

CHAPTER SEVENTEEN

"And come look at the inside! Miss Jessie gave us crates to hold the animals and food dishes and beds and all sorts of stuff," Anna said as she led them into the shed.

Will looked at Jessie and smiled. "That was very generous of you."

"It was my pleasure. The way these kids care about animals—it was the least I could do."

Everyone went inside and looked at the perfectly arranged crates and beds. There was even a little desk in the corner with file folders and pads of paper and pencils ready for their first customer.

"So that's where our missing office supplies went," Kate laughed and gave Anna a hug.

"I hope its okay, Grandma Kate," Anna said.

"Are you kidding, honey? You just tell me if you need more!"

Roberto walked into the shed and looked around. "I can't believe you did this all by yourself."

"Well, Mom helped me with the painting and she drew the sign for me," Anna said.

"Yeah, but this whole thing was your idea, Anna." Sofia smiled at her daughter. "I just did what you told me."

"Anna, this sign above the front door is really great!" Jonas said. "Where did you get the idea for it?"

Anna walked back over to the front door.

"I got the name from the Royal Society that Sir Benjamin belonged to in Scotland. Then, I thought it would be a good idea to put all the animals and the oak tree in the middle. The tree in the cemetery is kind of a symbol for this family. I guess Sir Benjamin thought so, too, because it's on our medallions. That tree seems to be the thing that ties this family together--everyone from the past and everyone here today."

Kate wiped her eyes and gave Anna a big hug.

"What a wonderful gift you've given us, Anna. You thought you were just putting together a summer project but did you stop to think how many lives will be changed in this little shed?"

"Yeah," Spencer whispered to Anna, "and what a great name for our new 'secret' club too. Not only can we rescue and take care of animals, but we can also protect the vortex. This could be our clubhouse!"

"Hey, yeah. That's a great idea, Spencer!"

Emily was staring at the oak tree in the sign.

"What's wrong, Em?" Spencer asked.

"There's something about that tree," she said as she looked closer. "I've got it! Sometimes the answers to things are in places we would never think to look!"

"What?" Spencer questioned.

"It's something Jessie told me. Come on, let's go!" she shouted as she went running through the backyard.

"Where are you going? Hey Gram, we'll be back in a minute!" he yelled as he ran after her.

Sully started to bark and raced after them. They ran all the way to the cemetery and when they got there, Emily swung open the gates and stood looking at the big oak tree.

"Why are we here?" Spencer asked, holding his side.

"Everyone has been saying that the deed to Sweetwater Farms is in the trunk. Well, we thought that meant Sir Benjamin's trunk, but there's another kind of trunk that we never even thought of," she said, pointing to the tree.

They both walked closer to the tree, but didn't see anything. Emily walked behind it and saw a split in the base of the trunk close to the ground.

"There!" she exclaimed as she reached into the hole and searched around. She felt something smooth and pulled it out. It was a wooden box with the initials—SL.

"Suri Lakena!" they both cried.

Emily opened the box. She pulled out the papers that were lying on the bottom against the red velvet lining and unfolded them. In big letters across the top was written: DEED OF OWNERSHIP.

She read:

"This Deed, made on the 6th day of June, 1838 hereby acknowledges that the property described as Sweetwater Valley has been conveyed free and clear to Benjamin and Lakena Sweetwater and this title will protect and defend said property from any unlawful claims."

"This is it!" Emily exclaimed. "It's the deed to Sweetwater Farms!"

"Great work, Em! I'd have never been able to figure that one out," Spencer said as he looked over the deed.

"I guess you have your special forces and I've got mine," she said, folding the papers and putting them back in the box.

"Hey, Em, will you tell everyone I'll be back in a minute? There's something else I need to do before I go home."

"Sure, Spencer. Do you need any help?"

"No, thanks. Me and Sully can handle this one," he said, and headed off to the Hidden Mountain.

❊ ❊ ❊ ❊ ❊ ❊ ❊ ❊ ❊ ❊ ❊

Spencer and Sully made it to the pine forest and waited for a Guardian. Soon Sully stood frozen next to Spencer as he watched the huge jaguar walk slowly toward them. She blinked her eyes at Spencer and rubbed against his leg like a big house cat.

"Hi, Kuma. Can you take us to the mountain?"

"It would be my pleasure, Sir Spencer," and she started to stroll through the maze of trees.

"Come on, boy!" he said to Sully.

When the mountain appeared Kuma left them and Spencer and Sully went up the trail. They made it to the top and went down the rock steps to the cave. When he saw the statue of Ayasha he compared his medallion to hers and stroked her head.

Once in the cave he and Sully stood at the fountain watching the water spew up to the ceiling. He heard the sound of bells and then

Takoda's howl. The vortex began to swirl upwards from the fountain and the purple and violet colors were stronger and more beautiful than ever before.

"The vortex has regained all of its power, my grandson," Suri Lakena said as she entered the cave. "And I believe we have you and Sully to thank."

Takoda walked up to Spencer and lay down next to Sully. Ayasha flew in and landed on Spencer's shoulder. Sully looked at the wolf and tried to get a whiff of him. Takoda turned to look at Sully and was unfazed by the yellow dog lying next to him.

"Well, I don't know if I'd say that. We had an awful lot of help," Spencer said as Suri Lakena walked over to him. "And we lost Billy."

"My dear grandson, Billy was a Knight and he knew the risks of being a protector of the vortex. He knew how important it was for all living things to live life in the positive stream of love."

"Still, I wish I would have had more time with him." Spencer sighed and hung his head.

"And you shall," Suri Lakena said as she lifted his chin with her fingertips.

"What do you mean?" he asked.

"Billy was a Knight of the Sword. There is a special energy that Knights possess that no one else has. It is an energy of purity and hope for the spirit of every living thing. They believe if the great planet is protected, it will always give us whatever we need. Because of this belief, Billy's energy will be born again. You will indeed see Billy Wynn again. I just cannot tell you where or when."

Spencer thought about her words and began to feel better. He was happy he might see Billy again and he remembered why he had come to the cave.

"So, Suri Lakena, how does all this work? I mean, now that I've agreed to become the new Gatekeeper, what do I do?"

She smiled at the innocence of the boy as she watched him pet the animals.

"You just continue being a little boy," she said, sitting on the rock next to him. "Now that Sir Benjamin and I have had our power restored, we will watch over the vortex until you are ready to take our place."

"When will that be?"

"When you are very old and you leave this energy field," she said, looking into his eyes. "And when you marry, your wife will have the choice to serve with you, just as Sir Benjamin chose to serve with me."

"Oh, I see," Spencer said. "So, I won't see you and Sir Benjamin for a long, long time then?"

"Oh, no, my grandson, we will be seeing a lot of each other. You will have lessons to do for your training."

"Lessons!" He was slightly alarmed. "Like school?"

"No, Spencer," she said laughing. "You will be taught by me and also the great planet."

"The planet will teach me things?"

"Oh, yes. The planet is a wonderful teacher—you just have to understand the language it is speaking."

"I know what that means!" Spencer exclaimed. "I have to watch what it does and pay attention to it."

"That's exactly right, Spencer."

"And so you will teach me things too?"

"Oh, yes. We will have many wonderful years together," she said, hugging him.

Spencer could hear the faint sounds of hoof beats coming down the corridor and Amadeus and Sir Benjamin entered the cave.

"Hello, laddie!" he said as he dismounted. "Me an' Amadeus wanted to give yeh our thanks fer the great job yeh did with tha' awful beast." The huge white stallion stretched out his left leg and bent back his right bowing to Spencer.

"It's okay," Spencer said feeling proud. "I had lots of help."

"Yeh, lad, but en the end it was jus' you an' yer dog. An' Billy was right—yeh are goin' to be a fine Gatekeeper!"

"How did you know what he said?"

"We were there, my grandson," Suri Lakena said as she stood by Sir Benjamin. "We always have been and always will be with you."

Spencer and Sully said goodbye to Suri Lakena and Sir Benjamin. Spencer petted each of the animals and started to leave the cave.

"Oh, Spencer, one more thing," Suri Lakena called out. "Sir Benjamin told me you were looking for the deed to Sweetwater Farms."

"Oh, yes ma'am, but Emily found it in the oak tree. She took it back home to Dad and Gram."

"Well, good. I put it there to keep it safe during the war."

Spencer thought for a moment and remembered his American History class. "Do you mean the Civil War?"

"Yes. I hope it didn't cause too much concern for your father."

"No, not much." Spencer smiled. "But I'm sure he'll be glad to see it when Emily gives it to him."

Spencer turned back to leave the cave. When he reached the cleared-out area on top of the mountain, he once again looked through the window in the rocks. He could see the horses grazing in the pasture and their white farmhouse and the apple orchard. He saw the balloons and streamers in the backyard and everyone having a good time. He looked down and saw the big, yellow dog lying at his feet. He realized all this was the language of the great planet—love, peace and contentment. A gentle breeze blew and he saw the moon just beginning to show itself. He could feel the energy that was coming from The Hidden Mountain and he was pleased that everything was as it should be—in the stream of the positive vortex.

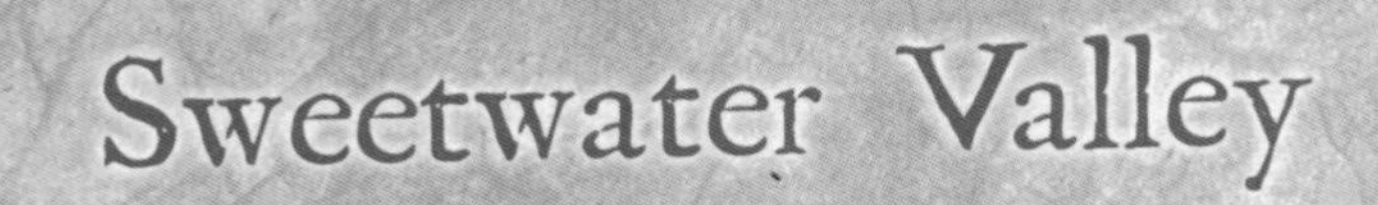
Sweetwater Valley

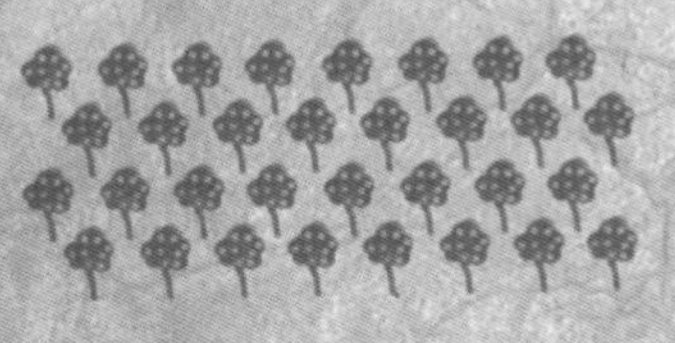

Sophia & Roberto's House

Sweetwater Animal
Society Clubhouse

Main House
Barn
Upper Horse Pasture